SUDDEN PERIL

INSIDE THE WAR AGAINST EVIL

SUDDEN PERIL

INSIDE THE WAR AGAINST EVIL

FRANK RICHARDSON

BONNEVILLE BOOKS
SPRINGVILLE, UTAH

ISBN 13: 978-1-59955-498-3
Published by Bonneville Books, an imprint of Cedar Fort, Inc.,
2373 W. 700 S., Springville, UT 84663
Distributed by Cedar Fort, Inc., www.cedarfort.com

LIBRARY OF CONGRESS CATALOGING-IN-PUBLICATION DATA

Richardson, Frank, 1943-
 Sudden peril / Frank Richardson.
   p. cm.
 Summary: An out-numbered group of patriots devoted to finding and exposing deadly secret organizations pays an unforeseen price for their patriotism.
 ISBN 978-1-59955-498-3
 1. Suspense fiction, American. 2. Adventure stories, American. 3. American fiction--21st century. 4. Undercover operations--Fiction. 5. National security--Fiction. I. Title.

 PS3618.I3446S83 2010
 813'.6--dc22

2010040936

Cover design by Danie Romrell
Cover design © 2011 by Lyle Mortimer
Edited and typeset by Melissa J. Caldwell
Printed in the United States of America
10 9 8 7 6 5 4 3 2 1
Printed on acid-free paper

ALSO BY
FRANK RICHARDSON

Where the Sun Rises

Acknowledgments

Thanks to my wife, Diane, fellow author Neil Newell, and story consultant Becki Richardson. Brad, Clark, Steph, Gregg, and Karen Richardson, Jon and Becca Willey, and Brandon and Emily LeFevre have all invested themselves in aspects of writing the story and deserve credit for anything positive resulting from the project.

I especially acknowledge support from the Glen L. and Marva Rudd family who read, commented, and urged me forward in submitting the story, and from Larry Crenshaw, Rich McKenna, Patrick Reese, Brett Bass, and Sharon Eubank for reader reactions.

A project like this would never come to fruition without the excellent guidance and support of the Cedar Fort editorial, design, and marketing teams.

ONE

The digital display on Sarah Rudman's wrist watch showed 9:55 p.m. as she stepped out of a taxi at 8th Avenue and West 91st Street, three blocks from her New York City apartment. She carried no handbag and no briefcase. She extracted a cell phone from her coat pocket and voice dialed an 800 number that rang into an electronic switching system in Denver.

When the recorded answer and menu played, Sarah keyed in a three-digit code. She listened for the beep indicating that a voice mail recorder was working and spoke quietly as she walked along. From memory, she recited the names of powerful and wealthy men and women, each with an organizational affiliation. She summarized financial transactions, speculated on upcoming events, and concluded the message cryptically with, "The Leopard has a first name: Ramon!" Pausing to remember any final bits of vital information, she signed off with her ID: "306 clear."

Her gloved hand hesitated briefly as she put the phone back into her pocket. She detected the sound of feet, leather soles on dry pavement, rushing toward her. Without looking toward the approaching figure, she angled across the street between two parked cars and quickened her pace. As she rounded the next corner, her apartment building came into view. She could tell by the sound that her pursuer was closing the distance between them.

At the far end of the block, a dark sedan turned toward her, its lights off. It moved slowly and almost silently. If Sarah hadn't heard the trademark clicking of studded snow tires on the pavement as the sedan rounded the corner, she'd have seen it too late.

Sarah's heart raced. Involuntarily, she glanced over her left shoulder to see her pursuer. The man was still walking but moving just slower than a run. He was a big man. No hat, long overcoat.

You've come a long way from the streets of Provo, Utah.

With a practiced eye, Sarah estimated the distance to the front door of her apartment building at forty yards. She knew she had a safety margin of about ten seconds. Ten seconds between her and— and what? Whatever lay ahead. She already held the house key in the hand inside her coat pocket.

Instinctively, she knew this was the moment. Further pretense was meaningless. She broke into a full run, leaping between two cars parked tightly together and darting into the street. As she expected, the driver of the sedan saw her and instantly accelerated. She could also hear the man behind her running.

Sarah stumbled briefly as she cleared the opposite curb and felt the naked branches of a decorative tree scratch at her face as she bolted for the steps leading to her apartment. She stumbled again as she tried to take the steps two at a time. As her hand with the key reached toward the door, the sedan screeched to a halt in the street only yards away. Dark figures flew from both sides, leaving the doors open.

Three seconds. That's all you've got. Key, don't fail me now!

As if guided by an unseen hand, the key slid smoothly into the lock. A quick twist and it clicked open. With all her strength, she pushed the heavy door open and moved inside, instantly turning her full weight against the door and feeling it shut and lock. Exhaling deeply, she turned and sprinted up the two flights of stairs to her apartment. The last thing she heard outside was the sound of feet hitting the stairs and the quiet curses of her pursuers.

Sarah leaned against her apartment door for a second or two to catch her breath but allowed herself no rest. She knew the next few minutes were vital to the cause. Entering the apartment without turning on a light, she moved quickly to a bedroom closet, where she removed and hung her overcoat. Reaching to a shelf above, she took down a hatbox and hastily removed the contents.

* * * * *

"What kept you, Tony?"

On the street in front of Sarah Rudman's apartment, four men talked in hushed tones.

"I didn't see her until she crossed 8th Ave. The cab must have dropped her there."

"We should have smoked her while she was still on the stoop," cursed a third man.

"Shut up, idiot! Our instructions were to bring her in. You two drive around to the alley and make sure she doesn't go out the back."

As the sedan pulled away, still without lights, the young Turk directing the operation paced back and forth in front of the stoop to the apartment building, deciding their next move.

"That chick can fly. I don't think I could run her down if I had to," said Tony.

"You couldn't run down my grandmother," replied the Turk. "We wait here for three minutes. If nobody goes in or out, we force the door."

As he spoke, a woman's voice could be heard within. Someone just inside the door. The Turk signaled to Tony, and each took up a station on either side of the door.

"So, give me a call first thing." The voice was low and gravelly with a stereotypical New York Jewish accent.

"No, no. I'll be okay. You worry too much," she apparently called behind her to the host or hostess she was bidding farewell. The door lock clicked and slowly opened to reveal an old lady dressed for a harsh winter night. She was badly stooped, and her white hair showed around the edges of a knit hat. She peered over wire rim spectacles.

The old woman flinched with surprise at seeing two men standing before her.

"Oh! My!" She peered up, her face gathering into a scowl. "You frightened me."

The Turk started past her so he could get a look inside. He forced the door open, causing the old woman to lose her grasp on the inside handle and upsetting her balance.

"Wait!" she barked. "What do you want? You can't come in here like that!"

The Turk turned his face away to avoid any problem of later identification and pushed into the entryway. Tony followed. The old woman braced herself against the doorjamb, sputtering and hurling threats after them as they passed the elevator lobby. They bounded up the stairs to the first landing and headed for apartment 211 on the floor above. The hallway on the second floor was well lit but not bright. The interior decor was upscale but not lush—all in all typical for that part of upper Manhattan. Without missing a beat, the Turk signaled for Tony to pick the lock. They had already lost too much time. He wasn't worried that the mark would call the cops. The client had dropped the phrase *industrial espionage*, so the Turk knew this was a business matter.

Tony had burgled his way through an already profitable career and had never done time. The door was open in twenty seconds. Both men entered with handguns drawn. Swiftly and silently they moved through the four-room apartment, checking in closets, out windows, under beds, even in the shower. As each possibility came up empty, the Turk felt the anger rising in him. He cursed under his breath and moved on silently. When it was clear that the mark had somehow eluded them, he put his hands to his temples and screamed silently.

"This is bad for business," he groaned. "Very bad for business."

"Maybe she didn't come to this apartment. Maybe she went to the roof," offered Tony.

"You two see anything in back?" asked the Turk into his cell phone.

"Nobody in the alley," came the hushed reply. "We can see the back of the building. Unless she split before we got here, she's still in there."

"Okay, drive on around the block. Let's get this broad."

"I don't think she came in here," persisted Tony, who was

scanning the bedroom. "Everything is in its place. No signs of a hasty exit."

"Would you please? I'm trying to think here," ordered Turk. "The hag in the lobby. Could it be the hag?"

"No way," Tony responded. "She was too small. Skinny face. Gnarled fingers. Couldn't be."

"Did you get a good look at the mark before she came in?"

"No. She fit the client's description. We know it was her because she came to the right address."

"We're missing something here. Let's go find the hag before she gets too far away."

"No way that can be her," Tony continued as they retraced their steps.

The entire search had been done expertly with businesslike precision, taking only three or four minutes.

"She can't be far down the block," the Turk muttered over his shoulder as they cleared the front entry and headed down the steps to the street.

Looking both ways they could see to the end of the block and beyond. Nothing. The old woman was nowhere to be seen.

"You two see anything on the streets?" asked the Turk into his phone one last time.

"Nothing here!"

"Aaarrghhh!" The Turk finally let out a cry of frustration. "This is bad for business. Very bad for business."

* * * * *

Three blocks away, a young woman, lightly dressed for such a cold winter evening, dropped a bundle into a trash bin just inside an alley off West End Avenue. Her crystallizing breath wreathed her short blond hair as she strode toward a nearby bus stop. She patted her breast pocket only once to reassure herself that an open-reservation airline ticket was still there.

TWO

A late afternoon storm was building over San Francisco Mountain north of Flagstaff as an old Ford pickup wheeled into the parking lot of a gas station and convenience store on the outskirts of town. A wiry youth emerged from the passenger side and threw a belated thanks through the truck door as he slammed it shut. He was handsome but wore a surly expression. Reaching into the truck bed for a dusty duffel bag, he turned to face the station as the truck merged back into rush hour traffic.

Jamie Louis Madero hastily surveyed the building and surrounding parking area, looking for someone fitting the description of the person he was to meet. Seeing no one, he walked toward the building and felt a welcomed blast of cool air as he shouldered his way through the door. Though it was still early summer, the ride from Winslow had been hot and uncomfortable.

Jamie searched for a sign directing him to the restrooms. After washing up, he gazed at his own image in the graffiti-laden mirror. A lanky Anglo in Levis and a western-cut shirt burst through the restroom door behind him. Reflexively, Jamie pulled back from the mirror and assumed a casual I-could-care-less-how-I-look pose. The intruder sidestepped him and headed for a urinal.

Making a last attempt to tame his unruly hair, Jamie eased out of the restroom, duffel over his shoulder, and headed out of the store. Still seeing no sign of the person he was to meet, he planted himself on a plank bench under the eave of the building to wait. Minutes later, the cowboy from the restroom took up a position on the other end of the bench and began leafing through a courtesy copy of the Nickel Ads.

Fifteen minutes passed with Jamie carefully noting each customer who came and went, looking for his expected host. By the time an hour had snailed past, Jamie was pacing. In truth, he didn't know who was to meet him. He extracted a letter from his duffel and reread for the tenth time the instructions bringing him to this unusual rendezvous.

It is my pleasure to welcome you as a summer intern with the Freemen Foundation. One of our representatives will meet you at 6:00 p.m. on Wednesday, June 22, at the convenience store located at the intersection of Smoke Rise Drive and Highway 89 in Flagstaff, Arizona. Please dress in the business attire outlined on the attached sheet. Bring with you the other essential items listed. A backpack or duffel may be easier to carry than a suitcase.

D. Jeffrey Gordon, Foundation Director, signed the letter.

The time was now long past 6:00 p.m. Jamie seldom resorted to profanity, but unable to restrain himself any longer, he exploded to his feet, employing one of his grandfather's favorite farm words. On the other end of the bench, the cowboy, who sat with his back against the building, legs stretched out to expose his dusty rough-out leather boots, raised the brim of his hat and gave Jamie a sidelong glance.

"Waiting for anybody in particular?" asked the cowboy.

"Yeah, and I wish to heck I knew where he was!" Jamie deliberately didn't look at the cowboy as he replied.

"Maybe I can help," the cowboy ventured.

Jamie was tempted to answer with a barb but managed to bridle his tongue. "Thanks anyway," he replied.

The cowboy was now leaning forward, elbows on his knees, hands clasped in front of him. Jamie could feel the cowboy's gaze.

"All right if I take a guess?" the cowboy persisted. Jamie groaned inwardly, conscious that the cowboy had paused to see if it was safe to go on.

"You're on your way to a new job," ventured the cowboy, "and you're not too sure you want to." It was a statement and not a question.

The pinpoint accuracy of the cowboy's insight rankled Jamie. For the first time, he turned and looked at the man sitting two arms' lengths away. Jamie had assumed that the cowboy was older, a transient ranch hand or day laborer. Looking now, Jamie could see that this man was only a few years older than he. While he had two or three days growth, the cowboy was essentially clean cut with sandy hair and clear gray eyes. The eyes were bright and unyielding. Steady. The face was thin but not gaunt and overall had a cheerful aspect to it.

"How would you know that?" Jamie asked.

"Only guessing," came the reply. "But if I'm right, and if I were you, and it was getting past my dinner time, and I was wondering where I would be sleeping tonight, I don't think I'd just sit and wait."

"Is that right?"

"Yep."

"What would you do?"

"Well," started the cowboy, revealing just a hint of a grin, "since you asked, I think I'd be pumping everybody in sight to find out if they'd seen my man, my meal ticket."

Jamie didn't look the cowboy directly in the eyes. He kept his own eyes moving.

"Like anybody in Flag is going to know an employee of the Free-men Foundation."

"You might be surprised," answered the cowboy.

"I doubt it."

"There's only one way to find out."

"And that would be?"

"Ask."

Jamie wiped his brow with the back of his hand.

"Do you know anybody who works for the Freemen Foundation in Flag?"

"Yep."

"Who?"

"Well, there's you." The cowboy nodded with half a smile. "And me."

That startled Jamie.

"You're the guy?"

"Yep."

"You don't look like a businessman."

"I'd bet there are a few who would surprise you."

"You're the person who's supposed to meet me?"

"I'm the guy," said the cowboy, grinning and extending a hand. "Chad Rowley. I'm glad we finally got to that," he said. "I'm hungry, and the prospect of sitting here all night waiting for you to make your move wasn't pretty."

"Why didn't you just tell me who you were an hour ago?" Jamie's voice was raised and had a definite edge to it.

The cowboy paused before answering, as if choosing his words carefully.

"Who do you want to be responsible for your comfort and happiness? You or me?" he asked.

Jamie pursed his lips as he exhaled.

"Let's get something to eat." The cowboy rose and started across the parking area. "We've got lots of time to discuss the finer points of personal responsibility."

Jamie hoisted his duffel and followed along, not a little confused at seeing that there was no car, van, bicycle, or other means of conveyance in the direction the cowboy was heading. The two walked side by side along Fort Valley Road leading north out of town.

* * * * *

Around the corner, just out of sight, a silver-gray Mercedes sedan with tinted windows waited in the dimming afternoon light, its engine running.

THREE

Next morning, Jamie awoke from a deep but troubled sleep. For several minutes he sifted through the remaining fragments of the night's dreams before he was awake enough to remember where he was. The smell of frying bacon finally pulled him back into the world.

A lump in the musty mattress reminded Jamie that he lay in an upper bunk on the back porch of the Bitter Root Trading Post in Gray Mountain, Arizona. The ceiling was low. As his eyes blinked open, he saw a hornet's nest the size of an orange only inches above his head, anchored to the exposed rafter. He hadn't seen it when he tumbled into bed during the early morning hours. Now he rolled carefully away to avoid disturbing the nest or the hornets that were milling around the opening.

As he tried to sit upright, he accidentally banged his head on the low-hanging rafter, setting off vibrations that stirred an unwanted flurry of activity among the hornets. In a heartbeat, a hornet attacked, stinging Jamie on the bridge of his nose. Jerking back reflexively, Jamie banged his head again. During the resulting flurry, he was stung twice: once on the forearm as he flailed to keep the insects away from his face, and once on the back of his neck.

In his effort to escape, Jamie rolled off the upper bunk. Trying to right himself as he fell, he barely managed to land on the side of one foot and crashed into a stack of empty cardboard boxes piled against the opposite wall. Fending off a cascade of falling boxes and fearing further attack by the hornets, Jamie finally came to rest on the uneven floorboards. The stings throbbed, and his eyes watered. He was light-headed and disoriented but definitely awake.

He gazed around to see if anyone had witnessed his ordeal and was relieved to see that he was alone. The lower bunk, where his traveling companion had spent the short night, was empty.

Jamie was still in his business attire. His pants and shirt were now rumpled and soiled from a long, dusty walk, a ride in the bed of a pickup truck, and a restless night on a dirty mattress.

As he rose to his feet, he remembered the two painful blisters, one on the heel of each foot. The events of the previous evening came back to him with painful clarity. His dress loafers had been new when he left home the day before. He and Chad had walked the better part of twelve miles along the dusty shoulder of Highway 89 before hitching a ride that brought them to the trading post.

Jamie was famished. The back door was open, so he went in, looking for the cowboy.

"In here," came a woman's voice.

The hallway led to a kitchen where he found a burly trader in western-cut clothing and a turquoise bolo tie, a woman, and Chad all seated around a kitchen table. Chad introduced the couple as old and dear friends.

Though the outside of the trading post had appeared shabby the night before, the kitchen was comfortably decorated with up-to-date appliances, an earth-colored tile floor, a large skylight in the ceiling, and a dozen hanging plants. The kitchen and living quarters behind the trading post were kept comfortable by a swamp cooler.

"Did the alarm clock finally go off?" chuckled the trader.

Jamie knew he was a sight. The trader's wife, Rita Carlson, showed Jamie to a bathroom where he could wash up. He returned to a hearty breakfast. Mrs. Carlson was generous with her helpings. She appeared to be a simple woman but very pleasant.

Chad visited quietly with Richard Carlson, and Jamie could hear only bits of their conversation. The Carlsons were kindly and hospitable people who had kept a trading post for many years, now hiring help to do most of the work.

Though the morning had started out poorly, the hour or so that Jamie and Chad spent with Richard and Rita Carlson gave Jamie's spirits a tremendous lift. He didn't want to leave.

"We'd better be on our way," Chad announced. Jamie was still in his stocking feet. He dreaded the ordeal of putting on his shoes.

"You folks have been very generous with us," said Chad. "There's one more favor we'd like to ask. My companion here didn't come too well prepared to enjoy his walk across northern Arizona, and I think his feet are hurting him a little. Would you have anything in the way of boots that might make the trip more enjoyable? Don't have to be anything fancy. I think we could find some way to repay you."

Richard fixed Jamie up with a pair of used but very serviceable boots, a pair of Levis already broken in, a long-sleeve western shirt, and a hat with several years' experience. All fit the young traveler, more or less.

When Rita had doctored the blisters, Jamie found that he could walk in reasonable comfort. They made arrangements to leave his duffel with the couple, promising to come back and get it later. Rita handed Chad a big sack lunch and gave Jamie two liters of bottled water to carry.

Jamie walked away from the Bitter Root Trading Post dreading the day ahead. He knew that if he had a ride back to Winslow, he'd take it in a heartbeat. In fact, he might even consider walking if he wouldn't have to face his mom and explain why he failed at his first real job.

FOUR

Gwen Fong seldom ate out. When she did, she tried to avoid Chinese food. It was widely known that Gwen had been born and reared in Hong Kong. Acquaintances who invited her to dine out naturally assumed she would prefer the fare from her native land. However, since few Chinese restaurants serve authentic Cantonese food, Gwen generally preferred to cook for herself.

In fact, she was battling a ferocious case of heartburn brought on by a luncheon at the Seven Seas, an inexpensive oriental restaurant near corporate headquarters in Brampton, a Toronto suburb. In a moment of weakness, Gwen ordered a plate of General Tsao's chicken. She hadn't specified the seasoning. The plate came extra spicy. Not wanting to attract undue attention to her displeasure, she ate some of it as she shared plates with others around the table.

Now she was paying for it. She had already chewed a fistful of antacids and still wasn't out of the woods. As executive secretary to the Chief Financial Officer (CFO) of Fletchner International, she was preparing copies of the preliminary year-end report emailed to her just minutes earlier from the comptroller's office. Two assistants were binding the reports in expensive, embossed covers while she recorded in a classified control log the number of each copy and the name of the board member who would receive it. The email transmission had come to her with a single-use password in print-only mode. That meant she could only open the file once. She couldn't save it to her computer's hard drive.

Having worked in the office for nearly three years, she wasn't surprised at the level of corporate security imposed. Though the corporate offices functioned under an impenetrable umbrella of secrecy, Gwen knew that the worldwide Fletchner enterprise owned huge assets. Because the parent company was not publicly traded, it enjoyed a degree of privacy uncommon among other companies its size. The incessant pressure and attention to detail imposed on employees were part of the cause for her stomach discomfort.

I must be getting an ulcer. Lucky me!

The intercom on Gwen's phone buzzed. "Yes, Mr. Stanley?"

"Miss Fong, get Reinhold Paul in Frankfurt for me on a secure line. While I'm talking to him, bring me my copy of the report." He hung up without waiting for a reply. A reply wasn't necessary since Stanley's instructions were never negotiable.

Gwen dialed the international call from memory as she invariably did. Then she stepped into the adjoining office where her assistants Charlotte LeMans and Mark Hart were busily assembling the reports.

"Attila wants his copy right now," she announced.

Mark swore. "Give us five minutes," he replied.

"Make it three."

Mark swore again.

"How long have you worked for Fletchner?" Gwen asked.

"Eight months."

"Starting to feel some burnout?"

Mark hesitated. "I'm not sure I want to talk about it."

"I understand."

Charlotte had left the room. Mark looked around cautiously as he continued to work.

"The pay is great," he said. "The perks are generous. But the treatment is just short of abusive. Sometimes I think it's not worth it. I can go anywhere and get this kind of abuse."

Gwen laughed as Charlotte returned. On top of the raging heartburn, the constant pressure from her boss, and a thousand other annoyances plaguing her at the moment, Gwen was fuming over Charlotte. Charlotte was involved with someone high up in the organization.

Don't ask me how I know. It couldn't be more obvious if she had it stamped on her forehead.

It's not that Gwen hated Charlotte or wished her ill. In fact, she felt some sympathy for Charlotte. Still, she was suspicious and somewhat fearful of Charlotte. Gwen knew that women who sleep with their bosses can't be trusted any more than the bosses can. Their adulteries predispose them to find and exploit weaknesses in others. Their inside link to wealth and power, no matter how tenuous, awakens greater ambitions. They become increasingly indifferent to the mangled bodies of those whom they use on their way to the top.

Gwen knew, therefore, that her own behavior in the office must be impeccable. Any infraction, however small, could provide the necessary fuel to launch the career of a mistress within the company. And Gwen's passion for her own cause dictated extreme caution. The stakes were high. Only constant vigilance would save her.

"Here's Mr. Stanley's copy," said Charlotte, too sweetly, as she delivered the freshly bound report. Then, as though it were an afterthought, she asked Gwen, "Where are you going on your vacation?"

"I'm going hiking in the Rockies." Gwen had hesitated too long, she was sure, while deciding how to answer.

"Oh, I love that," Charlotte continued. "Over near Waterton?"

Great. How do I get out of this conversation before it gets going?

"No, I'm staying with friends in Colorado," Gwen said, telling the truth.

"Too cool! Near Boulder? My boyfriend and I climbed Longs Peak last summer. It was a blast," Charlotte persisted. "Flying or driving?"

"Flying," Gwen answered as she rose from behind her desk. "I'd better take this report in to Mr. Stanley."

She moved toward Mr. Stanley's door across the hall, leafing through the copy to ensure that it was assembled properly. She could feel Charlotte's gaze as she walked away.

I've got to do something about that girl. A little time in the mailroom might be good for her career.

* * * * *

Gwen was still away from her desk when Mark and Charlotte finished binding the reports. Mark transported the booklets to the boardroom on a rolling cart, as instructed, leaving Charlotte to shred the throwaways.

Instead of starting the cleanup, Charlotte looked around to be sure she was alone and then began sifting through the discard reports. In a few minutes, she assembled a balance sheet and income statements showing the operating contribution of the major subsidiary companies. From a tiny pocket in the lining of her skirt, she extracted a storage card compatible with the digital camera Gwen kept in her office. Hastily, Charlotte took the camera from the drawer, inserted the card, and turned on the power switch. While the camera booted up, she arranged the discarded sheets on the worktable. She photographed them quickly at full zoom.

Having accomplished her task, Charlotte tossed the data sheets back into the discard pile and extracted the chip, replacing it in the hem of her skirt. Then she stepped to the work counter and took the staples out of an electric stapler, tossing them into the trash bin and making sure they fell out of sight to the bottom. Grabbing a wiping cloth, she hurried to Gwen's office, cleaning and replacing the camera. She was just leaving the office as Gwen returned.

* * * * *

Gwen blocked the door. Though she was much smaller than Charlotte, physical size meant nothing at the moment.

"What are you doing in my office?" Gwen asked directly.

"The stapler in the work area was out of staples, so I borrowed yours. I hope that was all right," replied Charlotte innocently.

Gwen knew it was a lie but was unsure how to answer. She knew that Charlotte was up to something and didn't want to give her a chance to clean up after herself.

"I see." Gwen stalled for time, considering her next move. "Please go up to the boardroom and make sure Mark has everything he needs."

"Sure, just let me finish my cleanup in here. I haven't shredded yet." Charlotte pushed past her and headed for the work area.

"I'll take care of it," said Gwen. "If we can get the boardroom prepared, you and Mark can get out of here on time this evening."

"Sounds good to me," said Charlotte. "But are you sure you don't want both of us present while you shred?"

Gwen knew well that the company policy required two employees to be present when financial documents were shredded.

"Of course, you're right," Gwen replied after thinking about it. "It's policy. Let's do it."

Together they gathered and shredded the discard pages and cleaned the area. The work proceeded quickly. Gwen was only able to glimpse the income statements. She knew she could recall at least five or six names of subsidiary companies. But there were many more that she couldn't read without appearing to be too interested.

They finished the shredding and entered the copy counter totals into the log. Gwen dismissed Charlotte and waited in her office for Mark to return.

On top of the heartburn, Gwen fought to suppress a definite feeling of foreboding. She couldn't put her finger on the exact cause, but Mark's unexpected delay wasn't helping.

FIVE

Mark Hart sat in the corporate security suite seven floors above. He watched as the security specialists replayed a video taken by a concealed camera in Gwen Fong's work area. The video showed Mark and Charlotte copying, assembling, and binding the reports. The staff heard Gwen refer to Mr. Stanley as Attila. They saw Charlotte photograph the income statements and watched while Gwen and Charlotte cleaned up.

"Good work," the head of corporate security commended Mark. Known to her security forces as "JR," Julienne Rostetter was seasoned, bright, aggressive, and hard as nails.

"It looks like Ms. LeMans is our girl. It doesn't matter who her playmates are. The Chairman will be very interested in this."

"Keep an eye on Ms. Fong as well," JR said to Mark. "If I were a betting woman, I'd say she's not clean either."

* * * * *

When Gwen Fong reached the office the next morning, her stomach was feeling better. The offending food was long digested, but the heartburn had persisted late into the evening.

It must be an ulcer. It's a good thing I'm going on vacation. Maybe I can have a doctor look at it.

Gwen was early as usual and worked for nearly an hour before

Mark came in. Charlotte, though usually punctual, was late.

She must have been out with a "friend." Gwen scolded herself for being catty.

Mark rushed through the door, his coat over his shoulder, and sweat evident on his forehead.

"Did you run up the stairs?" Gwen quizzed him. "Or are you being chased by a meter maid?"

Mark didn't answer. He stopped directly in front of Gwen's desk.

"Have you heard the news?" he asked breathlessly,

"What news?"

"Charlotte was killed in an auto accident last night. They think she missed a turn and drove her car into the river." He waited for a response that didn't come.

Gwen sat stunned and felt a wave of sorrow wash over her.

Someone should have warned the poor girl that powerful people have powerful enemies.

SIX

In the days that followed their visit to the Bitter Root Trading Post, Jamie Madero and his guide, Chad Rowley, fell into a tolerable routine. By a combination of walking and hitchhiking, they made their way northeast across the heart of the great Navajo reservation. The days were scorching. The two men took their water intake seriously, staying close to water or keeping water with them. They generally ate only at breakfast and in the evenings. As evening approached, they searched for shelter. If they couldn't find a Good Samaritan willing to put them up for a night, they located the cheapest room for rent.

They did their best to stay clean and presentable. Often those who put them up would let them shower and shave and occasionally wash the only clothes they owned.

It was a small thing, but as Jamie's blisters healed, he realized how valuable his boots were. They fit perfectly, and time showed that they were made of excellent leather that softened as it was worn. He now understood that Richard Carlson had given him a very expensive pair of boots.

The travel was no picnic for either of the men. Jamie blamed much of the discomfort on Chad. Jamie's experiences with the Freemen Foundation so far were totally different than anything he had expected. Still, there wasn't much he could do about it while they were on the road. His dark and sullen moods made communication difficult. Consequently, the pair walked for long periods in silence.

"Tell me about your family," Chad said.

"What do you want to know?" Jamie didn't much want to indulge Chad's attempts at being social.

"Do you have parents?"

"A mom. My parents divorced a long time ago. I only remember seeing my dad a few times."

"Marriage didn't work for them?"

"No. They came from totally different backgrounds. Dad's family is Catholic. Mom's is Mormon."

"Mormons and Catholics can get along," Chad said.

"Not in the same house."

"Any siblings?"

"My sister, Angie."

"Older or younger?"

"Are you writing a book?" asked Jamie.

"Nope. We just have a long way to go. Talking takes my mind off my aches and pains."

"Why are we walking? What's wrong with riding? Or flying?"

"I can't answer that right now," replied Chad. "This is the way the Foundation works."

"Stupid."

"The Foundation's paying you for this."

"Not enough."

"It'll work out."

"Right."

"So?"

"So what?"

"So older or younger?"

"Too young for you," Jamie answered.

"I'm not looking for a girlfriend." Chad laughed.

"She's younger. Two years."

"I understand you've got a little schooling under your belt."

"How do you know?"

"It was on your application."

"Oh, yeah. Almost two years."

"NAU?"

"Yeah."

"Have a major in mind?"

"Journalism."

"Your sparkling personality will make you a sure success in a media career."

"I'm smart enough to recognize sarcasm, thanks."

"No offense intended. I'm just sparring with you."

* * * * *

By July 2, Jamie and Chad had walked and hitchhiked about 235 miles in ten days. To Jamie it seemed like a lifetime. He could tell that life on the road was changing him. His constant exposure to Chad was beginning to influence the way he thought. In subtle ways, Jamie unintentionally began to model himself after Chad's mannerisms.

"What makes us any different from transients who go around living off handouts?" Jamie asked.

"We're just learning a few lessons here," said Chad. "Learning to read other people. Learning to trust our own abilities to survive. Making a few new friends. Believe me, as we get going, we'll earn our keep."

Late that afternoon, they passed the Cortez-Montezuma County Airport just south of Cortez, Colorado. It was a cloudless day. The temperature was in the high nineties even at Cortez's higher elevation. Neither doubted that the large western hats saved them from the relentless sun. The walk had been especially unpleasant, and Jamie was again in one of his foul moods.

They walked north with the traffic. Chad's head was down, as though lost in thought. Jamie glanced up just in time to see a silver-gray Mercedes sedan with tinted windows and California plates pass by. The sedan seemed to slow somewhat but then continued on.

"Recognize that car?" Chad asked, raising his head but not glancing behind them at the receding sedan.

"Don't think so. Nice car," said Jamie.

"Yeah, sure is."

The walk into Cortez took nearly an hour. In addition to his general irritability, Jamie sensed that Chad was preoccupied with something. Occasionally glancing over his shoulder, Chad explained the remainder of their journey.

"If we should get separated," said Chad, "there are a couple of things you may want to remember."

"Why would we get separated?"

"Probably won't," replied Chad. "But it never hurts to be prepared. Do you think you could pick these eyes out in a crowd?"

Chad stopped and looked Jamie directly in the eyes.

"What are you talking about?" Jamie asked.

"I just think it's wise to know who your friends are," replied Chad. "Do you see a black bar at one o'clock in my left eye?"

Jamie looked closely. The eyes were steel gray. Very clear and very bright. But after Chad mentioned it, Jamie saw a band of black pigment extending from the pupil through the iris to the white at about the one o'clock position in his eye. Jamie had never noticed it before, but it was very distinct when viewed up close. The right eye was perfectly clear.

"I see it."

"Study it carefully. It's sort of like a finger print," continued Chad. "You can always recognize me by that eye print."

During their days together, Jamie had recognized Chad's basically cheerful disposition. Chad tended to be light; he was often humorous, seldom sarcastic, and usually looked for the best in each situation. His serious tone now was in such contrast to what Jamie had become accustomed to that Jamie didn't quite know how to react.

"If for any reason we should get separated," Chad continued, "I want you to go to Telluride. It's about 100 miles up Highway 145. It used to be an old mining town, but it's a resort town now. Very nice place. You'd enjoy it there. If we get separated, I'll meet you at the Telluride post office."

All of this was said very matter-of-factly, as one person might say to another if they were parting in a shopping mall.

"Got that?" Chad asked. "Remember, Telluride!"

All this talk of separation did little to lift Jamie's already slumping mood.

On the outskirts of Cortez, they stopped at a convenience store not unlike the one where they had first met. Chad made a call at the pay phone, one of the few left in town. Then they visited the restroom. Chad seemed anxious and hurried to get them on the road again.

Jamie, being in a contrary mood, intentionally dragged his feet. Shortly after leaving the convenience store, they passed a little hamburger stand, a mom and pop operation where customers stood at the front window to place an order and waited while the burgers cooked. A faded product poster in the front window showed a burger with onions, lettuce, and tomatoes.

Jamie stopped to look. He longed for a burger with fries and a shake. They had been traveling for nearly two weeks, living about as sparsely as Jamie could imagine. He was terribly hungry. His Levis hung loose on his hipbones, and he was sure he'd lost fifteen pounds while traveling. Even though he knew they were on their way to find some dinner, he had to eat.

"Let's get a burger," he demanded. "I'm starving!"

Chad glanced from Jamie to the hamburger stand with a look of understanding but shook his head.

"Come on, Bud. I have a friend here in town. His wife is a great cook. She makes great pork chops, smothered in a cream sauce, topped with broccoli and cheese. Terrific! When you tie into one of those pork chops, you'll forget you ever heard the word *hungry.*"

But Jamie was not going to be put off easily.

"Is that who you tried to call back at the convenience store?"

"That's them," replied Chad.

"Were they home?" pressed Jamie.

"I'm sure they'll be there before long."

"Yeah, well, I'm hungry now. Let's get a burger. I could eat a hundred of them and still eat her pork chops."

"We'll be better off if we just keep walking. They only live a few blocks from here." Chad was visibly nervous about this delay.

"I'll make you a deal," pleaded Jamie. "Call again. If they're home, we'll keep walking. If nobody answers, we get a burger. Come on, I'm starving." He was talking so loudly that bystanders turned to look.

"Just take my word for it," Chad tried once more. "We need to keep moving. This isn't a good place for us to stop."

"No!" Jamie shouted. "I've had it! I'm tired of you making all the decisions. I'm tired of being hungry. I'm tired of—I'm just tired—and hungry. Come on. Please?"

Chad gave in with a gesture of resignation. They stepped to the window, and Jamie ordered his meal.

"I'll pass for now," said Chad when his turn came.

"Oh, man! You're something else," Jamie groaned, turning away to sit at one of two picnic tables just in front of the little stand.

"I'm not letting you ruin this for me. I'm going to eat it and enjoy it."

"Sounds good." Chad slowly sat beside him.

They spoke little as they waited for the burger and fries to cook. When delivered, the food was everything Jamie had hoped for. The fries were sizzling hot, the shake frosty, and the smell of the burger made his mouth water.

Jamie was just putting the first fry into his mouth when a battered pickup truck pulled up to the curb. Two surly characters stepped out and started toward them. If their appearance wasn't intimidating enough, one of the men was smashing a fist into his cupped hand, as though warming up for action.

"Uh-oh," moaned Chad. "I think we've got company."

Jamie looked up just in time to see the silver Mercedes pull up behind the truck. Without hesitation, Chad sprang to his feet and darted across the adjoining parking lot, dodging cars and pedestrians. One of the ruffians was after Chad before Jamie could react. The other sauntered over to Jamie.

"Stand up, kid!" he commanded.

Jamie rose unsteadily but couldn't turn to face his assailant because his legs were pinned by the attached bench of the picnic table at which he sat. He stepped over the bench awkwardly. His knees were trembling.

The man was Anglo, had a thick neck like a football player or Saturday night wrestler, and wore dirty jeans and a soiled T-shirt that showed off his expanding middle. Not a friendly sight. Jamie found that he could not even swallow.

"You should have never left Mexico," the thug sneered at Jamie.

In a flash, he drove a fist into Jamie's stomach just below the sternum. The blow came so unexpectedly that Jamie made no move to deflect it. He felt a sudden searing pain as all the air was driven from his lungs. He was sure that the fist went completely through him and struck his backbone from the inside.

Doubling over and clutching his stomach with his hands, Jamie couldn't even take a breath. He felt himself strangling as his whole body reacted with convulsive shock. Tears rushed from his eyes. He couldn't move. It was as though his feet were rooted in place.

The attacker stood there, watching Jamie struggle for breath. He walked away with a deep and disdainful laugh.

As soon as he could draw some air into his lungs, Jamie sat slowly on the bench behind him. He didn't know anything about what was going on around him. His entire focus at the moment was on breathing.

"You all right?" asked a male voice. Jamie eventually became aware of a person sitting beside him.

Jamie couldn't answer. So he shook his head.

"You took a pretty nasty shot. I don't envy your buddy, either. Doesn't look like a picnic for him." The man had emerged from the hamburger stand. Jamie figured he was the owner.

Jamie still couldn't speak, though he was at least beginning to catch some breath.

"Want me to call the cops?" the owner asked.

"I don't know," gasped Jamie. "I think I'll be okay. Who were those guys?"

"I have no idea," replied the owner. "Nasty bunch, though. I'd say the dude in the Mercedes was directing the action."

"Did you see him?" Jamie asked with difficulty.

"Yeah, he stepped out of the car for a second," replied the owner. "Fancy dresser. Black pants, black shirt, white tie. Hair slicked back in a ponytail. Wearing silver cuff links. He drove off in the direction where your friend and the two goons disappeared. I saw everything. Be glad to tell the cops."

Jamie sat for several minutes in stunned silence while he regained his composure. He was confused by what had happened. He knew he should go to Chad's rescue, but he didn't think he could catch them—and he didn't know what he would do if he actually *did* catch them. All he really knew for sure was that he didn't want to be sitting in the same spot if the attackers came back looking for him. At length, he gathered his few belongings, the uneaten burger and cooling fries, and fled. He didn't know where to go. But he knew he was going to put as much distance between himself and the attackers as he could.

SEVEN

I am most pleased," said the Chairman of Fletchner International, "that you and your team of professionals have intercepted and blocked a move by traitors in the organization to take over, shall we say, vital components in our corporate mix."

Julienne Rostetter watched the Chairman pace along the windows in his corporate suite looking south toward downtown Toronto. She recognized with deep discomfort that the Chairman's corporate jargon was another way of saying that an industrial thief had been caught red-handed and her convenient death had solved a problem for the organization.

"The LeMans girl was a fool," said the Chairman. "She probably wasn't bright enough to know that she was just being used. But if the information she was stealing had fallen into the wrong hands, one of our inner circle could have stolen vital company resources and maybe could have taken over a segment of the business. We couldn't allow that. LeMans was an unfortunate pawn in the game.

"You effectively blocked the move. My only regret is that we had to act so quickly. I would have liked to watch LeMans for a while—the little snitch might have led us to her benefactor. An earlier warning would have been helpful."

Julienne watched the Chairman retuck the back of his dress shirt snuggly inside his waistband, always careful to maintain his impeccable appearance.

You're smart, Mr. Chairman. Dangle the big praise out there, but always pull some of it back to keep an underling on her toes.

The Chairman fascinated Julienne. She knew him to be one of the richest and most powerful men in Canada—perhaps on the entire continent.

While she didn't find him attractive in any physical sense, she did admire his ambition and drive. He was also gifted at making money—vast sums of money. She often thought of him as the Donald Trump of Canada, realizing that a key difference between the two men was that the Chairman was careful to keep a low public profile.

"Art is a good man with a brilliant future," said the Chairman, referring to one of Julienne's subordinates. Art Warnock headed the Internal Security Division, responsible for safeguarding company assets, both material and intellectual, including the Chairman himself. The Chairman had recruited Art personally and sometimes dealt directly with Art, bypassing Julienne.

"I know you don't like Art, Julienne. I admit that he's little more than a gangster. I spend millions annually to buy the best security tools money can buy. Art doesn't know how to use them. He still rules with a .44, so to speak. If I wanted to kill every thief in the organization or wipe out every competitor, we could pave the streets with bodies. But I don't want them killed. I want them bought, won over—or compromised. We need to know what they know. We need to know *whom* they know.

"This is not the Mafia. We are not hoodlums. This is a business," continued the Chairman. "Information is the key. That's why I need you. You're smart. You're shrewd. You cover every inch, dot every 'i,' and cross every 't.' You don't have to solve every problem with a gun. I like that. Just don't go soft on me. You've got a great record. Keep up the good work and try not to count the losses, only the gains."

JR knew she was giving into one of her weaknesses by letting the Chairman sweet talk her. She saw through the thin veil of praise to the potentially deadly criticisms that lurked behind it. It was obvious that the Chairman had not trusted her to resolve the matter of Charlotte LeMans's theft, so he had turned it over to Warnock and his goons. Of course, JR would not have killed the girl. She'd have used those brains the Chairman was paying her for to find another way.

You've made a huge mistake, Mr. Chairman. You will pay for that.

Still, Julienne craved the Chairman's praise. She used it to vindicate herself and her decisions. She knew he probably discussed her defects in his conversations with Art Warnock. But she loved the thrill of having the upper hand, even if only for a moment.

"Stay in touch, JR," said the Chairman as he waved his dismissal.

* * * * *

Julienne gazed with satisfaction across the luxurious decor of her office in the security suite of the Fletchner International Building. She was a striking woman in her early forties. Though she was impressively feminine in both appearance and demeanor, neither she nor her office could be described as soft or frivolous. Rather, she exhibited a sleek elegance. She valued sharpness, crispness, and efficiency in everything around her. Seeing her in the surroundings of her office, it was easy to believe that she had always been photographed better in black and white than in color.

JR detested the male trademark golf mementos, sailing photos, shotguns, miniature sport cars, and pictures of the family complete with Irish setter. She found the upper crust with its good old boy network laughable, if not pathetic.

In fact, she detested most of the men she knew. They were self-serving and self-satisfied. Of course, they worked hard when they were young. She had long ago concluded that the masculine thing to do was to carve a niche for one's self in the company or industry, earn a name, feather the nest, and then sit back and enjoy it all. She couldn't count the number of business executives she knew whose energy and ambition were spent in a meteoric rise followed immediately by a flameout.

"Ms. Rostetter, Mr. Warnock is here to see you," reported her secretary.

"Give me five minutes and then send him in," JR replied, with an involuntary shudder.

By the time Warnock was shown in, JR was sitting at her computer terminal, reading the day's emails.

"You wanted to see me, JR?" Art asked, casually taking a seat in one of two overstuffed chairs facing her desk.

JR felt her blood pressure shoot up.

"Do you think you are so indispensable to this organization that you can sit in my presence without an invitation?" she drilled him.

Warnock locked his gaze with hers. He didn't respond and didn't move, addressing her with a half-insolent smirk.

"Get up!" JR shouted. "Until I tell you to sit."

As if considering his options and concluding that compliance was the best choice for the time being, Warnock slowly rose.

"Sorry," he apologized without sincerity.

But JR wasn't done. She wouldn't back down from this man. Wouldn't let his silent intimidation control her.

"You disgust me," she shot back at him unflinchingly. "I can't remove you, but I don't have to like you or what you do. Let me just make a suggestion: you may think you are the Chairman's pet, but just remember—those who grab up power in this organization ultimately become a threat to the Chairman. I've seen many of them come and go—or let me say, come and disappear.

"Now, sit down so we can get started!" she said after a pause. No profanity. No overt threats. Just JR's way of redirecting a person's attention. It could only be called castigation. She knew she couldn't frighten Warnock, but she could keep from becoming frightened by him.

"We have our fingers in pots everywhere in the world," she lectured. "When people get inside the organization and realize that they have potential access to Fletchner International's immense wealth, they naturally tend to want to dip into the bank. But the bank is closed. The bank is always closed, and we guard the vault.

"We have a great track record, but we can't afford any slips. And yet, so far this year, six people have managed to walk away from the company with potentially dangerous information. What do you have for me on these people?"

"We've looked into them all," Warnock responded with the same unyielding sneer. "Everything available on them. Four of them are typical thieves. Most have records of corporation hopping, carrying information to the highest bidder. We're on top of them. It will be a few weeks at most before we bring them in.

"Two of the six don't fit the pattern. The Rudman woman, the one who ran from a contractor in Manhattan last January hasn't resurfaced. No credit card expenditures. No car rentals. No airline tickets in her name. Nothing for over six months. We hired her through a headhunter. Career in international banking law. Never married. Speaks three languages. We found a Sarah Rudman at George Washington Law and at Bank One. But no record of her growing up."

He paused before proceeding. "Similar pattern for Chad Rowley, a short-term IS operative who walked away from the Phoenix field office in March. We've had a contractor out of California on him since. Tried to bring him in twice. He keeps appearing and disappearing. The contractor reported earlier this week that he had Rowley in his hand, but then lost him. He doesn't think Rowley will be easy to take and wants to bring back the body.

JR received Warnock's information with a grunt of disgust. "We don't want bodies! We want living, breathing, talking informants. This is a business, not a television show."

"We've compared all we know about these two," Warnock continued. "First, they weren't after salable assets. They seemed to be tracing corporate connections—mapping out the corporate network. Both were fairly new but had worked their way into secure positions. What puzzles us is the breadth of their contacts and their ability to disappear. Everybody has some vice that makes him or her easy to trace.

"I'd write them off as mavericks, except that there is a connecting link between them. The Mormon Church comes up somewhere in both of their profiles." He left the thought hanging.

"And your point is?" questioned JR.

"My point is that it may have something to do with their interest in the enterprise."

"How so?"

"I don't know. We're working on that. It just feels like more than coincidence."

"I don't see what religious affiliation has to do with industrial espionage," said JR. "Are you telling me the Mormons are trying to move into our markets? Not likely."

"I'm just saying," continued Art, "that when you find a thread, you follow it."

"Stay with it." JR rose to conclude the interview. "While you're at it, find out who else in the organization is Mormon. Get back to me as soon as you have something conclusive on any of our six thieves. I want to keep my eye on the scoreboard."

EIGHT

It was long after midnight. Jamie Madero walked alone. A waning moon was rising. He could see it occasionally through the tall pines as he followed the twisting road. He was grateful for the little light it shed on his surroundings.

He held the flaps of his coat closed in front of him to preserve precious warmth. He had found the old coat the day before, hanging from a fence post along the highway. He imagined some other traveler had left it. It was made of canvas and appeared to have once been a worthy coat.

The coat was thoroughly soiled with greasy stains along the collar and around the cuffs. The elbows were worn through. The lining was tattered. One of the large pockets at the waist had been ripped completely off. In the other pocket he had found some dirty tissues, a rusty pocket knife, eighteen cents, and a crumpled letter.

A girl named Kim had written it to her father.

Dad,

I hope you're OK. You said you were sick when you wrote that other time. We all miss you a lot. Even Mom said she thought it would be nice if you came to town for a while, but without your booze.

School just started. I'm in the ninth grade. It's really borrrrring. I guess it could be worse. Danny started the seventh grade. He's getting to be a snot. But I guess he's OK most of the time. Maya's still cute. She's a fun little sister.

We had to move again. That's hard, cuz then we have to change schools. But Mom said I could stay at JD Tanner Jr. High cuz I'll be going to high school next year.

Ron's not a good stepdad. He's really mean to Mom sometimes. I don't care if he's rude to me. But I can get really mad when he slaps Maya. Mom only stays with him cuz if they split she would have to give us up. That means foster homes. If we can make it until I get out of high school, I'll keep the other kids if I can.

I wish we could live with you. Please come back soon. I really love you.

Kim

Jamie was so discouraged by his personal circumstances and so homesick for his mom and Angie that the letter brought him to tears. He sat clutching the letter, sobbing for a long while. He refolded the worn letter and placed it back in the pocket of the coat. He felt guilty for depriving the owner of both the coat and the letter. But he didn't think the owner would return to claim the coat, and Jamie was definitely in need of it.

He walked along, thinking how need changes people. He would never have touched such a coat were it not for the fear of freezing. There was no telling where it had been, who had worn it, or what might still be living in the filthy fibers.

Jamie didn't know exactly where he was. Chad had told him to go to Telluride. Fortunately, the road signs along Highway 145 told him that the distance was more like seventy-five miles, not the expected hundred. Jamie thought he had covered about half the distance in two days—rather in two nights.

He had traveled at night because he was afraid. He had no idea who had attacked him and Chad. He didn't know who the man with the silver cuff links was or what he could possibly have against Chad. He still wasn't eager to meet his attackers again. But as the soreness in his chest and abdomen abated, it was replaced by growing anger. He had been wronged. He was not only hurt physically, but he also deeply resented the injustice and humiliation dealt him by the thug who hit him.

"Kid, you should have never left Mexico."

Jamie could still see the sneer and repeatedly heard his attacker's taunt. He doubted he'd ever see the man again. But if he did, he would be better prepared to defend himself.

His growing anger drove him on. Inwardly, the demand for justice overwhelmed his feelings of self-pity and the temptation to just turn around and head for home.

You're in trouble, he thought. *You're paying the price for your silly behavior and poor judgment. If you hadn't been so juvenile, this wouldn't have happened.*

Jamie rounded a bend in the road, no traffic in sight. He was walking up steep grades, approaching Lizard Head Pass, elevation 10,222 feet.

He stood alone in the dark, whistling wind, hugging himself for warmth. Never had he felt such aching emptiness. He couldn't stop. He couldn't go on. He prayed for help just to endure.

After some moments of indecision, he thought he saw headlights on one of the switchbacks below. Though he had been avoiding all traffic for nearly three days, he decided that he needed to take a chance on getting a ride. As the vehicle drew nearer, he walked to the edge of the pavement. He stepped out into the road, waving. He wanted to give the driver plenty of time to see him. The vehicle slowed to a stop. It was a flatbed truck with high tubular racking.

A cattle truck is just right for a guy in my condition.

Jamie watched the driver roll down his window. Clearly a rancher. He wore a full hat like Jamie's and spoke with a cigarette between his lips.

"What're you doin' out here in the middle of the night, boy? You're gonna freeze to death."

"This wind is pretty chilly. Could I get a lift? I'm trying for Telluride."

"Sure. Get in here!"

"Well, I probably don't smell too good. Could I just jump in back?"

"No, you couldn't jump in back. Get up here where the men ride. It don't matter how you smell. You can't have anything on you that I haven't had on me. Let's go. It's gettin' late. I got to be home in time to do my chores this morning."

As soon as Jamie sat down with the truck's heater blowing on him, he felt bone weary and sore all over.

"You okay?" asked the driver.

"I will be now. I sure appreciate this ride. You don't know how much."

"Well, now. People have to help each other out. Be a sad world if they didn't. You got a name?"

"Yeah, Jamie Madero."

"Nice name. Mine's Jake House. Short for Jacob."

And so the conversation went as they crossed Lizard Head Pass and headed down the other side. Jake was rough around the edges but good natured and generous. Jamie eventually lost the fight to stay awake.

A last thought passed through his mind as he dozed off.

Thanks for the cattle truck!

* * * * *

"Look, youngster, I'm sorry to drop you off here," said Jake. "Normally, I'd run you on into town, but my chores are waitin' on me, and I've still got a ways to go. I've enjoyed talkin' to you. Just a piece of free advice—if I was you, I'd try to find a place to wash up before you talk to anybody civilized. Take care!"

Jamie thanked him several times. He stood waving while Jake drove out of sight.

Following Jake's advice, Jamie left the Telluride road as soon as the sun was up. He found a hole in the San Miguel River where the rushing water slowed enough for him to wade out to his knees. Removing his boots, coat, and hat, he waded into the icy water. It was so cold that it hurt. His feet were numb in a minute. As quickly as he could, he washed his pant legs up to his thighs and then washed his hands, face, neck, and hair. He had no soap but cleaned himself as well as he could.

He had difficulty getting out of the water due to his numb feet. He sat on a rock and rubbed his feet to bring back some feeling. As soon as he could get his boots back on, he resumed his walk.

Jamie approached Telluride just as the morning sun crested the mountains to the east. He reached the post office as it opened at 9:00 a.m. and walked along the sidewalk once to see if by any chance Chad was around, not expecting to find him immediately.

There was no place to sit outside the post office. Jamie crossed the street and sat on a bench where he could see who came and went. He felt distinctly uneasy. He had tried hard to be invisible during his ordeal in getting to Telluride. Now he was out in the open where anyone who wished him ill could see him. On the other hand, he had to be visible so Chad could find him. He figured he was being watched.

Nearly an hour passed. Jamie had assumed the pose used by Chad on the day they met. With his hat pulled low over his eyes, he'd stretched out his legs and tried to appear as though he were sleeping. All the while, his eyes were in motion as he tried to take in as much of the scene as possible without moving his head. He watched especially for any sign of the silver Mercedes.

About mid-morning, three preteen girls approached from a nearby side street. They walked along, chatting about something of importance to them. As they passed Jamie, the girl closest to him dropped a piece of paper folded into a small square. It was heavy enough that it fell instantly to the ground right at his feet. The girls continued to walk as though nothing had happened.

Jamie dragged the note slowly toward him with the heel of his boot and picked it up. He stood, stretched, and turned down Colorado Avenue toward the filling station he passed as he came into town. He needed a restroom and wanted a secluded place where he could read the note.

He was shocked when he saw himself in the mirror. His hair was oily and unkempt. His beard was several days old. His clothes were filthy. He needed a shower in the worst way. But mostly, his black eyes had an intensity that he had never seen before. Just weeks earlier, he had known only the annoyances and discomforts of youth.

Now he knew what it was like to be stalked by fear, to go without sleep for several days, and to be weak with hunger. He had never been heavy, but now he was gaunt and hollow-eyed. He had to admit that he looked more than a little frightening.

He made sure he was alone, then extracted the note from his pocket. It was a half piece of lined notebook paper.

"Stay visible near the post office all day. Just after dark, meet me behind Nellie's Bakery."

There was no signature, only a crude drawing of an eye with a heavy line at the one o'clock position. Chad's eye print.

Jamie moaned. He had thoughtlessly left most of his money in the duffle at Gray Mountain two weeks earlier. He spent the little he had on his hamburger and shake in Cortez. Without Chad and with no way to buy food to sustain him, Jamie had no way to satisfy his overwhelming hunger. He thought he had reached the low point of his existence in the middle of the night before, but now he knew it was possible to go lower.

By the time darkness gathered over the tiny resort town, the temperature dropped again, and tourists hurried for shelter. Those out walking the streets were wearing jackets and long pants.

When Jamie judged the time to be about right, he stood, stretched thoroughly, and took a last look around. He walked slowly up the street toward Nellie's Bakery as though he didn't know where he would stay the night. He passed the bakery to the next cross street. Then he doubled back down the alley behind the buildings, pausing often to watch and listen. It was fully dark when he reached the back door. No one was there.

He noticed a sheet tacked to the back of the building near the door. Removing it, he stepped a few paces to a place where the street lamp out front cast back a shaft of light bright enough to read by.

"Wait here until you are contacted." The message ended with the same crude drawing of an eye with a line through the iris.

Jamie waited in the deep shadows. He could hear the traffic on Colorado Avenue, but no one ventured down the dark alley. He didn't see or hear anything to cause him concern. Nearly a half hour passed. Then, in the dark across the alley, Jamie heard the creaking of rusty hinges. An old shed the size of a large garage built of clap-boards stood at an awkward angle. The double doors were hung so as to swing outward on side hinges. The right-hand door was opening slowly, revealing a faint light inside. Jamie pressed back further into the deep shadows.

When the door was open enough to admit a single person, a girl looked out cautiously. She looked up and down the alley, then stepped forward. A second girl was behind her, carrying a flashlight with a handkerchief over the lens.

As the first girl stepped out into the alley, she accidentally kicked the shed door, and the sound reverberated within. Startled, both of the girls gasped. The girl inside hushed her friend, and both giggled. Then they stood silently as though waiting for something. Having gotten this far, they clearly didn't know what to do. Jamie could hear them whispering but couldn't make out what they were saying.

He knew he had to act. He didn't want to confuse or frighten the girls. He didn't think he could survive another day of waiting. He took one last look around to satisfy himself that all was clear before stepping out of the shadow.

What he saw made him freeze.

NINE

A ray of light from the street lamp on Colorado Avenue cast a shadow across the ground between Jamie and the open garage door—the shadow of a man standing partway between the street-light and Jamie.

No! Not now. Please don't let it be the guy with the cuff links.

Jamie couldn't tell from the shadow whether the man was facing down the alley in his direction or toward the street with his back to Jamie. He ached to race through the shaft of light and take refuge with the girls in the ancient garage. He wanted to get back to Chad and put the whole painful challenge that started in Cortez behind him.

I have to look. Can't afford to get caught at this point. If it's him, and he sees me, I'll be endangering the girls as well as Chad and myself.

Slowly, carefully, Jamie inched his way to the corner of the building and peered around the corner, gazing up the alley.

Dang! It's him.

Cautiously he sneaked another look to confirm his fears. Twenty feet up the alley, just off Colorado Avenue, stood a tall lanky figure. Jamie couldn't see facial details or tell much about the man's clothing. The man's back was toward him, at least for the moment. Jamie had only seen his enemy once, and even then only briefly. But there seemed to be no doubt that the man he now saw was the guy with the cuff links. Owner of the Mercedes.

Cufflinks.

Jamie cursed under his breath.

Cufflinks stood near the center of the alley, hidden from passers-by on the busy resort street. He smoked a cigarette, bringing the glowing weed rhythmically to his lips and then dropping it back to his hip as he exhaled his cloud of smoke upward.

Cufflinks was watching.

Jamie watched the watcher. He glanced back toward the garage that moments earlier had stood open. The door was now closed. No sign of the young girls.

Oh, no! Don't leave. Stay with me 'til I get past this gorilla. Please don't leave.

Once again, he peered toward the silent watcher but pulled his head back in alarm. He could see from the glowing arc of the cigarette that his pursuer was now moving in his direction.

Jamie groaned. With each passing minute, hope of getting to safety was waning.

Cufflinks came nearer. Jamie could hear him whistling lightly under his breath. He didn't dare look again but pressed back against the dark wall, wanting to become invisible. He prayed that the girls wouldn't choose this moment to open the squeaky door.

Cufflinks stopped almost exactly between Jamie and the garage. He lifted his head and dragged on his cigarette.

Jamie froze in place, hardly breathing. Afraid to blink.

After a seemingly eternal pause, Cufflinks turned back toward the street. Just as he did so, Jamie heard a muffled thud in the shed across the alley.

His heart stopped. So did Cufflinks.

Jamie knew if the girls were discovered, he would have to go to their defense. It meant a fight. He had no idea what his chances were against a man like Cufflinks. Was he armed? Could Jamie hold him off long enough for the girls to escape?

He braced himself, ready to spring.

Cufflinks took a step toward the shed and inclined his ear in its direction. He stood motionless for a full minute.

Cufflinks dropped his cigarette to the ground and crushed it with his foot. Taking another long look around him, he turned again and started slowly up the alley, away from Jamie and the girls.

Jamie felt faint. His knees shook as he leaned his head back into the wall and took a deep breath.

Allowing plenty of time for Cufflinks to gain some distance, Jamie gradually made his way to the corner of the building again and peered up. The alley was clear. No sign of his hated enemy.

Oh, thank heaven.

He stepped briskly through the light to the shadows opposite. Reaching the shed, he rapped gently, hoping he wasn't too late.

From within, he heard a tiny voice whisper, "Who's there?"

"Jamie Madero."

After another pause, the door began to move, opening slowly with a painful screech.

"Hi," said one of the girls. "We've been looking for you. Follow us."

They led him through the musty shed to the far corner, which was filled with scrap lumber and old crates. In the corner there was an open trap door. The girls started down a flight of steps below the door, beckoning him to follow.

The stairs descended about thirty feet in two flights. The walls were unfinished, carved into solid stone. When they reached the foot of the stairs, they were in a tunnel just tall enough for a man to stand. There were no lights. The tunnel was rough cut. It continued down a fairly steep incline. Every ten feet, ancient timbers supported the ceiling.

"This can't be safe," Jamie whispered. His two guides said nothing as they continued through the tunnel. He guessed their ages at about nine or ten years. It was too dark to really see their features.

They walked about twenty feet to where the tunnel opened into a larger shaft running crossways. Though Jamie had never been in a mine, he could tell that this was an abandoned shaft. The two girls turned right, and Jamie followed. Near as he could tell, they were now moving east.

Steel beams supported the ceiling of the shaft. He could tell that there had been electric lights in the shaft at one time; there were pieces of rail, mining tools, and equipment still lying around.

Jamie estimated that they walked no more than a hundred yards before the girls turned into a side tunnel on the right. They led him up a ramp like the one they had descended. Jamie's exhausted legs were like rubber, and his knees buckled as he climbed. When they reached the top, he found that they were at the bottom of another set of stairs, this time wooden. These eventually opened through a door into a cellar and up onto the back porch of a large Victorian home. The trio stepped immediately inside the house.

Jamie was suddenly in a different world. Though the home was likely a hundred years old, it had been fully restored. The floors were carpeted, the walls papered, and all the fixtures, furniture, and accessories reflected exquisite taste. Jamie could hear the sounds of diners in another room.

As soon as they entered, a handsome woman in her later thirties or early forties appeared. She was dressed in a long-sleeved, flower print dress that reached to her ankles. The shoulders were puffed, and the neck and sleeves were trimmed in simple lace. She wore an apron. Her hair was pulled back, with one or two rebellious wisps framing a pretty face. Jamie had the impression that she was in the middle of entertaining guests.

"Hi, Mom. We're back. This is Jamie Madero."

"Hello, Jamie," she extended her hand. "My name is Cherese. We've been waiting for you. You look like you could use a good meal and a warm bed."

"I'd be lying if I told you anything else." Jamie removed his hat and nodded a greeting.

"There's someone who wants to see you. Please come with me."

Jamie thanked the girls. They said good-bye and disappeared into another room, giggling and whispering excitedly as though they had just participated in a great adventure.

Jamie and his hostess climbed a set of stairs at the back of the house and walked along a hall with doors on both sides. Lettered on each door was the name of the room, "Aztec Room," "Cedar and Clover Room," "Columbine Room," and so on.

"This is very nice," offered Jamie. "Is this your home?"

"Yes," replied Cherese. "We operate it as a bed and breakfast."

That's just what I need. A bed and breakfast.

Cherese knocked softly on a door designated as the Aspen Room. Inside, Jamie heard a man's voice reply softly.

Cherese opened the door and moved aside so Jamie could enter. He stepped into a large bedroom, softly lit and furnished with a slowly turning ceiling fan and two queen beds. He could tell at a glance that the decor featured pine and aspens. It smelled wonderful, and the bed nearest the door was turned down invitingly. Jamie glanced to the other bed. It was occupied—by a man whose head and face were heavily bandaged.

"Hey, Bud," the man spoke with some difficulty. "Did you ever eat that hamburger?"

* * * * *

Out in the night, a solitary figure stood in shadow just off Colorado Avenue near Nellie's Bakery, speaking into a cell phone.

"The Mexican kid was met by a couple of girls. Can't tell you where they went, but I won't have any trouble finding the girls tomorrow. My guess is that he's meeting our boy here. Probably leave across the mountains."

He paused while listening.

"Seems like Rowley has contacts every place he goes," Cufflinks continued.

Again he listened. With a sinister glance toward Nellie's, he wrapped up the conversation.

"Rest easy. These are amateurs. Our boy's in the bag. His luck can't hold forever. But it would be easier for me and cheaper for you if we brought him back on ice."

TEN

Whoa, you're living close to the edge.
Sarah Rudman searched the street ahead, anxious to find an out—a doorway, a passing vehicle, some diversion that would allow her to disappear during a momentary distraction—away from the man tailing her. Actually, she wasn't certain that she was still being tailed. Months of covering her tracks and watching every move were beginning to wear on Sarah. Her vacation was approaching, and she knew how badly she needed it.

The possible tail was male, about forty-five. He wore dark glasses, a blue blazer, a red-and-white checked shirt, tan slacks, and boat shoes. All in all, he had the appearance of a leisure sailor. His hair was graying at the temples, and he carried a folded newspaper. He walked somewhat behind Sarah on the opposite side of the street, moving in the same direction along Seattle's Fifth Avenue near Seneca Street. His pace had matched hers since she exited the Rainier Building on an early afternoon lunch break. She had intended to hit the bagel shop a block and a half away for a quick bite and then return to work. She noticed him turn and walk in her direction as she exited the building.

You just broke rule number one, bozo. Never match pace with your prey.

She deliberately slowed, stopping briefly to inspect the contents of her clutch bag, as if to be sure that she had lunch money. Without looking in the direction of the tail, she noticed out of the corner of her eye that he had also adjusted his pace. He paused to glance at wares offered by a street vendor.

There goes rule number two. Never react to the prey's movements. Unless, of course, they're life threatening.

Sarah heard these words spoken in the voice of her father—the same gentle inflection, the same patient rhythm with which she had been schooled endlessly throughout her girlhood.

She resumed her pace until she reached the bagel shop. No easy avenue of escape had presented itself. Intending to return to work for the afternoon, she decided to carry through with her plans. She hoped that she was suffering from paranoid delusions or that, if this really were a tail, she would do nothing to reveal that she knew she was being followed.

Well, Skipper, I hope you're better at sailing than you are at spying.

She joined a line of lunchers at the order counter and looked back momentarily through the front windows just in time to see the Skipper disappear from view on the opposite sidewalk.

Okay. You got that one right. Never remain framed in view of your prey by a doorway, window, trees, or pillars. A framed object is always easier to distinguish from its background than an object in an open environment.

Sarah disciplined herself to eat at a leisurely pace while trying to determine if there was a back entrance to the store without actually going to the rear of the building to look. Seeing no possibilities there, she finished her lunch and left the same way she came in. She paused on the sidewalk, as if deciding which direction she would walk, and searched the street in both directions for any sign of the Skipper. Failing to see him, she walked back to work at a brisk pace, entering the building by the main entrance. She waited in the lobby while she counted to thirty, then walked back outside through the revolving door. It was a long shot. But she was rewarded for her extra caution. The Skipper was following her into the building on a fifteen-second delay.

Sarah had the clear advantage in this surprise encounter. She looked directly into his face for an instant and then let her eyes move beyond him as though she had no reason to notice him. She continued, without breaking stride, across the plaza and sidewalk.

The Skipper, on the other hand, reacted to the encounter by involuntarily raising the newspaper in his hand to shield his face from her view. He turned away without a clear destination in mind.

Sarah laughed to herself.

Oh, that has got to be embarrassing. You flubbed that, buster! Never react to being seen unless your life is being threatened.

However, as the cold reality of her situation set in, she admitted to herself that this was clearly a tail. A tail meant that her cover had worn thin and that she needed to make a move. The arrival of her new friend had to be related to the work she had done in New York City. Unfortunately, forcing the tail into an encounter removed any motive for further surveillance. The Skipper would now have to act. His options were abduction, violence, or breaking off the tail. She guessed that he probably wouldn't act until he contacted his client or handler. She didn't know if he was working alone. Scolding herself for acting so hastily—for forcing a showdown without making arrangements for her own escape—Sarah promised herself that she would remember this mistake. She would never make it again.

She now felt a rush of anxiety mounting within her. At moments like this, she always felt the desire to run. She had run to safety before and knew she could do so again if she had to. But at the moment, she worked to calm herself.

Running is the last resort. Only run when you have the advantages of speed and distance. To run and still fall into the hands of a pursuer only leaves you too exhausted to use other tools.

Standing near a bus stop, Sarah could still see the Skipper. He was talking on a cell phone, standing sideways to the scene so that he could monitor her movements. That confirmed her guess that he wasn't free to act until he checked with a handler. She now knew with growing certainty that going back to the office building was not an option. She would be at a disadvantage when she tried to come out again.

Never give your opponent control of the playing field. If you don't have a plan, keep moving while you create one. Force the opponent to react to your choices rather than giving him time to make choices for you.

She crossed the street in traffic, hoping a cab would come to her rescue. Reaching the other side, she turned to see the Skipper moving toward her. He was no longer shielding his face.

Uh-oh. He's got his marching orders. He doesn't care if I can identify him.

She knew there was no time to wait for a cab. Her pursuer was only sixty feet away across the street. He was close enough that she could see him clearly. His face bore an angry, vicious look—the face of a hunter.

Sarah discounted part of his bearing as the natural tendency of a predator. The idea was to intimidate a weaker prey, thereby robbing the prey of the ability to reason and forcing a fear response. She admitted her fear and cast a hasty glance in both directions for a safe haven.

A passing city bus held the Skipper at the curb for several moments and blocked his view of Sarah. With no avenue of escape in either direction, she instinctively turned the instant the bus passed between them. She threw the beige sweater she had carried over her arm around the shoulders of a passing female pedestrian. The woman squawked in surprise, turning to her left as Sarah disappeared to her right. The startled woman caused a small commotion among a group of passersby, some of whom may have seen Sarah and others who gestured about in confusion. In the melee, Sarah had two seconds to duck into a storefront. There was no way of knowing whether the Skipper had seen her enter the store. She only hoped that the commotion would distract him long enough for her to find an exit.

The instant she entered the store, she feigned a stumble and fell to the floor beneath the level of the street windows. Looking around, she realized that she had entered a tobacco shop.

Oh, great, Sarah. Couldn't you at least pick a place that had seen a woman in the last decade?

Two male customers watched in surprised silence as she crawled on her hands and knees around a self-standing display in the center of the sales floor. Blocked from view of the front windows, she rose to her feet and strolled confidently around the counter and through an open door bearing the sign *Employees Only*.

The elderly proprietor, a portly man with a near-white mustache and wavy frosted hair, followed her through the door calling, "Miss! How can I help you? Customers are not allowed back here."

"Please," Sarah pleaded once she was out of view from the front windows. "In less than a minute, a man is going to come through the front door. He's trying to kill me. Please help me!"

The kindly looking gentleman studied her for just a second or two and said, "I'll call the police."

"No, there isn't time. Please, go back. Distract him. While I go out the back way."

"There's an outside exit at the end of the hall," he replied, roused to action by the urgency in her voice. He turned immediately back into the store.

Bless you. I won't forget this.

As Sarah fled through the room, she could already hear a man's voice speaking in demanding tones out on the sales floor. She didn't pause to listen. Rushing toward the door, she grabbed a gray shop coat and a tan-colored straw hat from a coat rack.

I promise I'll bring these back.

She opened the door into an alley and looked for a way to get back into foot traffic immediately. Sliding into the shop coat as she jogged out to the street, she tucked her hair up under the hat. She was grateful she wore pants rather than a skirt.

Fortunately, the color match isn't that bad.

She paused briefly at the alley entrance to glance behind her and out along the sidewalk. Seeing no sign of the Skipper, she took up pace with a passing group of pedestrians and tried to vanish into the scene. Behind her, she could see the Skipper round the corner at the intersection only seconds later, searching the cross streets in both directions. Showing obvious signs of frustration, he stepped to the curb. A second later, a flashy red sports coupe pulled over to meet him. He slid quickly in, and the coupe turned the corner away from Sarah, merging into the flow of traffic as the Skipper and his handler likely searched both sides of the street for the elusive woman.

Knowing she was not safe on the street, Sarah walked a block before stepping into a thrift store where she bought two changes of clothes and a decent hat at bargain prices. She wore both changes out of the store, one over the other. She carried her own clothes, the shop coat, and the borrowed hat in a shopping bag.

She walked two blocks to a bus stop. She saw a bus approaching, so she slowed her pace to arrive at the stop just as the bus did. She stepped quickly on and moved to a seat away from other passengers. There she removed the outer layer of clothing and the hat, stuffing them under the seat.

She rode to Queen Anne and got off the bus several blocks from her apartment. She walked the rest of the way in a crisscross pattern, circling the blocks and doubling back, watching for any indication of a continuing tail. Once home, she called a friend who agreed to drive her down to SeaTac for an evening flight.

Sarah left the apartment just at dusk, carrying only a few items. She didn't intend to return. She was no longer Sarah Rudman. Her hair was now gray. She walked with a halting gait, dressed in matronly modesty. Her friend kissed her on the cheek and called her Mom as they walked arm in arm to the car at the curb. En route to the airport, the friend agreed to return the hat and shop coat. They bid each other farewell at the security gate—an affectionate parting of the daughter from her aging mother who boarded Delta 821, bound for Denver.

ELEVEN

When Jamie arrived in Telluride looking for Chad, he was exhausted and half-starved. However, a couple of good nights' rest in a real bed and a few hearty meals brought him nearly back to strength. He and Chad stayed at the Sunshine Bed & Breakfast for an entire week. Jamie enjoyed daily showers. His clothes were laundered. The bed was soft.

Because of his injuries, Chad couldn't move much at first and would not allow Jamie to go out into the town.

"We have friends out there looking for us," Chad said. "I think it's better for us if we let them look."

"Will you tell me what happened?" Jamie asked.

"Well, I was a little distracted and made one or two mistakes as we walked across Arizona. I underestimated how badly some former associates wanted to renew my acquaintance."

"Who are they?"

"I think the guy in the gray Mercedes works for my former employer." Chad coughed deeply. "Unfortunately, he's smarter than I gave him credit for. I guess he hired a couple of sales people to persuade me to go for a ride with him.

"I hoped I wasn't being too rude, but when I left you, I headed for the hills. I ran several blocks at top speed with one of these gentlemen right on my heels. He eventually got close enough to trip me up. We were in a little parking area just off the street between two stores. There were homes just across the fence. We wrestled around a little, and then his buddy came to the party. They worked me over pretty good. One of them kicked me in the side. That bruised my ribs. I think the other guy was trying to knock me out, but he couldn't hit me hard enough. He did manage to cut up my lips and black both eyes."

"Oh man," replied Jamie. "This was my fault. I wish I'd have been there to help."

"Not too much you could have done. These were pretty big boys."

"How did you get away from them?"

"In the end, my friend, Steve Allred, came to the rescue. Do you remember the man I told you about? The one whose wife cooked the pork chops? Steve's wife."

"I remember." Jamie had thought of those pork chops a thousand times as he walked along feeling his ribs bounce off his backbone.

"I know that sounds like a long shot," said Chad. "But when I could tell I was losing the argument with the muscle boys, I said a little prayer. Steve came. He almost ran the three of us over, tires screeching, horn blasting. He attracted a lot of attention from everyone within hearing distance. The two hired hands decided to wait for a return engagement and just walked away."

Chad coughed and doubled over, holding his ribs.

"Wow. Don't make me laugh. The worst thing is sneezing. Hurts the ribs big time."

"So?" asked Jamie.

"So?" replied Chad.

"So what happened next?"

"Oh—well it's a good thing the thugs moved on. Steve Allred isn't a very big guy, and I was in no shape to rescue my rescuer.

"The police came within minutes. I could still walk, and I couldn't pay for an ambulance ride. Steve drove me to the emergency room. They x-rayed me and bandaged me up. No concussion and no broken bones. But my shoulder was pretty badly wrenched, so they put me in a sling.

"We went back to the hamburger stand before we went to the emergency room, hoping to find you. The owner told us you had gone north. We searched for you most of the evening. Steve and Cynthia put me up for the night. Next day, Steve drove me to Telluride. We searched all along the way but couldn't see hide nor hair of you.

"I'd been recuperating at the Sunshine Bed & Breakfast for two or three days when you finally showed up."

"So how did Steve Allred know you needed help?"

"I asked him that. He didn't know I needed help. He left work a little early and was just driving home when he saw me losing a foot race. He turned around to see what was happening. By the time he located us, I was eating a knuckle sandwich. He thought he'd better break up the fun before somebody got hurt. Notably, me."

"Have you seen the Mercedes since the hamburger stand?"

"Nope. But that doesn't mean he isn't still out there. You can be sure he is. This guy won't give up. This is how he earns his living."

"What do they want from you?"

"I guess they think I have something that belongs to them."

"What would that be?"

"Information."

"Does this have anything to do with the Foundation?" asked Jamie.

"Probably."

"Could it happen again? If he won't give up, does that mean we'll see him again?"

"Probably."

"Can't you get a gun or something to defend yourself?" Jamie asked.

"No, Bud. That's not how the Foundation works."

* * * * *

Following their painful encounter with the opposition in Cortez, Jamie never looked back. He placed his trust in Chad's leadership. The nagging homesickness and resentment that he felt earlier in his pilgrimage no longer troubled him. In contrast to the strained relationship that marked their walk across Arizona, a real friendship grew between Jamie and Chad during the days in Telluride and on the long hike across Colorado.

The events in Cortez and Telluride now seemed like part of a distant memory. Jamie felt a sense of accomplishment as he and Chad approached Leadville. Their destination was a retreat center situated on eighty acres, stretching upward from a grassy meadow into the forested hills above.

A common building housed the center's offices and a dining hall. A couple of two-story dorms with open sleeping bays and modern bathrooms each provided lodging for up to sixty people. The structures reflected the rustic architecture typical of the area. Parking was located a quarter mile back toward the road to minimize dust. There were no hard surface roads or sidewalks on the property.

As Chad and Jamie strode into the common area among the buildings, only two people were visible. They were sitting just outside the door to the dining hall, peeling potatoes for dinner. As always, Jamie was hungry and looked for an opportunity to ask one of the cooks what time dinner would be served.

The cooks recognized Chad immediately and rose to greet him.

"Yo, Rowley, you finally made it!" exclaimed one cook who looked Chad's age but was taller. The two men embraced.

"Man, look what the wind blew in," said the cook to his companion.

"Kinda looks like you played your last game without a helmet," said the other, checking out the wounds still visible on Chad's face.

"Gentlemen, let me introduce our summer intern," said Chad. "Jamie Madero. From the great state of Arizona."

After many days feeling the need to always be alert and wishing he had eyes in the back of his head, Jamie felt like he was among friends for the first time. Sheltered from a dangerous world.

TWELVE

After dinner, Chad Rowley walked through the dorms, greeting the Founation associates as they arrived. The associates were divided into two groups. The couples and most of the older associates worked at what they called "arms-length" research. Most of their work was performed in offices, at libraries, or over the Internet.

A smaller group of mostly younger single associates performed inside or hands-on field research. They infiltrated organizations of interest and gathered information about the organizations' operations and contacts. They were employed by the organizations and performed legitimate employee functions.

All the associates referred to themselves as Insiders, a label that summed up their work and brought a sense of unity to the close-knit organization. Chad knew all the Insiders, some better than others. He was looking for one Insider in particular.

The sun had set over the high peaks to the west, and the evening light was waning. The air was cool, the smell of pine strong. Passing the upper end of the dining facility, Chad caught sight of an attractive blonde. She was heading for the women's dorm.

"Hi, 306. I hoped I might see you," he said.

"306? Do we know each other well enough to be so familiar?"

"Missed me, huh?" Chad grinned.

"Listen, Captain Marvel," she said, "I have a life. I don't wait for guys to come calling."

"Am I sensing that your fuse is lit?" asked Chad.

"You're sensing that I don't like to be managed. Especially from a distance. Especially like a puppet."

"I'm sorry," said Chad. "The transfer to Seattle was abrupt. We had an opening. We needed somebody inside the target organization. Seemed like a safe spot. We thought you might like a rest."

He waited. Sarah Rudman said nothing, just looked steadily into his eyes. Unblinking.

"Besides, Seattle can be beautiful," he added.

"When it's not raining," said Sarah. "But it's always raining in Seattle."

"Is that what's bothering you?"

"What makes you think anything is bothering me?"

"I can tell."

"Oh, you can tell. You think you know me that well?"

"Sweet. Even-tempered. Reasonable. Cooperative. Sure," he said, shrugging, "I can tell when there are ripples on the pond."

"You think you're so smart," said Sarah, a smile softening the lines of her face. "Well, let me tell you something, Einstein. I'll let you know when I need a rest."

"Okay," said Chad. "I get it."

"But I could use an assignment that lasts at least a year. Long enough for me to establish a normal routine. Maybe plant some flowers. Maybe find myself a boyfriend. Maybe get a regular hairdresser. Maybe have some mail delivered—my own mail."

"We thought Seattle could be that assignment," said Chad.

"Somebody found me in Seattle. I was being followed. I had to run. Again," said Sarah more seriously.

"Uh-oh. When did this happen?"

"Two days ago."

"Are you okay?"

"Of course I'm okay. I'm standing here, aren't I? Talking to you?"

Sarah paused, searching Chad's face. She reached a finger to the cut over his eye. Her gentle gesture caught him by surprise.

He flinched away. She dropped her hand.

"Did you think I was going to poke you in the eye?" She laughed.

"No," he said, reaching for her hand and guiding her fingers to the wound. "But don't be too tender with me. I spoil easily."

She laughed again.

Sarah traced the wounds on his face with her finger. Like many of his conversations with Sarah, this one held safely to the light side. Chad was familiar with this pattern. Sarah would warm to him. Then she'd back away. He'd tried talking openly about their relationship on past occasions. She got teary-eyed and pled for more time. He felt sure she loved him, but the mystery of her reluctance sometimes frustrated him. For his part, he'd wait forever, if need be, to have this woman's love.

"So we need to find you a new home?"

"If you still want me on the team," she said.

"Your tail in Seattle?" asked Chad. "Any idea who he or she might work for?"

"Not for sure. I didn't hang around to ask. My guess is that it goes back to Leopard."

Sarah had moved closer. Chad felt a charge of electricity.

"I worry about you," said Chad.

Sarah shook her head.

"I don't want you to worry about me," she said. "This isn't going to work if you start hovering over me. We're able people. We're involved in a good cause. What we're doing is important. We have to trust each other. It'll be okay."

"I can't help it," he said. "I don't want you to get hurt."

Sarah moved still closer. Their faces were only inches apart.

"I don't need a big brother. And I don't need another father," said Sarah. "I've already got the best. I need somebody strong who believes that I'm strong. Somebody who trusts me to come through."

Her lips moved to his, a space the thickness of a tissue separated them. Her open hands rested lightly on his chest. His hands went to her waist.

Chad blinked, then swallowed. Sarah's eyes searched him.

He pulled her to him.

At the instant their lips were to touch, Sarah turned away.

THIRTEEN

"That's a pretty classy outfit," said Chad Rowley to a middle-aged man dressed in exercise clothes.

The man wore a burgundy cotton sweatshirt emblazoned on the chest with a family coat of arms and the surname Gordon. The two men sat on cold metal folding chairs in a corner of the dining hall.

"How're your boys?" asked Chad.

"They're doing great," replied Jeff Gordon. "I was hoping they'd be with us for the week. But they both decided to stay at school for summer semester. I guess they're impatient to get on with their lives, careers, and whatnot."

"Sounds like they're following in your footsteps," said Chad. "Jason's at Cal Poly, right?"

"Yes. And Brett's at MIT. Both in engineering."

"You were Stanford?"

"Well, UC Irvine. Then Stanford for my MBA."

"Some pretty impressive credentials in the family."

"In truth, the smartest person in the family was Elise. When she passed away, the average IQ dropped dramatically."

"I'm sure that's not true. Anything new in Denver while I've been gone?" asked Chad.

"Things are going well. The only thing that's really new is a decision by the Foundation board to move our office to Port Townsend."

"Will that happen soon?"

"By the end of summer," answered Gordon. "We already own the property in Port Townsend. That'll help keep operating expenses close to the donations rate. That's always a good thing."

"It is. You don't think the Washington coast is too remote?"

"The facilities there are great. And it's important for us to stay out of the limelight. With today's technology, we could operate from anywhere and stay in touch. The only drawback is the long drive to SeaTac. We're looking at a helicopter for local trips and may consider opening a Seattle office."

"That sounds exciting."

Gordon inspected the deep laceration over Chad's eye and the extensive bruising still visible on his face.

"How are you feeling, Chad?" Gordon asked.

"Doing fine," answered Chad. "The incident was minor. I just hope it won't attract too much attention. We're on to something big here. It doesn't seem like a few cross words with the opposition should get in the way of our moving forward."

"It's hard to equate your injuries with a few cross words," said Gordon. "You're important to us—to me. Neither you nor any of our people is expendable. We've got to be careful. Are you aware of any other close calls?"

Chad paused.

"I talked to Sarah last night," he said. "She thinks she's being tailed and needs to make another move."

"How certain is she that they know her?"

"She was followed in Seattle. She hasn't had any direct contact with the opposition since she left New York. But I think we have to assume that they were able to trace her across the country. She thinks the people following her are contractors working for the Leopard."

"Have there been any overt acts, any threats of direct violence?" Gordon continued.

"She thinks her tail meant business."

"I'm sorry to hear that," said Gordon. "Some of these trends worry me, not the least of which is your being beaten. We need to be realistic in making decisions about our future steps."

Changing the subject, Gordon continued, "Jamie Madero seems

to be a likable young man. I had a nice visit with him last night. How did he do during your trip?"

"He did well. Giving him an extended trek experience by walking up here was a great idea. He seems to have matured a lot in that short time. In fact, after the scrape we got into at Cortez, he was on his own for a few days. I think the challenge has worked its magic on him. He's a bright kid. I've gotten attached to him."

"My brother said he was bright," said Gordon.

"I think he's right. Madero is gifted. But he was fairly petulant when we first connected. This internship is a good idea. I wouldn't count him out for the future."

"Dan has known Jamie since childhood. When he asked us to take Jamie on as a favor to him and Jamie's family, I just couldn't turn him down. I think he's counting on us to make a difference in Jamie's life."

"Sure. I understand. We'll have to see how it goes. For me, the big question is whether he's mature enough to make a contribution to our work. I think he needs to earn his way."

"Agreed."

Gordon glanced at his watch, rose, and stretched.

"Guess it's about time to start the morning. I wouldn't want to miss what comes next. You, however, had better sit this dance out. Get better. We've got important things for you to do."

FOURTEEN

Shortly before 6:00 a.m., twenty-six people gathered in the grassy area in front of the dining hall, dressed in a haphazard assortment of jogging and exercise outfits. They milled about in small groups, greeting one another with a mixture of good cheer and feigned resentment at being asked to assemble at such an unfriendly hour. The weather promised to give way to a typical, gorgeous midsummer day in the high Rockies.

"I think the women are faring worst," said the tall cook who had greeted Jamie and Chad when they first arrived the previous afternoon. Jamie still didn't know his name and was too timid to ask.

"It's cruel to make them show up in public without benefit of some serious in-front-of-the-mirror preparation," the cook said. "They look cold. You can tell by the glassy eyes."

Another young man with an athletic build stepped forward.

"Okay, rabble. Come to order. Time to pay our dues to the ultimate enemy—age."

"Morning, drill sergeant," called a bleary-eyed male without a smile.

Grunts and moans from others standing nearby swelled into a chorus.

"Let's get this over with so I can get back to bed," demanded another.

"All right, hold down the noise, you pansies!" bellowed the

drill instructor. "Our task is to rescue your oxygen-starved brains. I promise you'll be awake when I finish with you. First up is jumping jacks. Ready. One. Two. One. Two."

The jumping jacks led into something close to the Army's daily dozen. Push-ups, sit-ups, bend-and-reaches, squat-thrusts, arm and shoulder rolls, and on, and on.

Jamie joined in silently. Other than Chad and Jeff Gordon, he'd met only a few other members of the group before he fell asleep, exhausted, the evening before. During the exercise, he became aware for the first time that he was younger than the others in the group. Most appeared to be in their midtwenties. Some were older.

The drill sergeant was as good as his word. A half hour of calisthenics passed with increasing vigor. Everyone stopped complaining and bantering about. They were now going hard at the exercise regimen. No one wanted to surrender personal pride by giving up partway through. After a short breather, the drill sergeant, hands on hips, issued a vast smile and addressed the group in a broad Louisiana drawl.

"All right then! I thought y'all'd be curled up in a corner somewhere by now. I'm right glad to see that you ain't all turned to table fat since we met last."

That brought a chorus of challenges and derogatory remarks aimed at the character, upbringing, and geographic origin of their drillmaster. He was unruffled by the verbal abuse.

"Thanks," he replied. "That ought to do it for you mamma's boys. Y'all can sit out now while the rest of us do what we came for."

Again, a chorus of hoots and whistles.

"Don't call me a mamma's boy," answered one short, wiry twentysomething, her chin and chest out with hands on her hips in a gesture of clear defiance. "I used to whip the boys in my neighborhood. They were all bigger than you."

The exercise resumed in earnest. At length, Jeff Gordon called a halt to the festivities.

"That's enough for me," he gasped. "We could go on like this all day, but we have other important things to do."

Jamie was relieved and grateful.

"Let's go for a run," said Gordon.

Jamie's heart sank. The morning was starting off like the first day of track season. He didn't believe that these people, especially the older ones, could run after such a strenuous workout.

However, the invitation to run was met with a cheer. Led by Jeff Gordon, the entire group started around one of the bunkhouses to a forested trail leading up the hillside. At first the slope was gentle, but it then became increasingly steep. Though his stomach was a little upset by the early morning exertion, Jamie kept pace with the pack. The trail skirted the top of a long ridge and then descended in a winding fashion to the meadow below. In all, they ran about four miles.

Winded, tired, ready to be done, Jamie saw the group stop in front of him at the stream crossing on the way back to the common area. Rather than crossing the footbridge, they were shedding their sweats, hats, and shoes. In shorts and T-shirts, one at a time, they swam across a dark, swirling pool and emerged on the opposite side hopping and whooping next to Jeff Gordon, who had led the way.

Jamie's swim in the frigid water instantly swept away the heat of his exertion. Though shivering, he felt fully alive—and hungry.

* * * * *

Showered and dressed for the day, Jamie hurried to the dining hall for breakfast. The food looked great: French toast, slices of ham, scrambled eggs, fruit, and milk. Jamie helped himself to large servings of each. No one commented on his portions.

Looking around the room, the only person Jamie recognized was the cook from the previous afternoon, who sat at a table with two men and a woman, all about his age.

"Is it okay to sit here?" Jamie asked.

"Sure! Join us," replied the cook, pulling the chair out for Jamie. "Let me introduce Jeff Stillwell, Troy Johns, and Shelly Turner. I'm Justin Fisher. You're Jamie Madero, right?"

Jamie nodded.

"Did you come in with Rowley?" asked Shelly Turner.

"I did," Jamie replied as he shoved the first bite of French toast into his mouth.

"Do you know anything about him?" asked Justin.

"Not really," said Jamie. "He's just a cowboy to me."

There was a moment of silence as his eating companions processed this bit of information.

"A cowboy?" asked Justin.

"What makes you think he's a cowboy?" asked Shelly.

"I don't know. When we met in Flagstaff, he looked, acted, and talked like a cowboy." Jamie shrugged.

His breakfast companions laughed.

"I think that was just a disguise," said Shelly.

"Oh, this is rich. Where's the cowboy? I've got to ask him about this." Justin chuckled, searching the room for Chad.

"So why is it so unlikely that Rowley could be a cowboy?" Jamie asked.

"He's only twenty-five years old," said Troy Johns. "He served a Mormon mission in the Southwest, graduated from UC Berkley, and will be leaving the Foundation in January to accept a Fulbright Scholarship at Cambridge University."

Troy left the statement hanging in the air as though its ponderous importance would overwhelm the sensibilities of whatever listener might happen by. The others at the table all nodded gravely.

Jamie was eager to join in the praise since he had come to feel a close kinship with Chad. He tried to piece together the significance of what he had just learned. He didn't know where Cambridge University was. He had no idea what kind of scholarship Chad had qualified for. But he could see that his breakfast companions were awed by, or envious of, the achievement. Mostly, Jamie felt acute disappointment on learning that Chad would be leaving the Foundation.

Justin, seeing that Jamie had somehow missed the significance of all this adoration, shrugged and summed up the matter.

"Let's just say that Rowley can hold his own in pretty impressive company."

"So, you're saying he's too smart to be a cowboy?" Jamie asked, knowing he was baiting the others a little.

"No, nothing like that," answered Justin. "Rowley grew up in Anaheim—you know, Disneyland? Orange County? Next door to Hollywood? His father's a big movie producer. I'm quite sure that your cowboy has never been on a horse. I could be wrong, but I'd be willing to make a small wager that he doesn't know which end of a horse to saddle."

"You don't saddle either end of a horse, Fisher," commented Jeff Stillwell, who had been sitting silent. "You saddle the middle."

"You know what I mean. A motorcycle, yes. A sports car, sure. But a horse? Not even!"

"Here he comes now," declared Troy Johns. "Let's ask him."

"Rowley. Come sit with us!" called Troy, waving to Chad from where he sat.

Chad emerged from the kitchen carrying his breakfast plate and a glass of orange juice without the help of a tray. Juggling these items and his silverware, he moved around to an empty chair and set his place before greeting the others. He pointed at Jamie's plate.

"Well, Bud, a few meals like that ought to help you put back a few of the pounds you lost walking across the country," he said.

When Chad was seated, Justin broached the question of horses.

"Madero here thinks you're some kind of cowboy. The rest of us were just getting ready to take bets on whether you've ever been on a horse."

"Actually, I *am* something of a cowboy," Chad said, sensing immediately what was happening at the table.

"I had an older brother named Tom. Every summer from the time I was ten years old till I graduated from high school, our parents sent us to live with an aunt and uncle in Thayne, Wyoming. Uncle Les had about six hundred mother cows and their calves. Every June, we helped round up the cattle and truck them up to the summer range. We branded, inoculated, castrated—you name it, we did it."

He continued as he ate without interruption from the others. Jamie listened as though spellbound. He seldom heard Chad talk about his personal life and wondered why he had suddenly become so open.

"My parents wanted us to have the benefit of good education and opportunities for cultural development. But they hoped three months of hard work every summer would offset the influences we faced every day during the school year.

"They didn't have to worry about Tom." Chad's voice lowered as he spoke with obvious emotion. He stopped to cut into a juicy slab of ham topped with a canned peach half.

"Where's your brother now?" Troy asked during the pause.

Chad didn't answer immediately. He swallowed with difficulty, put down his fork, and folded his hands in front of him around his plate.

"I suppose he's serving a mission," said Chad. "During the summer before my senior year, Tom was getting ready to go on a mission. He wanted to stay home and work so he could pay part of his own way. I begged him to go back to Uncle Les's one last time. 'We'll never get to do this together again,' I told him."

Chad spoke slowly, the sentences separated by barely audible sighs.

"Finally, Tom agreed. But his heart wasn't in it. One night I scolded him, told him he was being selfish. Only thinking about himself. Of course, I was the one being selfish," Chad said after a long pause, with a catch in his voice.

"It was really a great summer. Tom made it great for me. He put his own feelings and desires aside to serve his little brother."

Tears formed in the corners of Chad's eyes, and he dabbed them away with a paper napkin.

"On July 24—about nine years ago—we went for a long ride after the family's Pioneer Day dinner. Tom's horse stumbled on a steep hillside and pitched him down the hill, then rolled over him. He passed away right there about a half hour later. Wouldn't let me go for help. Just he and I. Or rather, 'Just him and me,' as you'd say if you'd been riding a horse all day." Chad laughed a small, shallow laugh to cover his emotion.

"'You're a better man than I am,' he told me. 'Don't ever stray from the path, Bud.'

"He always called me Bud," Chad said, glancing briefly at Jamie, who looked away when their eyes met. "'Be true and faithful! True and faithful!' Those were his last words.

"Yeah," Chad concluded, "I'm pretty sure he's filling a mission in a world just beyond our view. He never seems very far away. I would surely love to see him again."

With that, Chad cut into the slab of ham once again. Amid the din of the dining hall, Jamie Madero found himself wrapped in an immense silence.

FIFTEEN

Jamie joined the other Insiders for the opening session of training. Refreshed from their exercise, they settled for a period of instruction. Chad conducted the opening session and sat beside Jeff Gordon at the speakers' stand. Jamie didn't know until the meeting started that Chad was the senior Insider over field operations. Working directly with Jeff, Chad determined Insider assignments and received reports. He often took the lead in meetings when Jeff was absent.

Chad covered a few items of business and introduced the new Insiders, including Jamie. He then turned the podium to Jeff Gordon. Jamie had met Jeff the previous evening. Handsome and athletic, Jeff had a full head of black hair with a distinctive white flash in the very front—a hereditary white lock. The men in his family called it the Duke's lock, reaching back to John Gordon, who was knighted by a Scottish king in the 1400s.

"Friends, you are so marvelous," said Jeff. "What a pleasure it is to share this important work with you. I think we should occasionally remind ourselves of the true nature of our work.

"The scriptures foretell a time of great adversity in the last days. One of the things we can do to prepare ourselves for those adversities is to get better acquainted with the villains who cause, or at least contribute, to the problems.

"The prophet Isaiah, in chapter 54, makes an important promise to those who try to maintain a state of righteousness. He writes, 'No weapon that is formed against thee shall prosper; and every tongue that shall rise against thee in judgment thou shalt condemn. This is the heritage of the servants of the Lord, and their righteousness is of me, saith the Lord.'

"In other words, the servants of the Lord, those trying to do right, will be entitled to his protection.

"In contrast to that reassuring promise are a number of scriptural passages that present sober warnings. As you know, the prophet who finished the Book of Mormon and hid it away lived about four hundred years after Christ. He saw our day in vision. What he saw disturbed him so deeply that he wrote about it at length. This prophet, Moroni, warned the people of our day to beware of what he called secret combinations. These organizations get their wealth and power by evil means. In the language of the scriptures, they '*murder to get gain*.' Further, the principals in these organizations bind themselves through oaths to support one another in their wickedness. The devil—Satan, or Lucifer—is the author of these oaths. Whether they recognize it or not, people who bind themselves together through evil acts are serving him.

"Moroni declared in the eighth chapter of Ether, 'Whatsoever nation shall uphold such secret combinations, to get power and gain, until they shall spread over the nation, behold, they shall be destroyed; for the Lord will not suffer that the blood of his saints, which shall be shed by them, shall always cry unto him from the ground for vengeance upon them and yet he avenge them not.'

"Moroni wrote further, 'Suffer not that these murderous combinations shall get above you, which are built up to get power and gain, and the work, yea, even the work of destruction come upon you.' Rather, Moroni wrote, 'When ye shall see these things come among you . . . ye shall awake to a sense of your awful situation, because of this secret combination which shall be among you.'

"We, as private citizens, need to awaken to these dangers. So do the governments of the world. If private citizens, community organizations, and governments would work together, they could take the steps needed to combat the threat that such organizations pose to our personal and political freedoms. Moroni does say, 'Therefore, O ye Gentiles, it is wisdom in God that these things should be shown unto you.'

"What can we do as private citizens? More important for our purposes here today, what can the Freemen Foundation do? Well, as you know, we are not in the law enforcement business. We leave that aspect of the work to established law enforcement agencies. But we can gather information to turn over to government agencies in such a way that we remain invisible. They can take legal measures to slow the growth of the largest of these combinations."

Jeff paused for a few moments and added in a somewhat mournful tone, "All of this presupposes, of course, that it isn't already too late to deflect some of these secret combinations from their aims.

"Who are these bad boys? As I've already suggested, they include all organizations that use illegal and especially violent means to gain wealth and power. In many nations they act with impunity. They're above the law—or they *are* the law. They include the Arab terrorists with whom we've been at war since September 11. These secret combinations exist among the citizens of many nations in Africa, Eastern Europe, and Latin America. Even in nations as advanced as Italy and Columbia, politicians, judges, and other civic officials are essentially held hostage by the immense wealth and power of such organizations, whether they be drug cartels or mobs. A quick look at what is happening along the US border with Mexico would serve as a good illustration.

"However, relatively few organizations have the scope and resources needed to corrupt or topple major governments. Few of them could set in motion forces great enough to destroy democracy and erase individual freedoms.

"*Gain* is the key word in this discussion. In scriptural language, gain means wealth or money—big money. Wealth comes before power, and without wealth, there is no power. Those who seek power need wealth to procure the means to wrest that power from the public and hold onto it. And none of these bad guys, these secret combinations, make money by hard work. They're social and economic parasites. They don't produce anything. They don't build houses or cars, make furniture or clothing, teach school, run hospitals or nursing homes, or put out fires.

"They hate productive work. They make their money in the industries that pedal various forms of death. Again, in the language of the scriptures, they *murder* to get gain and power. So these bad guys are into drugs, prostitution, gambling, weapons, theft, extortion, money laundering, and outright murder for profit.

"In democratic nations, they pose as reputable business institutions. They're importers and exporters, bankers, developers, investors, entertainment companies, labor organizations, and so on. They're not megalomaniacs trying to rule the world like the villains in a James Bond movie. They're not caricatures or cartoons. They're little criminals who have grown big—sometimes huge.

"Fortunately, if they don't receive widespread public support, the overall industries they promote grow slowly because the principle of competition is alive and well among them. And the means they use to carry out competitive transactions are brutal and permanent. They're like crabs in a pot. They don't cooperate to climb out. They consume one another until the survivors grow large enough to eat up the competition. Even in a pot with a hundred other crabs, one that weighs a ton will get its own way.

"One-ton crabs don't come along very often, and we'd better hold our breath that we don't see many of them very soon. Another prophet who saw our day and warned of these combinations was John, who wrote the book of Revelation. Let me note for your further reflection some of the imagery in the twelfth and thirteenth chapters of Revelation. No doubt these chapters are filled with symbolism. I think they're important for us because they mention two key latter-day figures. One is referred to as the Dragon. The Dragon is pretty clearly labeled as 'that old serpent,' called the Devil, and Satan. I think we have a good idea who that is.

"The other is called the Beast, a beast with seven heads and ten crowns. In the form of a leopard, the Beast derives power and authority directly from the Dragon. This Beast is invincible. It has power to regenerate itself when wounded. Sustained by the powers of evil, this Leopard or Beast will gain worldwide prominence and the power to make war with the Saints. To overcome them. In fact, according to Revelation, the Beast will gain power over all kindreds, tongues, and nations.

"Of course, we don't know who the Beast is," Jeff continued. He glanced around the room to judge how his listeners were receiving this information.

"We don't know if the Beast is an individual or group. It could be a larger organization, such as a national or international government, or an institution. As I read these passages, I imagine a world-wide organization controlled by a most powerful person. A secret combination.

"The scriptures we're talking about aren't always easy to understand. But I think they make the following points:

"One. There are organizations that exist to do evil.

"Two. They're all around us.

"Three. Many of them will self-destruct or be eaten up by others.

"Four. A few of them will grow large enough to constitute a serious threat to free government and democratic society.

"Five. If left unchecked, one will eventually grow to the point that it consumes all competition, including national governments.

"Six. The Saints of God won't be completely exempt from the consequences brought on the world by these secret combinations. The only hope that the Saints can cling to is the promise that no weapon formed against them shall prosper. Or as the book of Revelation puts it, 'He that leadeth into captivity shall go into captivity: he that killeth with the sword must be killed with the sword. Here is the patience and the faith of the saints.' In the end, the wicked will destroy each other.

"So, the mission of the Freemen Foundation is to sift through the organizations that are potential beastlings. Our job isn't to fight them. We don't interfere with their businesses. We just find them. Map the connections between them. Uncover information about their criminal activities that may lead to legal investigations.

"And, most important, everything we do must be done within the law."

Through Jeff's entire discourse on secret combinations, the room was intensely quiet. Even though the Insiders sat on metal folding chairs that grew harder as time passed, the listeners hardly stirred.

The meeting consumed the entire morning. As noon approached, Jeff Gordon closed.

"We want you to know how deeply your efforts are appreciated. We've already had some success in our work. Considerable success, in fact. And we'll have more if we persevere. Because you are our eyes and ears in the field, and our hands and feet, we have designed a week of training to help you become more proficient, even expert, in what you do."

* * * * *

Following the opening session and a light lunch, the Insiders changed clothes and went out into the field for confidence and team-building activities. The evening was devoted to a campfire assembly with skits, a few brief comments by Jeff Gordon, and a lingering sing-along.

The next three days seemed to pass in the blink of an eye for Jamie. They included daily physical training, problem-solving exercises, and an introduction to individual investigative skills. Jamie was especially intrigued by the training on memory systems— techniques for quickly organizing and memorizing information for later recall. In his free time, he practiced with strings of objects, numbers, or words, and associated mental pictures.

On Saturday, all Insiders took the day off to climb nearby Mount Massive, the state's second-highest peak.

SIXTEEN

Art Warnock fumed. He rode along beside one of his chief lieutenants in the plush rear seat of a chauffeur-driven Lincoln. His travel arrangements had been made hastily, and he had left important business in Toronto. The early-morning flight in one of the company jets had gone well, and he had been constantly in touch with his command center at Fletchner International. Now, however, he found himself outside cell coverage and could reach no one.

He disliked being pulled out of the comfort zone where he could maintain flawless control over a large contingent of field agents all over North America. Art was a headquarters man, not a field man. He was uncomfortable in strange surroundings. He was especially uncomfortable riding along Interstate 40 west of Denver through what he referred to as a frontier wilderness.

Art's regional security director, Phil Angelino, shook his head in disbelief. He was a good soldier, but not one to indulge the whims of his superiors.

"What wilderness?" Phil argued, gesturing broadly with his big hands. "Denver has two million people. What frontier?"

"We're a long way from Denver," countered Art sharply.

"So relax! Try to enjoy the beautiful scenery," Angelino hurled back at him.

"Shut up, Phil. I don't want to hear your crap this morning. I don't want to be here, okay? I couldn't care less about the scenery. If

I want scenery, I'll go down to the waterfront. And I'm furious at this Kilgrow character. We give him a simple job to do, and he can't pull it off without flying me out to this forsaken place to hold his hand. Fire the bum! Let's get somebody who can produce."

"Look, boss, you want him to pick up a defector. But you want it done with clean hands. It's not always that simple. You can't just drive by and pop a guy. And besides, the West is a big place. People can get lost out here."

"My point exactly," grumbled Art. "If we turned out the lights and shut off the sprinkling systems, the whole West would dry up and blow away. Good riddance!"

"Well, it's great to have you out here giving us some inspired leadership," Angelino replied.

"You're pretty mouthy for a little guy." Art shook his head again. He gazed out the window as they turned south on Highway 91, heading toward Leadville.

"You ain't looking too good in this gig either," he continued. "If I was you, I'd stop mouthing off and figure out how to save your fanny if we don't pick this Rowley kid up in the next twenty-four hours. The Chairman and Rostetter are both breathing fire, and I'm feeling the heat."

"Relax!" said Angelino. "Kilgrow has Rowley. But we think he might have the Rudman dame too. They could be a thing. He wants us to see the organization they work for."

"A thing. What's a thing? Speak English, will ya?"

"Relax, okay. No wonder you don't have a woman in your life. You're such a bad act. Nobody could stand to live with you."

"Shut up!" Art yelled. Then after a pause, "A bad act. What's that? You see. That's what I mean. Try to learn some English."

The hired chauffeur, watching this exchange in the rearview mirror also shook his head. The gesture didn't go unnoticed by Warnock.

"What are you looking at up there? Just mind your business and drive the car."

The haranguing continued as the car sped toward Leadville. By the time they arrived, Warnock, who was unaccustomed to traveling winding roads, was partially nauseated. If possible, his mood had grown even more sour.

They drove through town on Leadville's main and only street. Leadville lay in the Arkansas River Valley. Its altitude was over ten thousand feet, making it the highest incorporated municipality in the continental United States. The Arkansas River gurgled and bumped its way between the Collegiate Range and the Mosquito Range. Peaks on either side of the valley rose above fourteen thousand feet. The air was light and the temperatures cool, even in the middle of summer.

The chauffeur pulled into a dirt parking area behind an unused industrial shed on the south side of town. There sat, unseen from the highway, a silver-gray late model Mercedes sedan with tinted windows. A solitary figure emerged from the sedan as they came to a halt. The chauffeur got out of the Lincoln and walked around to Warnock's door without turning off the engine. When Warnock and Angelino were out of the car, the chauffeur sat back in his place behind the wheel and rolled up all the windows to shut out the details of the business meeting taking place beside his car.

Art Warnock and Phil Angelino stood side by side facing George Kilgrow. Kilgrow merely nodded a greeting, waiting for Angelino to conduct the business. Kilgrow was a stickler for protocol. He always observed good manners during business meetings.

Art Warnock studied Kilgrow with a measure of disdain.

He spoke to Angelino but looked directly at Kilgrow. "No wonder this clown can't carry out a simple assignment. He looks like someone out of *The Godfather*." Then addressing Kilgrow, "This is a very busy time. I've got a lot on my mind. What do you say we get this over with in about three minutes so I can get back to civilization and try to earn a living?"

Kilgrow appeared confused by Warnock's direct attack. He hesitated, as if trying to understand what was going down, but then shrugged and asked Angelino, "Is this your man?"

Angelino also wore a look of surprise as he witnessed Warnock's rudeness. Even those who conducted their transactions in a world of moral darkness held to certain protocols that allowed business to be carried on in a peaceable fashion.

"This is the man," Angelino replied, shaking his head. "The boss is under a little pressure right now. What do you have for us?"

Warnock cut in before Kilgrow could respond.

"Don't apologize for me to this sewer rat. He looks ridiculous. Besides, we're paying him, and he hasn't delivered."

Kilgrow's hand jerked toward his coat, and his eyes widened in a flash of instant anger. But Warnock held up a single finger, wagging it in front of Kilgrow's face.

"Don't even think of pulling a gun on me, sonny. You'll have more trouble than you ever dreamed of."

Kilgrow's hand rested on the grip of a pistol in his shoulder holster. At length, he broke the gaze that he had locked on Warnock. He glanced briefly at Angelino, who was nodding in assent.

"He can do it," Angelino testified.

Warnock knew what was going through Kilgrow's mind. Kilgrow had been shadowing the mark for weeks, working on a partial cash advance. If something went wrong with the job, he would not be paid. Much of what he had already invested would be lost. Warnock watched as Kilgrow drew a deep breath and forced himself to relax. With a face-saving sneer, he threw back his head in a laugh and smoothed his suit coat.

Nevertheless, when Kilgrow spoke, he spoke to Phil Angelino, who was his client contact.

"I've followed the mark all the way from Phoenix. He picked up a kid in Flagstaff. I have no idea what their connection is. Maybe the kid is a recruit.

"When we got a confirmation on the identity, I tried to pick up the mark in Cortez," said Kilgrow. "He resisted, so I worked him over good—hurt him bad. But a bystander came to his rescue and brought down a lot of public attention."

"You're really smooth there, fella," commented Warnock.

Kilgrow shot back a fierce look, visibly fighting to get himself under control.

"You know all this," he said to Angelino.

"I know. Keep going. I want Mr. Big Shot to hear it for himself," said Angelino.

Angelino's slur against Warnock wasn't overlooked by Warnock or by Kilgrow, who smiled faintly.

"The mark and the kid walked all the way up here from Flagstaff," Kilgrow said. "We lost them for a while in the mountains. But on the twenty-third, they showed up just outside of town here. They're over near Turquoise Lake at some sort of dude ranch." As he spoke he gestured toward the mountains on the west.

With obvious impatience, Warnock mimicked his gesture.

"Then go get them!" he shouted at Kilgrow.

In a flash, Kilgrow had a knife in his right hand and advanced ominously toward Warnock, brandishing it.

"I don't care who you are. You don't impress me. You don't scare me," he said as Warnock took a more respectful step backward. Angelino stepped out of the way as the two men faced off.

"You use that, and you're a dead man," Warnock threatened, "and so is everybody close to you—anybody who ever even knew you."

Again, appearing to weigh his alternatives, Kilgrow slowly backed down.

"The reason I invited you two gentlemen out here," Kilgrow began, resuming some of the etiquette of his trade, "is that the two of them are with a group. It looks like a church picnic. Men. Women. Grandparents. No kids, though.

"I couldn't believe they would walk all the way up here for a family reunion, so I checked at the courthouse and found out that the dude ranch is owned by an investment outfit. They rent it out. I called the owners. A Denver company has rented the whole facility for a week."

"What are they doing?" Warnock asked, interested for the first time since leaving the plane.

"Hard to tell. They meet a lot, talk a lot, go for walks in the trees, and swim in the stream. I don't know. We need some electronics up here. There's no way to snatch our mark while he's with thirty other people unless you want to change the ground rules."

"No, and stop asking to waste him. My orders are to bring him back for questioning. I'll tell you when and if those orders change," replied Warnock. "Let's go take a look at this place."

Leaving Kilgrow's sedan behind the shed, all three men climbed into the Lincoln. Kilgrow rode in the front seat where he could give instructions to the chauffeur. The drive took only a few minutes.

"Just beyond those trees is a parking area," explained Kilgrow. "From there it's a short walk to the buildings."

"Any way we can get close enough to take a look?" asked Warnock.

"Yeah, we can park up the road a ways and walk through the woods."

"No good," answered Warnock. "If anybody sees us in the woods, it'll be pretty tough to convince them that you're out hunting ducks in those clothes."

"In that case," replied Kilgrow, "take a look at these photos."

Kilgrow handed a stack of black and white 4x6-inch glossy prints to the men in the backseat. The photos had been taken by a professional photographer using a telephoto lens. Each shot was clear. Warnock leafed through them quickly. He hesitated only slightly when he saw photos of Chad Rowley and Sarah Rudman, two people in whom he was intensely interested. As he looked at each photo, he passed it to Angelino, who also recognized the marks quickly.

"Any signs of security?" asked Warnock.

"No," replied Kilgrow. "Like I said, it's a family reunion or company retreat or something. No muscle, no heat."

Warnock tapped his palm with the small stack of photos he still held.

"Okay, Phil. Slick here is definitely on to something," said Warnock to Angelino. "Get him some talent and the hardware he needs to find out what's going on here.

"Okay, Slick," he said, turning to Kilgrow. "Maybe you're earning your money. Don't screw this up. And don't let our boy get away again. I want him fast."

"Who's working the Rudman woman?" Warnock asked Angelino.

"I don't know," replied Angelino. "She's not in my ballpark."

"She is now," ordered Warnock. "Pick 'em both up."

"Like our friend here said," Angelino countered, "it's not going to be easy to make a clean snatch. They're never alone."

"Stay close to them. You'll get 'em," Warnock ordered.

"Is this the kid?" he asked, pausing on a photo of Jamie Madero.

"Yeah, that's him," replied Kilgrow, looking over the seat.

"What do you have on him?"

"Nothing yet. He hasn't been a factor."

"Get what you can on him too," ordered Warnock. "Let's find out how he fits in."

As the chauffeur wheeled the car around and headed back to Leadville, Warnock continued to study the photos, looking for familiar faces. The only person he thought he might recognize was an Asian woman with long black hair and a slender build. Though she looked familiar, he couldn't place her. But he'd get somebody on these photos as soon as he returned to civilization.

No one spoke all the way back to Leadville.

SEVENTEEN

That evening, before dark, an unmarked sedan pulled over to the curb where a couple waited for a city bus leaving downtown Cincinnati, Ohio. The couple glanced nervously at the car as two men exited the rear doors and moved toward them. Before either the young woman or her escort could react, one of the intruders hit the woman directly in the face, sending her sprawling. She came to rest against the wall of a nearby building, apparently unconscious.

"What the—?" her escort started to protest. Before he could say more, the other assailant pinned an arm behind his back. His scream of pain was cut short as the boxer who had hit his girlfriend hammered him in the stomach. His knees buckled, and he went limp, clutching at his stomach with his free hand. Both assailants grabbed him under the arms and dragged him into the waiting car, which squealed away from the curb even before the doors were completely closed. The entire incident lasted less than a minute.

* * * * *

Hours later, two men dressed in black, faces covered with ski masks, pried open the back door of an apartment in Redondo Beach, California, and burst inside. The resident, a young woman, ran to the back door to see the cause of the noise. She found the door standing open. As she moved forward to inspect it, she was pinned from behind by an arm around her waist. A gloved hand pressed a cloth over her mouth before she could scream. She felt the sharp prick of a needle inserted into her upper arm. All went black. One of the intruders helped the other hoist her limp body over his shoulder and carry her quickly to a car waiting in the alley. They left the door open. Just as they pulled away, the telephone in her apartment rang.

* * * * *

Before morning, similar abductions occurred in Worcester, Massachusetts and Meridian, Idaho.

Art Warnock slept well that night. He looked forward to work in the morning. Finally, he felt he was getting a few important things under control.

EIGHTEEN

By evening of the day following Art Warnock's trip to Colorado, he set up a meeting with Julienne Rostetter. He had managed the abduction of four people believed to have engaged in industrial espionage against Fletchner International. He had also set the wheels in motion during the trip to Leadville to bring in Chad Rowley and Sarah Rudman just as JR had ordered.

Furthermore, Warnock discovered through the visit to Colorado at least one additional employee who was linked to what he now called the "Mormon connection." Gwen Fong, executive secretary to the company's chief financial officer, had appeared in the Leadville photos.

This series of actions taken by Warnock constituted, in his mind, a major coup. Hungry as he was for recognition that would lead to his more rapid advancement within the company hierarchy, Warnock was savvy enough to avoid direct conflict with Rostetter. He was fairly certain that he could survive a showdown with her but knew there was little to be gained at the moment by doing so. Besides, he was feeling euphoric about the previous day's achievements. He wanted an opportunity to gloat.

Warnock knew that Rostetter detested him. He didn't care.

Her days at Fletchner International are numbered.

Warnock was initially confused by JR's seeming naïveté. How could anyone who had risen so high in the organization be ignorant of its true aims and methods? Furthermore, he was confused by the Chairman's tolerance of JR's unwillingness or inability to take care of the necessary dirty work. Every time the trigger had to be pulled, the assignment went to Warnock. Why not remove Rostetter from the picture and simplify the chain of command?

Warnock knew with growing certainty that, in time, the Chairman would gain sufficient confidence in Warnock's abilities and jettison Rostetter. He just needed to be patient and continue demonstrating his effectiveness.

He scheduled the meeting with Rostetter in a secure conference room rather than in her office. He wanted to meet her on neutral ground.

Rostetter arrived just in time, as he knew she would. She was an attractive woman, always meticulous in her appearance. Even though she was nearly a decade older than he, she aroused a physical desire in him that he found himself combating while he negotiated their never-ceasing power struggle.

"Thanks for finding time for me to debrief my trip and my latest findings," he started. She sat stoically, sending a clear signal that there would be no small talk between them.

"We brought in each of the four thieves that we know to have stolen and sold company information. All, of course, were pleased to cooperate," he lied with a sinister smile.

"Of course," JR echoed without smiling.

Her icy demeanor infuriated him.

Let the organizational theorists say what they want about gender issues in management. Gender is always an issue. If she weren't a woman, I would break her neck with my bare hands.

"We extracted the information we needed by nonconfrontational interrogation," he continued, knowing she would understand that he meant chemical interrogation.

Much of Warnock's report was given by one of his assistants, the young Mark Hart. Hart joined Warnock's staff after working for nearly a year with Gwen Fong.

Hart projected the digital images of the subjects during interrogation. He summarized the range of company secrets that they had, by their own drug-induced admissions, sold to competitors. He also reported to whom the secrets had been sold and how much the thieves realized from the sale.

"They were all solo acts. No connection among any of them," said Hart.

JR sat silently through the report. It was clear to Warnock that she had no stomach for the dirty work that protected the Fletchner Empire.

"And the thieves?" asked JR when the presentation ended.

"The thieves?" Warnock asked to be sure what she was driving at.

"What have you done with the thieves?"

"Of course," he replied as evasively as he could, "we sent them home."

"Sent them home!" Her disgust was palpable. He could feel himself getting hot behind the ears. He clenched his fists, the rage within him pushing the breaking point.

"And what of the other two?" she asked.

"As I told you before, Rowley and Rudman have a common connection with the Mormon Church."

"What of it?" JR asked.

"This photo shows Rowley at a retreat center near Leadville, Colorado. The company that rented the center for the week is called the Freemen Foundation," said Hart.

"A bunch of patriotic whackos," added Warnock.

"We took a look at the Foundation's website," Hart continued. "They cast themselves as defenders of individual rights. They're also heavy into fund raising and have a speaker's pool, do workshops, and so forth. They claim to be educating the public about threats to our freedoms."

"There's a problem with that?" asked JR.

"Not if you want a steady diet of Rush Limbaughs and Glen Becks," said Warnock.

"These are extreme right-wing Americans?" she asked.

"We're still checking them out," said Hart.

Hart pulled up another photo. "Here is Rowley again. The woman is Rudman. We're not sure whether they're romantically involved. They were employed at different Fletchner facilities. Both of them walked. Now, here they are together. That's more than coincidence."

"Okay. I still don't understand what their religion has to do with their interest in us," JR commented quietly.

"We don't know that yet, but we will soon," Warnock assured her. "I have ordered a bells-and-whistles stakeout of the little party in Leadville. In a day or two, we'll know everything there is to know about this group.

"Incidentally, you'll be interested to know that there is at least one additional connection between this group and Fletchner. This woman," he said, pointing to an image on the screen, "is Gwen Fong. She works in the CFO's office."

Warnock glanced at Hart, who stood looking at the carpet.

For the first time during the interview, Rostetter responded visibly.

"Yes, I know her. She showed up in the investigation of Charlotte LeMans. However, there was nothing we could hang her on."

"Not yet," Warnock agreed. "But she's still at the retreat. We plan to have a visit with her."

JR looked from Warnock to Hart and back.

"All right. Don't act on her until you're sure," she conceded. "But if she has her hand in the cookie jar, let's nail her." With that she rose.

"If you're finished," she said, "I still have lots to do. I'm sure the Chairman will be very interested in what you've done. I'll set up an appointment so you can trot out the dogs and ponies."

Without a word of praise, and with no acknowledgment to Hart, she left the room. Warnock stood for several minutes, analyzing the interaction in his own mind. He tried to figure out where he'd gained yardage and where he'd lost. In the end, he concluded that the best thing for the company would be to speed up Rostetter's demise. With her out of the way, security within the company could really be pushed to new levels. And he was just the man to do it.

"Syd!" he called through the still open door to his personal secretary. "See if you can get the Chairman on the phone."

"That's all for now, Hart," Warnock said, striding from the room. Hart tidied up the table and retrieved his information before leaving the room, turning out the lights behind him.

NINETEEN

I need a digital video setup with 100x zoom capability. Two directional mikes with 80 percent reliability up to a hundred meters. Better send thirty bug-type wireless mikes. And I need a team with two field specialists and a producer," George Kilgrow spoke methodically into his cell phone while sitting in his silver-gray Mercedes outside a motel in Buena Vista, Colorado.

Having received a green light from the client to intensify surveillance at the retreat facility near Leadville, Kilgrow wasted no time in ordering up first-rate electronic coverage.

"Have the talent and hardware here by this time tomorrow," he finished and cut off the call without saying good-bye.

When the order was placed, Kilgrow stretched the kinks out of his shoulders and back. He had been working long hours for eight weeks, living on the road with nothing but a change of suits and a toilet kit.

It's not that he would be missed at home. There was no one waiting in his Los Angeles apartment. And he'd been in the business long enough to know how to survive in relative comfort during endless days and nights of relentless snooping.

Kilgrow was a voyeur by nature. He loved to pierce the veil of privacy that most men and women drew over their personal lives. During his lucrative career, he had dogged politicians, celebrities, cheating husbands and wives, deadbeat spouses, and chiselers running from gambling debts. All in all, they were not a pretty lot, but their lives were certainly not dull.

His specialty was surveillance. He hired himself out to get the goods on people. He found the violence that often resulted from his snooping to be dirty and distasteful. He preferred to hire that work out to the muscle boys who make their living by various forms of persuasion—chemical, physical, psychological, and otherwise.

The talent and hardware arrived as ordered, and within thirty-six hours following the departure of Art Warnock and Philip Angelino, Kilgrow and his accomplices were on location designing their information-gathering setup.

As the team of electronics experts did their work, Kilgrow looked on, receiving reports and approving the placements. He thought about buying himself some appropriate field clothing to tramp around in the woods with the team but talked himself out of it.

Hey, why should I go out there and get dirty? That's what I'm paying these guys for.

They established a listening post in a rented panel van parked off a forested logging track. This undeveloped private land lay just outside the recreation property where the marks were meeting.

During the first full night they were on the job, the team crept into the unlocked dining facility. They didn't attempt to bug the dormitories until the following day. In broad daylight, they worked skillfully and silently while the residents were busy elsewhere. In less than twenty-four hours, they had arranged to capture on video or audio all that was said and done in the buildings and the grounds immediately around the dining hall.

Manning the listening post in shifts around the clock, they recorded and cataloged information on the activities and conversations that occurred among their targets. By the end of the second day, Kilgrow had seen and heard enough.

"Listen to that," he said, sitting at one of the desks in the crowded van, surrounded by sophisticated electronic equipment and stacks of steel-case luggage in which the team had transported the hardware from Los Angeles.

"These guys have got nothing," he said to Big Mike, the team member on duty. Mike was a hulking, overweight, unkempt, electronics wizard known for his resourcefulness in fabricating setups to meet unique surveillance needs.

"These guys are completely outclassed," continued Kilgrow, leaning back to stretch his legs. "They have no defense and very little talent. This is pathetic." He readjusted his headset as he continued to listen to a conversation occurring in the dining hall.

"Somebody's going to get hurt. I'm betting it's these guys."

"Any idea who the Leopard is?" Big Mike stirred restlessly beside him.

"No idea," replied Kilgrow. "Log it, and we'll pass it on."

TWENTY

The day following the group climb of Mount Massive was Sunday. Jeff Gordon led his people in a morning devotional service. The rest of the day was devoted to personal study, writing letters, and catching up on old friendships. Insiders could be seen reading on the lawn, visiting in small groups, and walking through the forest in twos and threes.

Jamie spent most of the afternoon writing his mother a lengthy letter, the first in more than a month since he left home. He realized that the letter was long overdue. He imagined his mother's anxiety and tried to make his report as detailed and positive as he could. He promised to email her often as soon as he was settled.

He spent much of the afternoon and early evening propped up against the trunk of a lodgepole pine a quarter mile up the hillside. He could look down on the buildings and see his companions moving about below him.

It had been a restful day, one Jamie felt he needed badly. The sun had set over the ridgeline behind him. Though it wasn't yet dark, the temperature started cooling. Jamie prepared to walk down through the trees to the dining room in search of an evening snack. He had just risen to his feet when he heard the call of a bird that he imagined to be the hooting of an owl. Curious, Jamie followed the call, hoping to catch a glimpse of an owl in the wild. He wandered through the forest along the hillside until the intensity of the call seemed to reach its peak.

There he stood, silently scanning the boughs of the trees around him. He couldn't tell exactly from which direction the call was coming. While engrossed in this visual search, he heard, not too far off to his right, the sound of a van door sliding shut. The noise wasn't loud, but it was distinct. The breeze blowing from that direction carried the sound of two male voices engaged in conversation. The sounds surprised Jamie. He had thought there was nothing but forest in that direction.

With no reason to suspect either danger or foul play, Jamie continued in the direction of the voices. He was off the slope now, walking through light undergrowth. He wore dark cotton pants and a plain flannel shirt borrowed from Justin Fisher. In the dusk, dressed in low tones as he was, he walked unseen to within just a few yards of the source of the voices before he stopped.

He instantly caught his breath when he saw the two men standing at the side door of the van. One of the men was still in shirtsleeves, despite the cooling temperature. Standing out on the cuffs of his black silk shirt were silver cuff links. They shone like miniature beacons. Without doubt, this was Cufflinks, the driver of the Mercedes. Jamie had seen him in Cortez and later in Telluride. He was certain he could pick this man out of a lineup.

Still partially hidden from the men by extending boughs, Jamie froze in his tracks. He couldn't move, even to back away, without his movements attracting their attention. As the remaining light faded, he stood so close to them that he was sure they would hear him breathing.

Jamie felt suddenly aggressive. He had a score to settle with Cufflinks. The more converted he became to the Foundation's cause, the more eager he was to confront the sinister figure. Still, he had an eavesdropping advantage, and he wanted to learn all he could about the two men before announcing his presence.

"We've got what we came for," Cufflinks said to a shorter, wiry man standing next to him. His listener was dressed in a dark green jumpsuit and wore comfortable hiking shoes.

"The client wants us to bring in three of these jokers who all have something that belongs to him. He also wants us to send a message to their friends," said Cufflinks. "You and your boys clean up here. Send all the data over the secure line to the client number I gave you. Remember, I don't transfer the funds until I have a copy of everything you collected."

Jamie watched as the two men parted, trying to make sense of their conversation. Cufflinks walked down the logging track through the trees as his contact climbed into the van and started the engine. As they moved away, Jamie slipped back into the trees. He followed Cufflinks on a parallel course until he was out of sight of the van. Then he carefully stepped out into the logging track, keeping the disappearing figure of Cufflinks barely in sight.

Cufflinks reached the paved road and turned left. Jamie followed carefully, ever conscious that the van might come up behind him. He had walked only a tenth of a mile further when he heard the sound of an automobile engine starting somewhere ahead of him. He hurried forward until he was hidden in the trees just off the road where he last saw Cufflinks. In just moments, he saw the Mercedes, using only parking lights, pull past him headed toward Leadville. Before he could move from his concealed spot, the van pulled up on the logging road behind him and turned out onto the hard surface. There was now a passenger along with the driver. Using the memory system the Insiders learned a couple of days earlier, Jamie committed both license numbers to memory.

He rehearsed the events of this encounter in the woods as he hurried back to the dining hall, knowing that he needed to find Chad as soon as possible and relate the information to him.

Chad listened without comment or question.

"Good job, Bud! Let's go see if we can find Jeff," he said, clapping Jamie on the shoulder.

Jamie recited the matter a second time to Gordon, who listened intently, making occasional notes. Jeff and Chad then questioned Jamie for additional details.

"What do you think this means?" Jamie asked Chad. Jeff sat silently, pondering the gravity of the information Jamie had just revealed.

"I think it could be serious. I believe we should take a careful look at the location of the van tomorrow to see if anything was left behind. However, I'm not sure we should act right away. It seems unlikely that these people, whoever they are, would try anything in this setting with so many of us around."

"I agree," replied Jeff. "Let's find out what we can without alarming the others unduly. This may give us some additional leads to follow after training."

Reluctant to challenge the judgment of his more seasoned leaders, Jamie still felt alarmed by Cufflinks's declaration about sending the Insiders a message.

"Don't you think we should tell the police—or maybe put out a guard or something?" asked Jamie.

"You're right to be concerned," Jeff said, pausing for a long moment before replying. "But based on what you heard and observed, I don't think they'll be in a position to do anything about their threats tonight. Let's sleep on it and see how things look tomorrow."

Jamie continued to feel uneasy as he lay on his bunk that evening. Eventually, he slipped on his jacket and shoes and passed an hour or two walking noiselessly around the compound. The moon was past full. Jamie could see from where he stood in the shadows that all was peaceful. When he felt better, he went inside but slept little until morning.

TWENTY-ONE

After the customary exercise period and a pleasant breakfast the next morning, the Insiders gathered indoors for the day's classes. The sky had grown overcast, the weather cooled, and a light drizzle started falling and would continue through the day and into the night.

The Insiders met in an open bay in one of the dorms. They sat on rows of folding chairs arranged in a semicircle.

The instructor for the session was Sarah Rudman. Jamie knew her only slightly. He was impressed by her poise and stunning sense of self-assurance.

Unlike the other Insiders who were dressed down for comfort, Sarah was dressed up for the occasion. She wore a taupe pleated skirt reaching just below the knees, a tailored navy blazer, an off-white blouse, and a paisley necktie. Navy flats completed the outfit and added comfort as she strolled back and forth in front of the other Insiders.

She asked the class to take a careful look at her. She walked back and forth across the room, turning so that the students could see her from various angles.

Then she strode confidently behind a blanket hung from the ceiling. A minute or two later she emerged wearing a flowered, casual skirt that flared at the knees. She wore a tight white T-shirt with a scooped neckline, large hoop earrings, a short blonde wig, and long brightly painted nails with matching lipstick. She chewed a huge wad of gum. She talked teen babble nonstop. Somehow in the midst of an unending stream of syllables, she told the Insiders, "I will show you today that you can be nearly anybody you want to be."

Jamie was amazed at the difference two minutes made in her appearance and mannerisms. He would not have believed her to be the same woman.

She then stepped behind the blanket again. This time boots replaced her shoes, and she donned camouflage pants. She emerged wearing a short, shaggy wig with matching mustache, and a ball cap with the bill turned backwards. She moved differently, more like a young man would move. Again the transformation was remarkable.

"Of course, *you* know that I'm not a man," she said in a deeper, rougher voice. "And if you look carefully, you can obviously see the difference. But, at a distance, or if you have no reason to look carefully, by changing sounds, profiles, colors, and textures, I appear to be a different person.

"We're trained from birth to scan our environment and the objects in it, looking for recognizable patterns," she continued. "Once we see a few characteristics of a familiar pattern, we automatically fill in all the blanks. We think we're seeing an instance of a pattern we already recognize."

She stepped behind the blanket for another minute. She emerged this time as an elderly woman. In that minute, she added forty pounds and forty years.

"Effective disguise is mostly a matter of minimizing features, playing down the unexpected, and emphasizing the expected," said Sarah. "In the next hour, we'll introduce and demonstrate the basic principles of disguise."

On her signal, two or three Insiders brought in boxes and bags filled with dress-up items. These included clothing of all kinds and in all colors, eyeglasses, hairpieces, handbags, props, clutches, and a huge makeup kit. The Insiders were free to go to work on themselves. Sarah circulated among them, coaching their disguise efforts.

"Begin with the overall appearance, and move from there to the details," she instructed. "Remember, you're not covering yourselves up, you're remaking yourselves from the inside out. Good disguise needs a solid foundation. You can't just try to look like a new person. You have to become a new person temporarily."

Sarah's manner was so confident and her rapport with each of the Insiders so personal, that Jamie, though thoroughly enjoying the challenge of remaking himself, could hardly take his eyes off her. He also became aware as the morning wore on that the other young men in the room were having the same difficulty. He took special note of Chad Rowley.

"What do you make of Rowley and Sarah? He's not acting like himself," Jamie said to Justin Fisher, who at that moment was working on variations of mustaches.

Fisher viewed his profile in the mirror.

"You're just noticing? I'd say the worst kept secret in the Foundation is that the Big Guy is gaga over Her Highness. The poor boy is smitten. He's taken the bait," said Fisher. "The only question remaining is whether or not Her Majesty wants to reel him in."

Jamie continued to watch. In a short time, it became clear to Jamie that these two impressive people, Chad and Sarah, had more than a passing interest in each other. She exhibited a measure of coyness, seeming to toy a bit with Chad's awkwardness. There was little doubt that she encouraged and enjoyed his attention.

Jamie noticed in Sarah an endearing mannerism. Despite her commanding public confidence, in personal settings, she sometimes swept her blonde hair back behind her right ear with a single finger. The gesture was very feminine. But it also hinted that she could feel self-conscious and vulnerable. It contributed to the allure she exercised over Chad and the other young men in the room.

Jamie became engrossed in the art of disguise. Throughout the morning and into the afternoon, the Insiders tried out different disguises, like players in an ever-changing kaleidoscope of images. Jamie became more convinced, with each new effort, that disguise could be a powerful weapon in the battle between good and evil. He thought often of the day of reckoning when he would again face the enemy. He took seriously each new tool that might give him greater advantage when the showdown finally came.

* * * * *

Just before dinner, Chad announced that the Foundation leadership had decided to shorten the training by a day. He assured his friends that there was no cause for alarm. The move was simply a precautionary measure. He asked them to be ready for the buses by midmorning the next day.

Jamie received the news with mixed feelings. He was terribly disappointed to cut short his chance to rub shoulders with this exciting group of young adults. At the same time, he was relieved that Jeff Gordon and Chad were responding to what might be a serious threat to the group's well-being. Jamie joined willingly in the cleanup and preparations for departure. After dinner, Chad dropped by to tell Jamie he was driving into Denver on assignment from Jeff and would return early the next morning.

* * * * *

"Hi, beautiful!" Chad whispered as he stepped beside Sarah, who was wiping dishes and stowing them in the dining hall cupboards. They weren't alone in the kitchen, but no one was paying attention to them.

"Do you talk to all the girls that way?"

"Not a chance. One in a lifetime," said Chad.

"Then why are you whispering?"

"I'm trying to protect your good name and reputation."

"There are no secrets in a house full of budding spies."

"Maybe not. In that case, let's just make a public announcement."

"What shall we tell them?"

"Let's tell them we're getting married and going to England together."

After a pause, Sarah said, "Okay. Way to call my bluff."

"What's wrong?" asked Chad. "I think it sounds like a splendid idea."

Sarah put away a water pitcher and reached for a pan to dry.

"What makes you think I'm going to fall for you just because you're gorgeous, brainy, the kind of man every woman desires, and standing in line for a juicy inheritance?" she asked.

"Try not to think of it that way," said Chad. He picked up a spare towel and joined in the dish chores. "Think of a tiny cottage with flowers in the window boxes, the laughter of children, and a male slave to do your bidding."

"Tempting," said Sarah. "But a girl has to think of her career before she throws it away on frivolity."

"You're saying that you have some unfulfilled dreams? You need to live them out before you can settle down?"

Sarah kept working.

"Or are you saying that you just don't think I can make the grade?"

"I don't know what I'm saying," she answered. "I guess you'd have to know what it was like growing up with my father to really understand."

"Would it help if I took some lessons from your father?"

"No, I'm sure you'll do fine on your own." She laughed. "Let's get back to the male slave bit."

Both were silent. The dishes were almost finished. Other Insiders kept coming and going from the kitchen.

"Well, there's no rush," said Chad. "We don't have to make a public announcement tonight. It can wait till morning."

Sarah smiled.

"We'll take our time," he said. "When you're ready. But know this. In the end, I'll do anything I have to, to win you over."

"Is that a promise?" she asked.

"A promise."

"Will you go to England without me?" she asked.

"Yes," said Chad.

"What if you come home, and I'm married to somebody else?"

"That would hurt," he answered. "But, honestly, where would you find a man who'd make a better male slave?"

Chad reached up, gently taking Sarah's face in his hands. He kissed her. Not hastily. Not timidly.

"Can't make up your mind?" he asked.

Sarah sighed.

"Chad, you know I like you. More than like you. And I love the romance. It's so easy for me to get caught up in it. But when I honestly ask myself if I'm ready to take the leap, I get all confused. I think I just need a little more time."

TWENTY-TWO

Less than a quarter mile from the dorms where Jamie Madero and his fellow Insiders slept after their last day of training, a figure clothed in black from head to foot and equipped with climbing spikes ascended a telephone pole just inside the boundary of the retreat center property. He clipped the telephone circuits and electrical feeds into the building. The digital display in the dining hall blinked out at exactly 11:38 p.m.

Jeff Gordon, one of the few Insiders still awake, continued typing as the tiny fan in his laptop computer ran off the internal battery. He was just finishing an entry into his personal journal when the door behind him shattered inward, splintering the doorjamb and crashing against the wall.

Instantly, two black-clad figures, both wielding assault weapons, their faces covered by black masks and eyes hidden by infrared night vision goggles, stepped methodically into the room. A single swipe of a gun butt struck Gordon in the back of the head before he could react. He collapsed onto the desk, still sitting in his chair. The second attacker touched the mike switch on the radio attached to his shoulder harness. He spoke into the mouthpiece on his headset, "The lights are out on number one."

At the same time, intruder teams entered the darkened bays in each of the dorms. In a booming, electronically amplified voice, the intruder team chief called out into the bay where the couples slept,

"You are covered. Don't move. Don't think. Don't breathe." And then he added caustically, "Unless you are prepared to die."

Four intruders covered the occupants of each of the bays. One of the women in the couples dorm, frightened awake by the voice, called out to her husband who had been sleeping on the bunk above her.

"Silence!" screamed the intruder team chief with ear-splitting amplification.

One of the more elderly Insiders spoke out.

"My wife suffers from heart—"

His words were cut off by a crashing blow from the fist of an intruder standing just beside his bed. The man fell back, clutching at his mouth and gasping for air.

When it was clear that all of the Insiders were going to comply, the team leader spoke in a calmer, but not softer, voice.

"All right. Roll out of bed. Top bunks to your left side. Bottom bunks to the right. Lie face down on the floor. Arms out straight above your heads. Remember, you can't see us, but we can see you."

All of the Insiders moved to comply. One elderly woman began sobbing, unable to control herself. An intruder kicked her on the bottom of her outstretched foot as she lay face down on the floor.

"Shut up, or you'll never see your grandchildren again."

"Now then," the team leader barked, "stand and face your beds with your arms over your heads."

The Insiders were then instructed to move out into the center of the bay. They lined up single file, hands still held high. They marched down the stairs in near pitch darkness. Some stumbled. Others stubbed toes and cried out sharply. Each mistake was met by a corresponding act of coercion.

The captors led the barefoot Insiders across the open area to the dining hall under a moonless and overcast sky. The going was torturous on their tender feet. With merciless precision, the intruders herded the couples into the dining area, where they joined the single Insiders, who had been roused in similar fashion from the other dorm bays. Still in total darkness, the Insiders were at a complete disadvantage to their captors, whose night-vision equipment allowed them to see in the dark.

The intruders separated the women from the men by shoving, prodding, and overcoming any resistance by sudden force. One of the women flailed about her in the darkness for her husband as he was torn away from her. Instantly, an intruder grabbed a handful of her hair and wrenched the woman to her knees.

As she cried out in pain, her husband stepped toward the sound of her voice in the darkness, calling her by name. An instant later, the Insiders saw the muted flash of a silenced assault weapon and heard its distinctive report. The husband crumpled to the floor without a word. A young male Insider standing near him also twisted in pain and fell.

Unable to see clearly what was happening but knowing that her husband had been shot, the elderly woman cried out.

"What have you done? You brute! Oh, Fred, where are you?"

"Silence!" screamed the intruder leader through his amplifier. "Be absolutely still."

His thick eastern-European accent was slightly discernible despite the amplification system that gave his voice an electronic quality.

"This is the last time we will tell you. We are out of patience. The next person who talks or moves will be shot! Do you understand me?" He shouted to make his point absolutely clear.

The room was silent except for the crying woman, who had now located her fallen husband. The intruder chief spoke briefly to his associates in a foreign tongue. He then snapped on a bright handheld light, its narrow beam illuminating the woman and the lifeless form of her husband. The light emitted a focused beam so that the forms of those standing just outside the beam were barely visible. It was as though this couple was spotlighted on a stage.

The woman, who was slight of build and possessed refined features, knelt with great dignity and cradled the head of her lifeless husband in her lap. She turned her face toward the light, though its brightness was blinding, and with her eyes closed, spoke in the direction of the light and the intruder's voice.

"You have done a terrible thing!"

"Silence! " screamed the intruder as he stepped toward her, the light shining directly into her face.

"I will *not* be silent! There is a God in the heavens," she persisted, her voice becoming stronger with each word. "I hope that someday in the eternities, he will forgive you for your horrible cruelty."

Without further comment from the intruder, a black-gloved hand, holding a pistol with a long, ugly silencer cylinder, reached into the circle of light. Placing the silencer next to this courageous woman's head, the unseen intruder methodically pulled the trigger.

The captives in the room closed their eyes or turned their heads, clearly not wanting to record these images in their minds or hearts. The women clung to one another. The men stood with bowed heads. Stunned silence prevailed. For a few moments it was as though eternity were frozen.

The intruder chief broke the silence.

"That is right. Now I believe you understand what you are to do."

While his command of English was good, his accent lent a bizarre echo to this scene of horror.

"I assume that we now have a working agreement. When I tell you what to do, you will do it without question."

He snapped his light off again, plunging the room into blackness.

* * * * *

Now that the worst conceivable thing had happened—the taking of a human life—a sense of calm settled over the gathering, a calm that Jamie felt strongly. Minutes earlier, as the attack commenced, he scolded himself for relaxing the vigilance he had maintained the night before. He had sworn that he would be prepared for the next encounter with the forces of evil. He had tried to imagine how that encounter might come about and what he would do. Since Cortez, he had been trying to steel himself for the moment. But he had never imagined any peril this sudden and lethal.

Jamie couldn't see much of what had transpired, but he could feel the presence of death and felt the wave of calm assurance that settled over the Insiders. He knew that his life and the lives of his companions were now in the hands of God. The anger growing within him since Cortez now swelled into a sort of rage. Not a mindless, self-destructive rage, but a hot, unflinching determination to set things right, to protect the innocent, and to bring the offenders to justice.

He thought of King David as a boy, facing the seemingly unbeatable Goliath.

"Who is this uncircumcised Philistine," David asked in righteous indignation, "that he should defy the armies of the living God?"

But for now, the path of duty was clear. Jamie Madero must do as he was told. He must leave retribution in the hands of the Almighty.

Minutes passed as Jamie stood silently in the darkness. Though there was activity all around him, he could see almost nothing. The only sounds were from the movements of the intruders and occasional, barely audible comments among them in their own language.

At length, the intruder leader instructed the Insiders to lie on the floor, face down, with their hands behind their backs. Quickly, the intruders moved up and down the rows, taping the mouth, wrists, and feet of each captive.

Jamie listened as the sounds of movement in the dining hall gradually diminished, an indication that the intruders were leaving. He lay still for a long time to be sure that they had left. He didn't need to wonder why they had come. Cufflinks had said his client wanted to snatch three of them and send a message to their friends. He didn't know which three were to be taken. But he did know that the message had been sent.

When it was clear that the intruders had departed, Jamie tried to work his hands and feet loose. He gradually gave up the effort. The small gains he made didn't warrant the resulting pain or fatigue. He wiggled himself over next to one of his companions with the idea of freeing the other who could then free him. However, in the pitch black, he was unable to communicate what he intended or how to cooperate.

Finally, overcome by fatigue and feelings of deep frustration, Jamie lay still and tried to rest. Sleep wouldn't come. Whenever his mind was at rest, the images and sounds of the gleaming sidearm and the old woman's words flooded back to him.

* * * * *

While the Insiders in Leadville lay helplessly in the dark, awaiting rescue, three vans sped toward a private airfield where a small business jet stood refueled and prepared for takeoff. The pilot had filed no flight plan for the final leg of the trip. The flight and its occupants would be nearly impossible to trace.

TWENTY-THREE

Jeff Gordon awoke slowly from a nightmare, overwhelmed by feelings of foreboding. Shooting pains pierced the back of his skull, and occasional bright flashes inside his head left his senses reeling. He was surprised to find himself sitting in his chair, lying over the desk rather than in bed. He searched his memory in vain to remember how he came to be there.

When he could move, he rose on unsteady legs and stumbled to the door behind him, reaching for the light switch. Several flips of the switch convinced him that the power was off. He seemed to recall that it was out but didn't remember why he should know that.

He returned to his desk and fumbled around in the single drawer, looking for a pen light that he knew was there somewhere. He thought of his laptop computer and searched the desktop with his hands, but he couldn't find that either, nor could he remember where he had put it.

The back of Jeff's head and neck were so painful to the touch that he winced when he reached back to feel the injury. Dried blood matted the hair around a gaping wound. He wondered if there had been an earthquake and if some part of the ceiling had fallen in and struck him on the back of the head. He could make no sense of his situation, and his head hurt so badly that he was content to defer thinking about the puzzle until later.

Jeff stepped cautiously into the hall and moved toward the

kitchen, feeling his way along the wall. The kitchen was separated from the dining room by a long, folding door. He thought he could hear movement out in the dining room, but there were no voices and no way to turn on a light to check the security.

He moved along the countertops until he felt the top of the propane range. He reached into the cupboard above, where he remembered having placed a box of matches while taking his turn at meal preparation the day before. Finding the box and fumbling with it in the dark, he struck a match. Looking around in the cupboard by match light, he also found a partially burned candle that had perhaps been used during an earlier power outage. He lit the candle and carried it before him as he slowly walked back out into the hallway from the kitchen.

In the hallway, he was sure that he could hear movement in the dining room, so he turned in that direction. What awaited him in the dining room was a scene he would never forget in time or eternity. In the candlelit cavern of the dining hall, where so much good had happened during the week of training, all of his associates were gathered. Some lay on the floor. Some sat back to back. One of the younger men was moving by tiny, shuffling steps from one person to another, attempting to give comfort, though he could do no more than mumble behind his taped lips.

"Oh, my," Jeff muttered.

Though still in great personal pain, he comprehended immediately that a tragedy had occurred. He stepped as quickly as he could to a young woman sitting upright, her wrists, feet, and mouth taped.

Setting the candle beside her, Jeff removed the tape from her mouth slowly and with great care. He knew he was hurting her, but she didn't utter a sound of complaint. She just looked plaintively into his eyes.

When the last bit of adhesive tape snapped loose, he asked, "Brittany, are you all right? What happened?"

Tears of relief flooded her eyes.

"Oh, thank heaven you've come. It was so terrible! I think some of our Insiders are dead."

Jeff Gordon felt as though he had been struck in the chest by a hammer.

"Dead?" he gasped. "Who—what—what happened? Where?"

He couldn't finish his thoughts. They came racing with lightning speed.

"One of the couples," Brittany replied. "Go help them first."

Jeff picked up the candle. Searching the room, he realized that the men and women had been divided. He rushed to the other side of the dining room and there found several of the brethren sitting near two prostrate forms.

With unbelieving eyes, Jeff Gordon saw what he knew could be the end of the Foundation's work. Suddenly descending upon him like a great weight was the realization that he had failed these wonderful people whom he had come to love. He had misjudged the danger and placed their lives in jeopardy. And now, visible beyond all denial was the evidence that a couple, and perhaps others, had paid for his folly with their precious lives.

TWENTY-FOUR

Three state police cars were parked in a tight cluster at the service station convenience store on the south side of town as Chad Rowley drove by on his way back through Leadville toward the center. He had made an early start from Denver, where he completed the tasks assigned by Jeff Gordon the evening before. Turning toward the Turquoise Lake area, he passed two ambulances, their sirens blaring. He felt more and more uneasy when he saw ahead, near the turnoff to the center, a knot of emergency and law enforcement vehicles.

As he approached the center, a uniformed county sheriff's deputy waved him to a stop. Walking toward Chad's driver-side window, the deputy's right hand rested on the butt of his service revolver. Powering down the window, Chad nodded a greeting.

"Morning, officer. What's going on here?"

The officer had moved around so that he was standing behind Chad's left shoulder.

"Could you show me some identification, sir?"

Chad fished out his driver's license and handed it to the officer, who studied it carefully for a moment and handed it back.

"Where are you headed, Mr. Rowley?"

"I'm an employee of the Freemen Foundation. I'm just returning from Denver to the retreat center over there in the trees. Is something wrong?"

"I'm afraid you can't go in just yet," responded the officer. "Please pull your car over by those two Sheriff's Department vehicles. We'll let you know when you can proceed up the road."

"Officer, I'm one of the Foundation's senior officers. I'm returning from an assignment. I know my boss will want to see me as soon as possible."

"Sorry, sir. Please pull your car over there out of the way. We need to let emergency vehicles pass." The deputy walked off without further comment.

Chad pulled the car away as instructed. Getting out of the car, he stepped over to an unmarked sedan with government plates. The county sheriff and two men wearing blue FBI windbreakers were bent over the rear deck of the car, studying a map. Chad stood quietly a pace distant from them, hoping they would see him.

"Excuse me, gentlemen," he said finally.

"What do you need?" the sheriff replied in a somewhat unsociable tone.

"Sheriff, I'm Chad Rowley, a senior officer of the Freemen Foundation, which is holding a retreat and training session at this retreat facility. I've been in Denver overnight and was told to report back immediately to our director—who's up there." Chad pointed up the road in the direction he so badly wanted to go.

"Please contact Mr. Jeff Gordon," he continued. "He's the director. He'll confirm what I say."

"I'm sorry, sir," replied the sheriff. "This is a crime scene under my control." Then, glancing at the field agents, he added, "At least for the moment. We can't allow anyone in there."

The reference to a crime scene further heightened Chad's anxiety.

"Please, sheriff," he pleaded. In a gentler voice, he added, "The people up there are my friends. I need to see them."

The sheriff considered Chad for a moment.

"Deputy McGloughlin," he said to a nearby deputy, "call up to the house and get a confirmation on . . . what's your name again?"

"Chad Rowley."

"Call up to the house and get a confirmation that Chad Rowley is one of their people."

"Do you have some ID, sir?" asked Deputy McGloughlin, unclipping a mike from his lapel.

Again, Chad produced his driver's license, which the officer studied carefully, comparing the photo to the man in front of him.

"Lake 25, this is 15, over," called McGloughlin. "Contact Jeff Gordon on your end. Get us a confirm on a Chad D. Rowley as a guest at the retreat center. Rowley wants access. Let me know what you find—15 out."

Nearly fifteen painful minutes passed. Chad paced back and forth only feet away from the sheriff and the two FBI field agents. During the minutes that he waited, a steady flow of emergency and law enforcement vehicles, some using sirens, streamed into the area. Teams of officers received instructions and entered the woods. Two officers bearing a roll of plastic marking tape cordoned off the area by stringing the tape from tree to tree.

A helicopter could be heard flying down the valley from the north and hovered in an open field just off the Turquoise Lake road.

"Tell those news guys they cannot do a flyover yet," yelled the sheriff into his mike over the clamor. "Set it down in the flat. We'll give them the word when it's clear to go."

He stopped to listen.

"I don't care. We haven't finished our initial recon of the area yet. Tell them to set it down!"

Chad also noticed a woman, apparently from the press, who made her way from officer to officer, asking questions that they clearly declined to answer. Undeterred by their rejections, she moved toward Chad. She was about Chad's age, dressed in tailored slacks and a forest green windbreaker with a Channel 9 News logo embroidered onto the chest. She carried a recorder in one hand and a cell phone in the other. She walked directly to Chad and addressed him without hesitating in the least.

"Can you tell me how many people have been killed here?"

Chad was taken back by her assertiveness. Even more, the possibility that someone might have been killed stunned him.

"I'm sorry . . . I'm just a bystander here," he stammered.

"Do you know who owns the house?" she asked.

"I don't know that there is a house," he answered.

"Do you live nearby?" she continued.

"No. I'm just a visitor."

"Whom are you visiting?"

"I—uh—" hesitated Chad, not wanting to talk to this woman. He hoped with nagging impatience that clearance would come soon, allowing him to walk up to the dining hall.

The news lady brought him back to the conversation.

"You said that you're visiting. Who are you visiting?"

"I'm here to visit friends."

"Where are your friends?" she pressed. "Are they up that road?" She was standing directly in front of him and was close enough that he felt uncomfortable and wanted to inch away. The news lady pursued him.

"What did you say your name was?" she asked.

"I didn't say," Chad replied as quietly as he could, looking past her in the direction of the recreation property.

"Please, Mr. Whoever-You-Are. Something big has happened here. It's on all the police nets. Nothing this big has happened in Lake County since the Gold Rush. And our viewers have a right to know what's going on."

Chad was losing ground in this uninvited interview. He tried to excuse himself, but the news lady wouldn't relent.

He turned away from her and walked toward his car. She followed.

"Is this your car?" she asked.

Chad said nothing.

"Find the owner of a late-model Ford, Colorado license." She spoke the number into her recorder. "Who do you work for?" she asked.

Finally, out of hearing range from others, Chad turned to look the woman in the eyes.

"Look, miss, I'm trying not to be rude. I'm not a spokesman for anyone. I just got here fifteen minutes ago. I don't know whether anything happened. And even if I knew something, it wouldn't be my place to talk to you about it."

Seeming to sense that she had finally pushed about as far as this source was willing to go, she blew out a deep breath. The breath stirred the wisps of hair framing her face.

"Okay, *mister*," she said. "I know that you know something. I can feel it. I'll find out who you are, and I'll find out what you know." She crowded closer until he could feel her breath in his face.

Just then, the sheriff's deputy, standing thirty feet away, called him.

"Okay, Mr. Rowley. You're cleared to go up. Follow me."

The news lady smiled.

"Well, Mr. Rowley. I was right, wasn't I? Go up where? What is this place? Is this a private home? A business? Mr. Rowley, you can tell me."

Chad strode forward, taking steps as long as he could manage, forcing her to run in order to keep up with him.

"Who do you work for, Mr. Rowley? Where do you live? Why are you here?"

Reaching the side of the deputy, who had already started up the road, Chad felt himself blushing. The deputy, seeing that Chad was outgunned in this standoff, took pity on the younger man. With an understanding grin, he extended his arm to bar the reporter's advance.

"Sorry, ma'am. This is as far as you go. The press is not allowed into the crime scene yet."

"So it *is* a crime scene," she spoke into her handheld recorder.

"Ma'am, we'll let you know when you're cleared to go in. The sheriff will make a statement as soon as there's a statement to make. Please stay behind the line."

"I'm with Mr. Rowley," she said, stepping beside Chad and taking his arm. "Isn't that right, dear?" she asked Chad with a straight face.

That brought a laugh from both Chad and the deputy. As they walked away, the woman called after Chad while extending her business card.

"Please, Mr. Rowley. I need your help. And if you find that you need mine, please call me. Kathleen Taylor. Channel 9 News. This story will be all over the country on the evening news. I want to be the one who tells it."

Chad took the offered business card, put it into his shirt pocket, and rejoined the deputy on the walk up to the center just visible through the trees.

"Timid little gal, isn't she?" said the deputy. "I was worried about you there for a minute. Didn't get any teeth marks on your fanny, did you?"

Both men laughed. Chad could feel his tension easing a little. He was grateful Kathleen Taylor had come along to take his mind off the difficulties that surely lay ahead.

TWENTY-FIVE

As Chad reached the dining hall and dorms, he knew with sickening certainty that something terrible had happened. An ambulance, several more law enforcement vehicles, and a chartered bus had driven into the courtyard among the buildings.

His colleagues were already loading their personal possessions into the bus to return to Denver. They nodded their acknowledgment to Chad. No one spoke. The usual sociable air was completely missing. A palpable cloud of gloom seemed to hang over the scene. Still, underlying the somber mood, there was an atmosphere of quiet assurance. The Insiders moved with purpose. They appeared to be a people subdued but not beaten.

Chad found Jeff Gordon in the dining hall lying on a gurney, his eyes shut, being attended by a paramedic. Restraining his inclination to question everyone around him with the same intrepid urgency he had observed in Kathleen Taylor, Chad stepped up to the paramedic.

"How's he doing?"

The paramedic replied without looking up, taking an IV from his partner on the other side of the gurney.

"We've given him a sedative. He's lost quite a bit of blood from the severe laceration at the base of his skull, and he likely has a concussion."

"Do you know how this happened?" asked Chad.

"Nope," replied the paramedic as he swabbed off Gordon's arm to insert the IV.

"Is he going to be okay?" asked Chad.

"We're going to get him to the hospital as fast as we can.

"Okay, Larry," the paramedic said to his partner. "Let's roll him."

As they guided the gurney toward the door to the courtyard, Chad looked around for someone else to talk to. As he walked back toward the kitchen and office, his eyes were drawn to chalk marks and several large blood stains on the floor. Photographers and forensics experts were at work documenting the scene.

No one was in the kitchen. The office was empty. With his head bowed and expecting the worst, Chad walked out of the dining hall toward his dorm just as Jamie Madero came out of the building. Chad was struck by the difference he saw in Jamie's countenance as he walked directly toward Chad. Jamie put down a suitcase and duffel he was carrying.

"Hi, Bud," said Chad with all the restraint he could muster. "How're you doin'?"

Jamie reached his arms around Chad's shoulders and hugged him with a manly embrace. Then he pulled himself back, wearing a forced and sad smile.

"They caught us off guard again, didn't they?" he asked.

Chad followed him to the bus, where Jamie handed up the articles he was carrying.

"Let's go sit down for a few minutes. I need to ask you some questions," said Chad. He steered Jamie toward the dining hall. But as they approached the door, Jamie stopped.

"I can't go in there," Jamie whispered. "Not ever!"

"Sit here with me," said Chad, gesturing to a nearby bench. "Tell me what happened."

"You don't know?"

"Just tell me what happened."

"I don't even know where to start," replied Jamie.

Fatigue and emotion were clearly etched into Jamie's youthful face. He related the events of the nightmare, including the staggering revelation that the terrorists had taken Sarah Rudman and Gwen Fong.

Chad stopped breathing, his eyes widening in alarm. The color slowly drained from his face as the impact of this revelation registered.

Jamie continued his narrative, elbows on his knees and face in his hands. He wiped his nose and eyes on the long sleeve of his shirt.

"I'm sorry I wasn't here," said Chad.

"I'm glad you weren't here," replied Jamie. "I never thought I'd see anything like this. I feel sorry for the Spencers, and for Stu Atcheson. I'm worried about the missing women. But I felt like we were being protected. I know we were. What I don't understand is why these people had to die."

Chad nodded.

"What do you think about it all?" Jamie asked.

"Probably about the same as you, Bud. It's horrible. We've got to find those women. What did Jeff say?"

"He told us to pack our things. Said a bus would take us to the Denver office. He told us to cooperate with the law enforcement people and not to talk to anybody else about it. He said he'd be in touch as soon as he could. He was really sad. He didn't seem like himself," answered Jamie.

"Well, Bud," replied Chad, "he had a pretty good whack on the head. He'll be back. Jeff Gordon is a survivor.

"Any idea where they took Sarah and Gwen?" Chad asked. "Did they say anything? Drop any hints?"

"No," said Jamie. "They were animals. I'd say they knew exactly what they were doing. We didn't have a chance."

Insiders began to board the bus.

"Looks like it's about time to go," said Chad. "Guess you'd better jump on the bus."

"Where are you going?" asked Jamie.

"I'm not sure. These bad guys have got something I really want."

"And that would be Sarah?" Jamie ventured.

"Yeah, it would," said Chad.

"So, what are you going to do now?" Jamie persisted.

"I don't know, but I can't just sit and wait."

"I'm with you," said Jamie, a light of understanding kindling in his eyes. "Wherever you go, I go."

"No way," replied Chad. "You'd better do what Jeff said."

Jamie stood silently for half a minute.

"This goes both ways," he said resolutely. "I came here to become an Insider. You're an Insider. If I have to follow Jeff's instructions, seems like you do too. Besides, I don't have a home or apartment to go to. And who's to say that if I wander around without supervision I won't compromise the Foundation in some way without even knowing it? But most of all, I want to be there the next time we meet these guys."

Chad looked at Jamie for a moment, mentally comparing the boy he first met in Flagstaff to the young man standing in front of him now.

"Guess you're right," said Chad. He turned toward the bus to see that all of the Insiders were accounted for. They retrieved Jamie's few belongings. Then Chad gave the signal for the bus to depart, and he and Jamie waved to their departing friends.

The pair waited until the caretaker arrived and Chad turned the keys over to him. The place was still abuzz with law enforcement activities. The sheriff told Chad and Jamie to stay in touch with the Foundation's Denver office so that Jamie could be questioned further when detectives began their full investigation.

The pair left the center much the way they came in. Jamie still wore the boots given him by Richard Carlson at Gray Mountain Trading Post a lifetime earlier. This time they had the advantage of Jeff Gordon's auto, which would get them to Denver much quicker than going on foot.

With great effort they escaped Kathleen Taylor, now accompanied by a cameraman who rolled footage as she grilled them about their involvement. She asked about the bus loaded with people who had left earlier. She asked about the ambulances. She asked where they were going next, and on and on.

"Our viewers have a right to know," were Kathleen's parting words.

* * * * *

As Kathleen Taylor had predicted, the story made the evening news all over the country.

"Terrorists gun down three at a private retreat center high in the Rockies. Two women are reported missing after terrorists storm the center in an unprovoked nighttime attack. Channel 9 correspondent Kathleen Taylor will join us live from Leadville with more on that story following this message."

TWENTY-SIX

Get Art Warnock up here right now! I don't care where he is or what he's doing. I want him here this instant!"

Julienne Rostetter was furious. She fairly screamed into the intercom connection to her secretary. As Fletchner International's head of corporate security, the report she held in her hand should have come directly to her. Instead, Art had sent it directly to the Chairman and had merely copied her. She was livid at his insubordination. She wanted to tear him apart with her bare hands before she went to the Chairman and demanded that Warnock be removed from his position. She could not control him. She knew that he was doing terrible, illegal things.

The report was a follow-up on the questioning of four suspected industrial thieves late last week. It also detailed Warnock's successes in bringing in an additional suspect and a headquarters employee whom he claimed was linked directly to a theft ring. She had specifically ordered him not to move on Gwen Fong without consulting her. He had completely disobeyed her instructions.

While not stated specifically in the report, it was clear to JR that Art's methods were nothing short of illegal abduction. The interrogations were unduly violent. The entire operation may actually have included murder. Further, the report jumped to conclusions that JR was not willing to support.

Like the rest of the country, JR had heard of the terrorist attack in Colorado on the news the night before. No terrorist organization had yet claimed responsibility. JR knew that Warnock had been investigating the link between Rowley, Rudman, and Gwen Fong. She was convinced that Warnock was behind the foolish attack. It would eventually lead investigators to Fletchner International's doorstep. She had tried to warn the Chairman but he had waved her off with a patronizing pat on the head, as if saying, "Now, be a good girl and go back to work."

JR was a professional. She was happy to use her considerable talents to achieve business aims, to deter theft, and to gain an advantage for her organization, but she would not be a party to murder. Though she had long suspected foul play in the Internal Security division, it was now clear that Warnock had gone beyond anything she previously imagined.

"I know you think you're untouchable, but—" she said to Warnock when he arrived. The insolent expression on his face heated the hatred she felt for this man.

I don't just hate you; I despise you.

Warnock was not cowed by her fury. He barely paid attention as she spelled out in graphic detail the consequences of his continued insubordination. He laughed openly when she threatened to ask the Chairman to remove him. After listening impatiently for several minutes, Warnock finally stood up.

"Can it! If you've got a beef with me, take it up with the Chairman. In fact, I *want* you to take it to the Chairman. I've got something so hot that he'll be lapping from my bowl. It's you, not me, whose neck is in the noose. You're a weak link, and the Chairman knows it. If I were you, I'd buy a ticket to the last stop on the line, change my name, have a little cosmetic surgery, and try to forget I ever knew the Chairman or anything about his organization."

There was just enough truth to what Warnock said that JR lost all control.

"Get out of here!" she screamed.

The instant that Warnock left the office, JR grabbed a notebook and headed for the Chairman's office.

Striding along the hallway, she met Mark Hart, one of Warnock's lieutenants, coming in her direction.

"JR, I guess I'm a little out of place in this, but I thought I'd apologize for breaking protocol," Hart commented with a degree of sincerity. "I prepared the report for Art. I didn't know what he was going to do with it. I really thought it was going straight to you."

JR looked at the younger man, attempting to decide if he was actually making an effort at conciliation. Or was Hart feathering every nest in sight? Was he trying to make sure that when the dust settled he would have a job, no matter who won the battle between her and Warnock?

"Well, aren't you a good little Boy Scout," JR said. "If you're too dense to see the real issues here, let me tell you that I'm repulsed by the content of the report and by the sick and vicious methods you slimeballs use."

Hart didn't strike back or try to excuse himself. He lowered his gaze and stepped aside to let her pass. On impulse, wanting to leave him a little wiggle room in case he was being sincere, she said, "Let me know when you come down on one side or the other."

* * * * *

"The Chairman is in a meeting that will last another half hour," said his secretary. She was a mousy little bimbo with artificial red hair who took every occasion to speak down to those who came and went.

"I have to see him now," said JR, subduing her distaste for the woman.

"I'm sorry, Ms. Rostetter. He told me that under no circumstances was he to be interrupted. I'll be happy to let you know when he's available."

You do that—you ninny.

JR seethed at Mark Hart. He had delayed her long enough to let his boss get to the Chairman.

So much for apologies, Mr. Hart. Say good-bye to your career at Fletchner International.

Arriving at her office, she slammed the inner door and threw herself into the comfortable black leather chair behind her glass-topped desk. She spent the next five minutes trying to bring her anger under control. JR felt suddenly weary and vulnerable, feelings she hadn't known since she was a girl. She didn't fear for her life—at least not at the moment. But she knew with growing certainty that she had lost an important battle, a battle from which she might never recover. Feeling empty, she knew she couldn't allow herself to think about her life from any vantage point except her professional ambitions. There was nothing else.

You resort to anger, ambition, and intrigue because they give you purpose. You'll never be happy working in a flower garden or walking the dog. Keep fighting, girl. You'd better fight until there's nothing left to fight for. What then? Death? Oblivion? I can't imagine. I really don't want to think about it.

For the first time in as long as she could remember, JR leaned back in her chair and tried to think about nothing at all.

TWENTY-SEVEN

Art Warnock had hit the jackpot. With the instinct of a hustler who knows he's found a fat purse with loose strings, he relished the Chairman's full attention. He recited the information he'd gotten by chemical interrogation from the two women abducted from Leadville. He knew, but didn't tell the Chairman, that his imported strike team missed the third target, Chad Rowley. Actually, Warnock had everything he needed. But just to keep things nice and tidy, he'd already put out a contract on Rowley.

In this business, it doesn't pay to leave the opposition a leg to stand on.

"We're dealing with a group of amateur detectives," he reported to the Chairman. "Part-timers. Mostly they're students. Some are retired attorneys, CPAs, and computer people. They call themselves the Freemen Foundation. It's kind of a watchdog outfit. They look for organizations that have the wealth and power to buy government influence to change the laws to favor their own ends."

"Buying government influence? Change the laws? Those sound like good ideas to me," said the Chairman with obvious sarcasm but without even a hint of a smile. "How can we get into that kind of business?"

Warnock chuckled politely.

"This Freemen Foundation is a bunch of super patriots," Art continued. "Most of them are Mormons. The guy who put the thing together is a Mormon. He seeks out like-minded people."

"Do they have formal ties to the Mormon church?"

"No. They gather evidence and turn it over to the police or to the Feds. Their whole idea is to penetrate target organizations while maintaining a low profile."

"Doesn't look like they're that low profile. They've made the national news," said the Chairman.

Warnock laughed.

"You're right there. Sounds like they took a serious hit. I'm betting they back way off, if they don't go out of business all together."

The Chairman was up, pacing.

"Why do they care how we earn our money?"

"They see themselves as guardians of free government—and truth—and motherhood—and apple pie," replied Warnock.

"What do they get for their pains?" asked the Chairman.

"Nothing," said the head of Internal Security. "It's just a duty they feel they owe to society."

"Right-wing whackos!" mumbled the Chairman. "You say you've got everything under control?"

"Completely," replied Warnock.

"You've found all their infiltrators and given them walking papers?"

"I think so."

"Is that a yes or a no?"

"It's a yes."

"Do we have anything that belongs to them?" asked the Chairman. "Anything they are likely to come looking for?"

"No," returned Warnock, shaking his head. "We don't have anything to worry about from them. This is a little group of busybodies, not a military organization."

"You obviously don't know all there is to know about the history of religion." The Chairman absently tapped a pen against the palm of his hand as his thoughts ranged elsewhere.

Warnock was unsure where the Chairman's thoughts were headed. He remained silent.

"Some of the most effective military organizations in the history of the world have been instruments of churches. The history of Europe up through the emergence of modern nationalism was shaped almost completely by the armies of the Roman Church. Think of the Crusades. Think of the secret Muslim brotherhoods.

"Furthermore, remember that many of the armed conflicts raging today are carried on by adherents of various religions. It was true in Ireland. It's the source of the continuing conflict between India and Pakistan. Religion isolates Israel.

"Religions and armies operate on the same principles—discipline, sacrifice, obedience, and the rule of law. Don't mistakenly think that because religious people espouse faith, hope, and charity, they are incapable of decisive and combative action."

Warnock knew he was out of his depth in any discussion with the Chairman about something as abstract as world religion.

"Their little excursion into our territory has cost them big time," said Warnock. "I expect them to fold their tents and go home."

"That same attitude cost Napoleon his empire," replied the Chairman. "So you're telling me that they will have no further interest in us?"

"Well," Warnock hesitated, "there is the small matter of the two women who have helped us out."

The Chairman wheeled toward Warnock with a look that could wilt a cactus.

"When I ask you a question," the Chairman's words smoked like a hot poker, "I want you to tell me what I want to know, not what you want me to know. I asked you a minute ago if we have anything that belongs to them. When I ask a question, I want a straight answer, not a load of bull. Don't ever make me ask twice."

Warnock blinked and found it difficult to swallow.

"I saw the thing on the news last night about Leadville," said the Chairman. "Nasty stuff! I don't know what animal would do something like that. I felt especially . . . especially, ah, compassionate—yes, compassionate—toward the women who were abducted. A terrible thing! I would certainly hate to read in the newspapers that anything bad happened to those two women."

The Chairman looked directly at Warnock.

"There's not much I can do for the unfortunate ladies who were abducted, and I don't want to know if you had anything to do with that. I'm sure you didn't, being the upstanding man you are. But these other two women who have helped you out with a little information, I want you to watch out for them. Take good care of them. Make them comfortable. You never know when making friends like these women can be helpful to the organization.

"That's it, Art," the Chairman concluded as he rose and showed Warnock to the door. "Stay in touch."

Warnock left the interview feeling less confident than he had when he entered. He hurriedly withdrew a cell phone as he stepped to the elevator.

"Where do we stand with the two women?" he asked one of his henchmen. He listened briefly.

"Put the women up somewhere comfortable and make sure nobody lays a finger on them. I think the Chairman sees them as bargaining chips."

TWENTY-EIGHT

When the secretary finally ushered Julienne Rostetter into the Chairman's palatial office, JR could hardly wait to start talking.

"Sit down, Julienne," said the Chairman before she could speak. "Can I get you a drink?"

His every movement was deliberate, clearly trying to slow JR down.

"I can tell that you have a few things you would like to get off your chest," he said. "Before you say anything, let me give you a piece of advice. You're a bright woman. You've come a long way in the industry. I know you and Warnock aren't getting along right now. That will improve with time. Don't burn any bridges. Don't take any stands you can't back away from."

The Chairman strolled slowly along the glass wall that overlooked the grounds twenty-two stories below. He had his hands in his pockets. His suit coat hung on a valet nearby. As he talked to JR, he looked out toward the city, as one would inspect his own property.

"Above all," he said, "I don't want to hear you say that Warnock has to go. Don't say that it's either him or you. And don't tell me that you believe Warnock is doing illegal and brutal things. Or that what he's doing is bad for the organization—and that it'll come back to haunt us down the road. Okay? Don't say those things. But anything else you want to say, that I want to hear. Okay? Now, tell me why you were in such a hurry to get in here and visit with me." The Chairman stopped, saying no more.

JR stared at the Chairman in disbelief. She didn't know whether he was reading her mind or whether he'd been around so long that he'd experienced everything before.

"Well, I guess I just came to say hello," she answered meekly.

"How very thoughtful of you." The Chairman threw back his head and laughed, something not often witnessed by those who worked with him.

"Julienne, you're a very bright woman. I like you." The comment actually came with a degree of warmth.

It was the first statement the Chairman had ever made to JR that reflected any personal feeling toward her. Though she confessed to herself that she had coveted his approval through the years, this statement awakened in her a sudden sense of foreboding. She was unsure how to respond.

"I like these neighborly visits. Let's do this often," the Chairman continued in a somewhat strained fashion. JR knew that nothing could be further from the truth. Neighborly visits with the Chairman were among the last things she desired.

"You know that Warnock has dreamed up a connection between some of our wayward children and the Mormons. Now I know that can't be true," the Chairman said without conviction. "It must be his imagination. And his timing isn't very good in light of the terrible thing that happened in Colorado yesterday.

"Disgusting," he continued. "Makes me worry about this world we live in. At any rate, if we were to have some contact with this Freemen Foundation, Warnock is the last person in the world I would send to talk to them. He's not very good with public relations. But he seems to have a pretty good head for sizing up the competition.

"I want you to take the lead in this matter. I want you to find out all you can about the Freemen Foundation. Find out what there is in Mormonism that would encourage a group of their adherents to take up a cause like this. What are these people really up to? What motivates them? Why would they have an interest in us? What are their weaknesses? You know, general things like that. And don't let too much time pass while you're looking into it. Get back to me with something in two days."

The Chairman's eyes grew distant.

"I'm very curious about this," he said.

As had been the case so often before, JR left the Chairman's office disarmed and with a new set of marching orders.

At least he gives me a reason to keep living.

TWENTY-NINE

It had been a long morning. JR returned to her office just after 1:00 p.m. from an international meeting with security heads from the Fletchner subsidiaries. The key topic was hemorrhaging in the bottom line for operations in Russia, where a government crackdown on organized crime was finally getting underway. JR sat uncomfortably through the entire meeting, saying as little as possible and mostly asking questions.

As always, the discussions were conducted in the language of modern business. The reports were replete with euphemisms and understatement. They cast the best possible light on what were probably illegal activities.

The excitement of working for a company with huge resources and unbelievably nice salaries had kept JR from ever probing too deeply into the Chairman's business portfolio. But on this day, she found herself thinking that the time had come to leave Fletchner International. She would proceed carefully, putting out a few feelers, contacting a few headhunters with whom she had dealt before. She was suddenly very weary.

Oh, wake up, woman. What's wrong with you today?

Heidi, JR's secretary for the past three years, greeted her as usual.

"Good afternoon, Ms. Rostetter. Your mother has called three times. Celeste Hughes left a package for you. I have some information about the Mormons that you asked for."

133

"You may as well come in," JR replied. "I'm famished. Could you bring me a small pasta salad, a cup of yogurt, and one of those flaky rolls—plain? You can tell me what you've found while I eat."

JR busied herself for a few minutes until Heidi returned. She sat savoring her lunch while Heidi summarized the information she had gathered about the Freemen Foundation and the Mormons. The pasta salad was excellent—the low-cal Italian dressing was just tart enough.

"Okay," began Heidi, "first the Mormons. I've gone to all the usual sources. The Mormon Church has an extensive website. I got a few things from an online encyclopedia, and others from a cute guy in my apartment complex who's a Mormon. I called their mission headquarters in Toronto. They wanted to send a couple of representatives out to talk to us. I told them to put together some pamphlets and stuff. And I had the company courier stop and pick them up."

Heidi was a thirty-three-year-old single mother with a daughter in middle school and a son in elementary school. JR liked her for her efficiency. She always kept a cool head when JR was under pressure or on the edge of losing personal control.

"I suppose you know that the real name of the Mormon Church is The Church of Jesus Christ of Latter-day Saints," said Heidi. "Their world headquarters are in Salt Lake City, Utah. They have about fourteen million members worldwide. I found quite a few celebrity names affiliated with the Church: J. Willard Marriott, Jr., chairman of the board of Marriott Corporation; John Huntsman of Huntsman Chemical and Huntsman Cancer Institutes; Senator Orrin Hatch of Utah; Steve Young, former quarterback of the San Francisco 49ers; Donny and Marie Osmond; Gladys Knight of rock and roll fame; and Harrison Ford."

JR had been peeling off flakes from her dinner roll and letting them melt in her mouth. From childhood, she had disciplined herself to eat slowly. She considered that to be one of two keys to staying slim throughout life.

Eat slowly and exercise daily.

"Wait," she interrupted Heidi's report. "Harrison Ford? I don't think so. I've met him. He's not the type."

"Well, that's what Jerry, the guy in my apartment complex, told me." Heidi shrugged. "Sounded good to me."

"Let's try to stick to the facts here," instructed JR as she raised another fork of pasta salad to her lips.

"Okay, well," continued Heidi, "Latter-day Saints are known for their health code. They don't drink alcohol or smoke, and they stay away from other legally addictive stimulants. According to Jerry, because they have so few other vices, they eat—a lot. He thinks the residents of Utah consume more ice cream, cookies, and soft drinks per capita than any other place in the United States."

"I'm sure the Chairman will be interested in that bit of trivia," JR commented without trying to conceal the annoyance in her voice.

"Latter-day Saints emphasize family solidarity," said Heidi. "They have their own university system. They have one former Miss America. Their leaders are all old men. They have their own scripture that they call the Book of Mormon."

JR listened with little interest, knowing that Heidi had not yet begun to answer the Chairman's questions. JR would need something better than this before she could report back to him.

"What makes them tick?" she asked. "What are they after? What are they trying to accomplish? These are the kinds of things I need to know." JR got up and started pacing around the office.

"Well," Heidi hesitated, "they're after religion. They're trying to get people—you know. They're trying to get people . . . to . . . religion, I guess."

"Great! That's a lot of help. What does that mean?"

"I don't know," Heidi replied.

"Have you read all of that stuff?"

"A lot of it. There are things in here about how they started. You know, the pioneers."

Heidi squirmed as JR bore down on her with the beginning of what Heidi could tell was one of her boss's typical interrogations.

"I need to know what is at the heart of this religious movement. Why do people do this? What do they get out of it? How do they see the world? What interest do they have in politics? Or business?" Then she added, "How do they view crime?"

Heidi hesitated to answer. "Well, there's nothing like that in any of these materials."

"Can't your boyfriend tell us this stuff?" JR quizzed.

"He's not my boyfriend." Heidi blushed a little. "I just said he's a cute guy. I wouldn't personally have any interest in somebody who's—religious. You know what I mean?"

"We need more answers," said JR. "Call the Mormon Church in Toronto and have them send over a representative so we can get more in-depth information."

"Are you sure that's what you want?" Heidi blinked.

"Why not?" asked JR.

"Well, you've heard about Mormon missionaries."

"Heard what?"

"Well, I mean, if you—uh—if I call and ask for a representative, they're going to send a couple of Mormon missionaries. You know, the young men in white shirts and ties. They ride bicycles and wear little name tags on their shirt pockets." Heidi was demonstrating all of this with her hands as she talked.

"They're going to put the moves on you, like—try to get you to join their Church." Heidi shook her head as if warning JR away from danger.

JR had finished her lunch. Seeing a solitary crumb that fell on her desktop, she cleared it away.

"Tell them we don't want any proselytizers. We just have a few questions to ask. Maybe we can get our hands on a copy of their book."

With that, JR retrieved her suit coat and checked the computer for the location of her 2:00 p.m. meeting.

"Harrison Ford? I can see why you don't make your living as an investigator," JR said over her shoulder as she headed out the door.

THIRTY

Representatives of The Church of Jesus Christ of Latter-day Saints arrived at the Fletchner International Building in Brampton, Ontario at 6:30 p.m., just as Heidi was gathering her things to go home for the evening. JR had just returned from a late afternoon meeting and was settled down in front of her computer, answering the day's emails. Heidi rapped lightly on the door to announce the arrival of JR's visitors.

"Just show our guests in, Heidi," JR called.

She continued what she was doing for a minute or two before turning to find two young women standing in front of her desk. JR blinked in momentary surprise. She had assumed that the Church representatives would be men.

"Hello," she said. "I'm Julienne Rostetter." She gestured the two young women to the seats nearest the desk.

One of the young women, perhaps the senior of the two, stepped around the side of the desk and extended her hand.

"Hello, Ms. Rostetter. I'm Sister Phillips and this is my companion, Sister Hanford."

JR found herself a bit confused by the introductions. She wasn't accustomed to shaking hands and certainly not with women.

"Please sit down, ladies," she invited.

JR estimated the age of the older woman at twenty-three or twenty-four, and the other perhaps a year or two younger. Both were attractive. The older woman, Sister Phillips, had a touch of natural glamour. They were somewhat windblown and sweaty from the afternoon heat.

"Did you ladies ride your . . . ," JR hesitated, "your bicycles out here?"

"No," replied Sister Phillips with an easy smile. "We have a car."

"I see," JR continued, not quite knowing where to go with the conversation. So, in her usual straightforward manner, she launched into her agenda for the meeting.

"I need some quick answers about your denomination. I think I already have most of your publicity information in hand," she said. "Please tell me—what is it that makes you people tick?"

"That's a wonderful question," Sister Phillips spoke up. "Not one we hear often, but it gets right to the heart of the matter. What makes us tick and sets us apart from many other people in our world is that we know who we are. We're children of God. And we know who he is. He is a personal, lovable father. The creator. The source of all light, knowledge, and goodness in the universe. And we know why we're here. We know what he expects of us while we're here. We know where we're going when we die, if—" she paused for emphasis, "—if we're willing to live according to God's plan."

This was all said so quickly that JR had to sort through the series of assertions and decide whether any of the information was helpful to her.

"I would venture to say that there are many people," said Sister Phillips, "perhaps you know some, who are glad to be caught up in the rat race of life because they don't have any other reason to live." The missionary paused again.

"That reason to live is what makes us tick."

Sister Phillips spoke with a force that unsettled JR. While she found such assertiveness in a woman as young as Sister Phillips to be a little offensive, what unsettled JR most was the fact that Sister Philip's opening statement addressed the very feelings JR had struggled with since her interview with the Chairman the day before. She had been fighting off the nagging realization that if it weren't for the adrenaline rush she felt every day as part of the investigation business, there would be nothing else to interest her. Nothing else she could give herself to. Nothing else worth living for! While it bothered her so much that she preferred not to think about it, Sister Phillips's statement struck at the heart of her internal conflict.

"I see. And can you tell me what that reason for living is?" asked JR.

"Yes, we can," replied Sister Phillips. "We would love to."

What followed was a discussion lasting nearly an hour, about what the sister missionaries called the "plan of happiness." Repeatedly throughout the discussion, alarms went off in JR's mind. She objected to what these young women were saying solely on the basis that she had always considered herself agnostic. She objected because she had instructed Heidi to tell them that she didn't want to be proselytized. She objected because she didn't want to accept or believe anything taught by those on the lunatic fringe of religion. And she objected because she had always been brighter, quicker, and more insightful than anyone around her. But here she sat with two women not even finished with college who were teaching her about the purpose of life.

JR wanted to voice her objections and end this conversation with one quick and decisive stroke. But she found herself unable to do so. What stopped her was not the fear of hurting their feelings. She'd have done that in an instant and without remorse.

What confused JR, unsettled her and frightened her, was the feeling that everything they were saying was true, and she knew it. And she hated it!

JR, wake up. This can't be true! You don't want it to be true. It means that everything you've done with your life has been a waste!

She wanted to get away and think. She had never heard that a person's spirit is eternal, that she had lived in a spirit world long before her birth. She had never considered that she came to the earth with a specific mission. Or that fulfilling her mission would bring happiness. Or that family relationships formed in mortality would go on into the eternities. Or that a loving God would reward his children for the good they do by multiplying their happiness endlessly into the future.

After forty-five minutes, JR was hardly hearing anything the missionaries were saying. She responded mechanically. She was experiencing too much inner turmoil to focus on anything else.

"Ms. Rostetter, are you okay?"

The two lady missionaries stopped their presentation. Julienne realized that she had completely fazed out. She needed to be alone until she could pull herself together.

"I'm fine," she replied. "I may be a bit tired. I still need to ask some specific questions, but maybe we should do that at a later time."

"Sure," replied Sister Phillips. Sister Hanford nodded her agreement.

The lady missionaries rose and moved toward the door. Sister Phillips turned back.

"Ms. Rostetter, the voice you hear in your mind that tells you not to believe what we say is not your own. It's the voice of a being that wants you to be miserable and lonely. He wants you to waste your life. He wants you to fail in the mission you came here to perform. But you've also had feelings that the things we're saying are true. Those come from a Heavenly Father who loves you and wants you to succeed. To be wonderfully happy. Thank you for your hospitality. We can find our way out."

Julienne Rostetter, woman of steel, stood speechless at the door to her office. She felt like a little girl. Suddenly, she felt a desire to visit her mother.

THIRTY-ONE

Sarah Rudman lay uneasily on her flimsy bed, gazing with deep concern at her roommate, Gwen Fong. At least six days and nights had passed since their horrible ordeal in Leadville. Both women were present when their unidentified abductors killed at least one—and possibly more—of their friends. The hours following the abduction were a blur in Sarah's mind. As soon as the women were led to a waiting van with their wrists and mouths taped, the abductors had injected them with some drug that had brought unwelcome oblivion.

Sarah was unsure how long she remained in a state of drug-induced unconsciousness. She had no idea what had happened to her or Gwen during that time. However, she did know that her captors took no precautions to observe sterile procedures in giving the injections. Two or three spots on her upper arms were inflamed and sore. Sarah knew enough about medicine to fear that non-sterile injections could bring deadly infections. She knew that both she and Gwen needed medical attention desperately.

Gwen appeared to be discouraged and disheartened. That was not surprising. More important, she seemed to be feverish. All day, she had lain listlessly upon her bed. Sarah could hear Gwen breathing heavily through her nose. She could suffocate if the tape weren't soon removed from her mouth.

Sarah knew she needed to act soon to save them both. Her

captors had forbidden any communication between the women. They threatened death if the women tried to escape or attract any rescue. Sarah couldn't reach Gwen's bedside because the women were tethered with strong nylon cord. It was just long enough to allow them to lie down and move around on their beds, but not long enough to move about within the room.

Sarah resolved to act. She had to attract the attention of her captors and alert them to Gwen's condition. She could only hope that doing so would result in help for Gwen and not worsen their situation.

Sarah lay on her back and raised her bound feet to thump repeatedly on the wall. The walls were of hollow construction and each strike of her heels raised a long, resonant thump. She lowered her feet to the bed and turned to await the arrival of her captors.

She didn't have to wait long. No sooner had she righted herself on the bed, than the door flew open and a hooded captor stepped into the room. He scanned the room quickly. He could obviously see that Sarah was awake and that Gwen Fong was not. He moved swiftly and ominously toward Sarah, producing an ugly knife as he advanced.

Sarah gestured wildly with her head toward Gwen. She looked toward the sick woman and did all she could in her restrained state to direct the captor's attention toward Gwen. Her heart pounded as he reached her bed in three long steps. Sarah was not easily frightened, but she found herself wanting to close her eyes and scream for help.

Sarah willed herself to turn her gaze toward Gwen, expecting to feel the knife cutting into her throat in the next instant. Every nerve in Sarah's body tensed. When the pain did not come, she allowed herself to breathe out. Then she felt the warm steel against her throat and pressed her head back further into the pillow. There was still no cutting sensation. She allowed herself to turn her eyes up toward her captor. He was looking toward Gwen.

After a long moment's hesitation, he seemed to understand what Sarah was trying to do. He slowly withdrew the knife, stood upright, stepped to the other bed, and shook Gwen firmly. Detecting no response, he raised one of her eyelids to check the pupil. To Sarah's immense relief, he felt the unconscious woman's forehead.

As Sarah looked on, the captor strode purposefully from the room, replacing his knife and closing the door behind him. Her heart still pounded wildly, and her entire body quivered.

Oh, thank you, thank you, she prayed.

Sarah was startled to see Gwen's eyes flutter open. The older woman turned her head toward Sarah. Though Gwen's mouth was taped, Sarah could see a distinct smile in the corners of her eyes. She could almost hear Gwen speaking to her.

Thank you. Please don't worry about me. I'll be all right. Adversity makes sisters of us all. You are my sister, and I love you.

A sudden and powerful assurance swept over Sarah that Gwen Fong was not helpless. Though she hadn't known Gwen well before the abduction, Sarah felt the other woman's quiet resolve. Sarah knew that when the moment for action arrived, Gwen would be a strong and resourceful companion. For the millionth time, Sarah Rudman regretted never having a sister of her own.

Sarah brimmed with frustration. *If only we could talk to each other. Of course, that's exactly why they won't let us talk. They keep us together for ease of control but completely isolated so we can't strengthen each other—and can't plan anything.*

A few minutes later, the captor returned to the room. This time, he walked to Sarah and blindfolded her. She then heard someone else enter the room and could tell by the sound that he or she was standing over Gwen's bed. Of course, no one spoke. A minute or two later, there was a rustling of bed linen and the springs of Gwen's bed squeaked as she either rose from the bed or was lifted. A shuffling of feet and other involuntary noises by the captors followed. Sarah could only interpret the sounds as their exertions to carry Gwen from the room. They closed the door behind them but didn't lock it. Sarah assumed they either had their hands full with Gwen or they intended to return her soon. Eventually, she heard someone relock the door.

The captors didn't return that evening. Sarah lay there, still blindfolded, hungry, and thirsty. Alone and bedsore in total darkness, Sarah had never felt so helpless.

In the midst of her privation, she again turned her thoughts heavenward. The acute frustration boiling inside her diminished as she prayed. As she grew sleepy, her thoughts turned to her father. Sarah tried to imagine what he might be doing this evening. Recalling with never-lessening fondness the feeling of being near to him, she knew how he cherished and admired her. Just thinking of him brought Sarah comfort and strength. She could still hear his voice in her mind as it sounded down through the years.

"Princess, it's just you and me till we meet Mom in the other world. Let's enjoy each other while we're here," he often said.

Dad, I wish you could find me. I know you'd come and get me. In the meantime, I won't disappoint you.

Sarah thought about Chad Rowley, freely admitting her love for him. She knew he felt the same way about her. He was everything she wanted. In fact, she felt desperately foolish as she lay there in miserable captivity and remembered declining his offer of marriage so she could pursue her career ambitions. Would she give up a chance to be with him so she could endure more of this? Not likely.

Sarah knew her choice was in part driven by an unpaid debt to her father. He was all a father could be to her. In some way she couldn't fully explain, following in his footsteps seemed to be the only way she could repay his tenderness and absolute devotion to her for so many years. She didn't know if this life was what he'd want for her, but regardless, it was her gift to him. Not knowing how long it would take her to repay her debt, she couldn't move forward with Chad. However, she would enjoy his affection so long as he understood her reservations.

No doubt Chad would be consumed with anguish for her safety. He would do everything humanly possible to find and rescue her. In so many ways, he was like her father. She tried to imagine what would happen if Ike Rudman and Chad Rowley met in the present circumstances. Alone, uncomfortable—even miserable—she knew she wasn't forgotten by either.

THIRTY-TWO

Sarah didn't so much fall asleep as slide into a state between sleep and waking. She was conscious of being in the same cheap motel room, and she thought she could feel the blindfold she wore. But she felt an oppressive darkness surrounding her—a sinister presence in the room. Her head was spinning, filled with surreal voices.

In this semi-conscious state, Sarah concluded that this was a side effect of drugs that had been administered to her without medical supervision. She didn't panic, but feelings of impending doom washed repeatedly over her.

As the blackness deepened, she saw, once more replayed from lower levels of her consciousness, the scenes of the killing at Leadville. She could see as clearly as if it were happening again—Irene Spencer kneeling beside her fallen husband. Sarah could feel Irene's goodness. She admired the serenity and peaceful strength with which Irene testified to the man who was about to take her life.

I will not be silent. There is a God in the heavens. I hope that someday in the eternities, he will forgive you for this.

Then with sickening clarity, Sarah saw the black-gloved hand reach into the circle of light.

No, please!

Sarah couldn't tell whether she was dreaming or whether her captors would hear her muffled cry and punish her for breaking the command of silence. Yet she couldn't restrain her cries. Though she, like so many of her companions, had turned her eyes away to avoid seeing the slaying of Irene Spencer, Sarah now saw the gun placed to Irene's head. Sarah tried to turn her gaze. She willed herself to stop thinking about this.

I don't want to see this.

But her resistance was to no avail. As if in slow motion, she saw the gun at Irene Spencer's temple.

No, no. Please! Nooooooo—

Irene Spencer's eyes were open, and her lips moved slightly as she uttered a silent prayer. She was the picture of perfect calm. She fairly glowed within the bright circle of light. Sarah knew she couldn't witness this vicious act and go on living, but she was powerless to look away.

With mounting alarm, Sarah watched the gun jump as Irene's slayer pulled the trigger. Every nerve in Sarah's body recoiled in a mighty jolt as though a tremendous surge of electricity coursed through her. Her chest constricted, and with a mighty gasp, she screamed out in agony.

Oh, Heavenly Father, no! Don't let this happen. Please, oh please. Oh please!

Sarah sobbed. From the depths of her soul, her grief poured out. For Irene Spencer. For her own mother who left a weeping husband and a bewildered infant daughter as death wrapped its silent shroud around her. For a lonely girl abroad in a vast and shadowy world, always anxious for the safety of her doting father. For every living soul who ever suffered, or longed, or feared, or wept, or knew the piercing agony of loss or failure or hopelessness. For all of these, and many more, Sarah sobbed until her hot tears soaked the blindfold.

As she gained control of her feelings, her focus returned to the scene of Irene Spencer's death. She was startled to see the scene mostly changed. The gun had been withdrawn, and the remainder of the room outside the circle of light around Irene was now totally black. Irene was still kneeling over her husband, looking very much alive, as though nothing had happened to her. Irene kissed her husband's lifeless form tenderly. With a sweet and imperturbable smile, she then rose and, looking about her, smiled in recognition toward that person she seemed to be seeking.

Irene was now clad in white, her countenance radiant. The years seemed to melt off her as Sarah looked on. Now reaching into the light were the hands and arms of a man also clad in white. They were the hands of a younger man, and indeed, as this newcomer stepped fully into the circle of light, Sarah could see that he was a man in his prime. He gently encircled Irene in his arms and pulled her to him in a familiar embrace. This was not the DeLoy Spencer that Sarah had known. This man was much younger. Sarah was somewhat confused, wondering if perhaps this were a son.

But shortly, Sarah could see that the woman in white was also not the Irene Spencer she had known, though a faint resemblance remained. This younger woman was gloriously beautiful. She radiated light. Sarah could see that the flashlight of the terrorists and all of the surroundings of the dining hall in Leadville were now gone from the scene. The light in which these two young lovers basked came from within them.

Sarah Rudman, who only moments before was lost in the depths of terror and grief, felt her heart melt within her. Despite her sophisticated exterior, she had always been a softie. She could cry at anything. That is, if she were alone or with her father, who was also an old softie.

Now, she cried the cry of joy. Her sorrow in knowing that DeLoy Spencer had also been killed was swallowed up in the realization that this wonderful couple was blissfully reunited in the realms beyond the veil of death. Surely, if no terrorist's bullet could spoil this scene, then what was there to fear in the mortal world?

DeLoy and Irene Spencer faded slowly from Sarah's view, still locked in their familiar embrace. To Sarah, it seemed as though they were one rather than two. As they faded from view, she could hear music. It wasn't loud or stirring, but it gently breathed peace into her soul. She felt as though she were being lifted from her bed of affliction.

THIRTY-THREE

Kathleen Taylor of Channel 9 News arrived early at the LDS church meetinghouse in Boulder, Colorado, where the funeral for DeLoy and Irene Spencer was to be held. Nearly a week had passed since the Spencers and another young man were killed in the unexplained terrorist attack at Leadville. Kathleen considered herself fortunate to have been staying with friends in Dillon the night before. She received an early call from the news editor asking her to rush over to Leadville to check out a tip that multiple shootings had occurred.

In her three years as a television reporter, Kathleen had posted a number of impressive stories. But she hadn't yet had a really big break, one that made national news. Instinct told her that this might be the story. Driving at speeds approaching lunacy, she arrived at the crime scene while the law enforcement agencies were still responding. The early tip allowed her to break the story, reporting live from the crime scene. The story contained two newsworthy angles. First, it involved terrorist activities in America's heartland—always a hot topic. Second, it raised the prospect of controversy about a private foundation doing investigative work, possibly a spin-off of industrial espionage.

Though the story raised more questions than answers, it ran well, and to Kathleen's ecstasy, it made the national news that evening. She returned to the Channel 9 newsroom late to something of a hero's welcome.

"Hit the big time, huh?" commented Roy Sanders, Channel 9 longtime anchor. "Way to go, kid."

It felt great. Kathleen had worked hard, been aggressive, asked the right questions, and had the maturity to present the killings as a tragedy demanding answers. She resisted the temptation to leap to any unsupported conclusions.

"There's more to this than we can tell at the moment. But stay tuned, and we'll bring you the rest of the story," Kathleen had finished with her favorite closing lines.

"I'm sure you've made Paul Harvey proud," quipped Stacy Quinn, a co-anchor whose on-the-air warmth faded as quickly as the lights on the set at the end of a newscast.

Kathleen smoldered for three days over that little crack. Not that she minded being compared to Paul Harvey. She considered him one of the great storytellers in the news business. But the jab came from phony Stacy. Stacy had never been a reporter. She'd never dug for a story or crusaded for the rights of viewers. To Kathleen, Stacy Quinn was just a pretty face. Nevertheless, Kathleen bit her tongue. She would bide her time, trusting that in the end, talent and hard work would win out over looks and politics.

If not, then I really don't want to be a part of this industry anyway.

But the story that began so strongly had not developed as Kathleen hoped. Other than the information released by the sheriff's department and the local color that Kathleen had woven into the original newscast, she'd only found a few additional leads.

The Freemen Foundation operatives who survived the ordeal were a close-mouthed lot. They had been instructed to leave all interaction with the media in the hands of the Foundation's public affairs consultant. Furthermore, aside from their firsthand knowledge of what transpired during the attack, the victims knew little else. They were unable to identify or even speculate about the identity or motives of the terrorists. Everything had happened in the dark. Even the terrorists' voices had been electronically modified.

Kathleen had met and interviewed one person at Leadville who might be a knowledgeable source—if she could get him to talk. She knew him only as Mr. Rowley. But after he'd made the required statements to the sheriff's department and the FBI, he disappeared.

Because the attack occurred in Leadville and away from Denver, Kathleen was unacquainted with the sheriff's department sources there. She had also hit a stone wall with the Foundation's director. She knew Jeffrey Gordon was a multi-millionaire entrepreneur from California turned philanthropist. She knew he'd been badly injured by a blow to the head during the attack. Like Mr. Rowley, Jeffrey Gordon had disappeared as soon as federal and local investigators released him.

Kathleen's editor gave her plenty of time and support to pursue the story further. But he drew the line when she asked him to finance her trip to Chapel Hill, North Carolina, where a funeral was to be held for Dennis Stuart Atcheson, the third Freemen Foundation employee killed in Leadville. Kathleen had begged, threatened, and thrown a fit in the newsroom. She had even declared that she would fly to North Carolina at her own expense.

"Go right ahead," replied her editor with an offhand shrug. "And I might suggest that when you return, you seek employment with one of our competitors. You're acting like a woman whose only real interest is her own career and not the profitability of the station. I'd like to see our competitors hire a whole army of people like that." He walked away without further comment.

"What are we going to do about this story? It's too good to lose," she called after him.

"Contact the network affiliate in Raleigh and have them send a reporter out to the funeral. Tell them what you want to know," he suggested matter-of-factly as he sorted through a stack of copy.

"But to show you that I'm on your side," he continued, "I'll let you take a crew to Boulder on Friday to cover the local angle on the double funeral for the couple."

At least that's something.

The report back from Raleigh was disappointing, as Kathleen knew it would be. So she had to make this day count. The story was already old news. Unless she could revive it here in Boulder, she'd have to write it off and move on to other assignments.

When she arrived at the chapel for the funeral, the Freemen

Foundation had a public affairs representative in attendance to handle media inquiries. The representative was a woman who knew the ins and outs of working with the media. She was prepared with a news release containing obituary material and a statement by the Foundation's board condemning wanton violence, appealing for the release of the abducted women, and casting the Foundation's mission into the most publicly laudable verbiage possible.

Media representatives were reminded that the funeral was a private religious service. They were invited to attend the service but had to leave their gear outside. Interviews must wait until later. Media personnel were placed on their honor to observe these restrictions.

"Keep your eyes open for the guy with the white hash mark in the front of his hair," Kathleen instructed her cameraman, Doby. She showed Doby a somewhat dated press photo of Jeffrey Gordon.

"He's the director of the Freemen Foundation. I've got to find out from him what they were doing in Leadville. I need to get the truth about what they do overall. And if you hear the name Rowley, let me know immediately."

Kathleen always requested Doby for her assignments because he was alert to story angles on location. He often handed her unexpected enrichment material. He had gained an excellent sense of composition while working as an apprentice cinematographer at a film studio. He was drawn to news because he craved the thrill of capturing events while they were happening.

Kathleen and Doby stood outside a back entrance to the church, where many of the guests were entering. She did several man-on-the-street interviews while waiting, but she cut the last one short to go inside when the signal came that the funeral was about to begin.

"Wait out here," she told Doby. "When it's over, I'll meet you right here. I have no idea how long it's supposed to last. While I'm in there, I'll try to locate the people we need to talk to after the service."

* * * * *

Jeff Gordon had already been in the chapel for twenty minutes when the funeral service began. After meeting with and expressing his condolences to the children of DeLoy and Irene Spencer, Jeff visited quietly with some of the Insiders who were gathered in a section of seats to one side of the chapel. The mood among them was sober. All had suspended their Foundation activities and were awaiting further direction from Jeff. Following the shooting, Jeff had been advised by FBI investigators to keep a low profile. Once the Freemen were settled after the attack, he quietly boarded a private business jet and flew to California, where he passed the week with one of his sons.

"Mr. Gordon, Brother and Sister Spencer's children wanted me to invite you to join us on the stand. If you'd like to, you can sit here in the row behind me," said the bishop who was conducting the funeral.

In his seat on the second row of the stand, Jeff Gordon sat uncomfortably through the service. Despite his love for DeLoy and Irene Spencer, his mind was often elsewhere.

* * * * *

Kathleen Taylor also sat uncomfortably through much of the funeral. She wracked her brain, looking for an angle that would make attending this funeral seem worthwhile. It was a lovely service, she admitted. The music was pleasant, and the speeches were short with a down-to-earth quality.

This is all fine and well. But how is it newsworthy?

She was about to throw up her hands in defeat and send Doby out to the graveside service alone for a parting shot when the audience rose at the conclusion of the service. As if by a miracle, she was saved. Not by the doctrine that had been preached. Definitely not by some miraculous conversion. But by a head of rich black hair with a white streak over the forehead.

There he was. He had been sitting directly behind the pulpit, blocking him from Kathleen's view during the entire service. She had to restrain herself from leaping to her feet, sprinting to the front of the chapel, and grilling Mr. Gordon right in front of the entire audience.

Kathleen knew she had to find Doby and get to the side door through which the family and dignitaries would exit. She excused herself as quietly as possible, sliding between the pews and leaving the chapel through a rear door. She fairly ran down the hallway to the back of the building. Seeing Doby standing by the funeral hearse, she shouted to him.

"He's coming out the side door to your right!"

"Who?" Doby asked.

"Gordon! The Foundation director." She sprinted around the building, her blonde hair trailing behind, with Doby close on her heels.

With time to spare, Kathleen grabbed her handheld mike and looked about quickly for the right position. The honorary pallbearers were already out the exit door, followed by the family. She expected the other funeral participants to follow but was disappointed. The audience was pouring out through the door, but Gordon was not among them.

"Great, just great!" she barked. "Come on, Doby. He's not getting away from us."

They retraced their steps to the rear of the building only to find many of the mourners already in their cars and pulling out from the curb.

Where are you, Gordon?

"Okay, Doby, you go back to the right around the building. I'll go left. We'll meet in front. If you see Gordon, stop him. Do anything. Trip him if you have to. He can't get away from us."

Kathleen worked her way through the dispersing crowd, looking for the man with the white lock of hair. Her anxiety mounted. People were leaving in all directions, and cars were now lining up for the traditional procession to the cemetery.

When she arrived in the front of the building, Doby was already there.

"We missed him, boss," Doby declared.

"No!" shouted Kathleen. "No! Where is he? Where did he go?"

"He was just getting into his car when I came around the corner. I got a shot of him over the roof of his car. Didn't last long, maybe a three or four count, but he looked right at me. I think it will be a decent image."

"That's great, Doby. But I have to talk to him. Did he drive off?" she demanded. "Which direction?"

"He turned right along Canyon Drive."

"Come on," she called, running toward the van. "We're going to catch him."

* * * * *

Jeff Gordon drove only two blocks north along Canyon Drive, then turned onto a residential side street and parked along the curb in front of another car. He watched out the driver-side rearview mirror for several minutes as most of the funeral traffic and media vans passed by on the main street behind him. Then he dialed an unlisted telephone number, which rang in Seattle, Washington.

THIRTY-FOUR

Chad Rowley sat silently in an overstuffed chair on the second floor of the Freemen Foundation offices in Denver. Just inside the entrance was a spacious reception area. Parallel hallways ran toward the rear of the floor from the reception area and were joined at the back by another crossing hallway. Individual offices were situated around the perimeter of the floor outside this square of hallways. Inside the square were a large conference room, a workroom, and a smaller break room.

Normally a beehive of continuous activity, the offices were now deserted except for Chad and an office couple who answered the telephones during business hours.

Chad reflected on the maddening delays and inactivity of the past week. Jeff Gordon had arranged for Jamie Madero to work temporarily with proselyting missionaries from the Denver Colorado mission. He instructed Chad to stay in Denver and out of sight.

In the midst of reanalyzing the situation, Chad became aware that someone had entered the reception area just outside Jeff Gordon's office. He stepped to the door of the office to find a deliveryman with a bottle of purified water on his shoulder getting directions from Evan and Ida Rast, the office couple. Chad could not see the man's face. But he had been around the Foundation office enough to recognize the blue-and-white-striped uniform shirt worn by deliverymen from the water company.

Evan Rast led the deliveryman around the corner to the opposite hallway where the break room was located.

Because of the attack the previous week, Chad was more suspicious of ordinary events. In this instance, instinct told him that all was not as it should be with the delivery. For one thing, the office received two bottles of water a week. For another, all of the deliverymen from the water vendor knew exactly where the dispenser was. Also, the company hired only young men who would work at entry-level pay to do the physically demanding job. The man Chad had just seen had a more mature physique. Though clearly strong enough to handle the heavy bottles, he was far beyond his prime.

Without drawing the attention of Ida Rast, who was still in the reception area, Chad slid into the hallway on his left, moving noiselessly along until he reached the back hall. He arrived at the far corner of the floor in time to see Evan Rast leave the break room and return to the front desk. The deliveryman was now alone, removing the expended bottle in preparation to replace it. His back was to Chad, who could see through the door the deliveryman's close-cropped hair streaked with gray. Setting the expended bottle aside, the deliveryman made no attempt to replace it. Instead, he drew a handgun from the front of his shirt. He then reached into his pants pocket and extracted a silencer that he mounted on the barrel.

Alarmed but not completely surprised by this move, Chad had seen all he needed. He turned and sprinted back through the cross hall as silently as he could and then down to the reception area.

"Evan. Ida," Chad called in a hoarse whisper. "Quick, in here."

The couple was startled. But the look on Chad's face and the urgency with which he gestured them into Jeff Gordon's office roused them to action.

"Get down behind the desk and stay out of sight," Chad ordered.

When the couple was safely in the office, Chad closed the door behind him. He remained in the hall, where he could see to the back on his left and across the reception area in front of him. His plan was to draw the gunman away from the office in either direction, depending on which way he came. With his attention fixed on both hallways, Chad was startled to see, out of the corner of his eye, the front door to the office swing open and two hooded men step in.

Having no time to plan his actions, Chad dove into the hallway to his left. Recovering his footing, he flew down to the cross hall. He knew he was running back toward the man with the gun, who was probably an accomplice to these two intruders, but he had no time to reconsider. With no other avenue of escape, Chad moved to the door of the break room and found it empty. Knowing that he had to draw the assailants away from Jeff Gordon's office at all costs, he continued up the hallway, approaching the reception area from the opposite side.

The scene that met him there could only be duplicated on a movie set. The two hooded assailants lay prostrate on the floor of the reception area, both clearly dead. Standing midway between them, a silenced handgun at his side, was the deliveryman. He looked up as Chad peered around the corner from the far hallway.

"Hello, young man. I thought I might find you here."

Chad froze. "Who are you?"

"I'm Ike Rudman," the man said.

THIRTY-FIVE

van and Ida Rast were clearly shaken when they left the
Freemen Foundation offices. Having survived the ordeal in Leadville and a shoot-out that claimed the lives of two would-be assassins,
the Rasts left the office as soon as they were released by the FBI. As
Evan followed his wife out, he turned to Chad, who stood in obvious
dismay, watching the forensics experts documenting the crime scene.

"You fellas sure know how to throw a party," said Evan with half
a smile. "If things keep going as they are, we'll have some exciting
stories to tell the folks at home—if we get there."

"You'll get there, Evan," replied Chad. "It's been a bad week.
Jeff'll be back soon, and we'll get things rolling in a more positive
direction. Thanks for all you do."

Nearly three hours had passed since Ike Rudman's confrontation
with the two hooded gunmen. He was now in Jeff Gordon's office on
a conference call with FBI agents from the Denver field office and at
FBI headquarters in Washington DC. Silvan Ortega, the FBI agent
in charge, asked Chad to leave the office before the call began. The
door closed solidly behind Chad as he walked away.

Watching Ike Rudman and the FBI agents as they went through
their paces, Chad felt increasingly deflated. He knew, of course, that
the Foundation carried out its investigative efforts at an elementary
level. The Insiders had attempted to achieve a level of professional-
ism equal to the lofty aims of their endeavor. However, he now saw

more clearly than ever how extensive the resources and abilities were of those men and women who made a career of this kind of work.

Ike Rudman had talked little with Chad before the FBI arrived, and now he moved among the law enforcement professionals with the ease of a veteran. He identified himself to the federal authorities and was immediately accorded every privilege and regarded with obvious deference by the agents. Watching Ike at work reminded Chad how little he actually knew about Sarah and her family. However, he contented himself with trying to learn what he could about the management of a crime scene until the opportunity presented itself for Chad to get better acquainted with Ike.

In the midst of Chad's reflection, Jeff Gordon walked through the entry door. Stepping around an FBI photographer, he headed toward Chad. One look at Jeff convinced Chad that the director was both tired and distressed.

"Sorry I didn't get to you and let you know where I've been." Jeff greeted his operations chief with a familiar handshake and hasty apology. "This has been a day to remember."

"I'm happy to see you safe and sound. You've spoiled us," Chad replied. "When you didn't call, I wondered if you'd been in an accident—or something worse."

"I tried to call in at 2:00 p.m. but got an FBI operator intercept," said Jeff.

"Did the funeral go well?" asked Chad.

"It did," answered the director. "I think the family was greatly comforted. Let's go into my office where we can talk. I've got some important news."

"Your office is being used by the FBI and our guest."

"Our guest?" asked Jeff.

"Ike Rudman. Our own Sarah's father."

Jeff was silent for a few moments while he processed that bit of information.

"How did he get here?"

"I have no idea. Maybe a more important question is why he's here. And more important still, who is he? I mean professionally. I would guess from watching him with the FBI that he moves in very high circles. I'm sure you'll want to get acquainted with him."

"Indeed," replied Jeff with a slight shake of his head. "Let's sit down in the break room until they finish. Give me just a minute to freshen up."

The conference call apparently had not ended when Jeff sat down across the table from Chad.

"After the funeral, I telephoned the chairman of the Foundation's Board of Directors. He told me the Board met in an emergency session yesterday to discuss our fate."

Jeff leaned forward for a minute or two, head in his hands, rubbing his eyes.

"The Board chair told me that he and the other board members are deeply troubled by the turn of events and are considering whether they want to withdraw their support from Insider operations. That would, in effect, disband the Freemen Foundation for the time being—at least until they reconsider the possible risks."

"Does the board think we are in any further danger?" asked Chad.

"Well, our enemy has shown that he can reach out and harm us at will. I suppose he has the means to identify anybody involved with the Foundation, including anyone who has made a financial contribution."

"So what if the board decides the risk is too great?" asked Chad.

"Many of our Insiders would need to move on to other employment. It would set us back significantly. Without the financial backing of board members and their support in circles of influence, we couldn't keep going long." Jeff said no more and gradually lifted his head to gaze directly at Chad.

The news didn't surprise Chad. He would have been surprised to hear anything else. But it saddened him when he reflected on how much he and the other Insiders had invested. Some had paid a great price—the ultimate price.

"I'm sorry to hear that," said Chad. "I know that must be a big disappointment to you. It certainly is for me."

"Frankly, it is," Jeff agreed. "I'm not at odds with their thinking and would have to go along with their decision. But it will be difficult for me to walk away from this. I have seen what our enemy can do. There is something in my makeup that resents bullies. The Leopard has hit us hard—and way below the belt. We still have those two wonderful women out there somewhere. I trust that they're still alive, but I'm sure they're suffering." Jeff rose and paced the small workroom as he continued, now pouring out his own feelings.

"I can't walk away. I won't walk away. If the Board abandons us, I'll have to find another way to carry the work forward."

"What do you propose?" asked Chad.

"I'm not sure. I hope the Board will take a courageous stance and recognize that this is a time to push forward rather than retreat. If not, I'll use all my personal resources if need be. I have other friends and like-minded acquaintances. I'll see if I can generate additional interest among those who are looking for ways to make the world a better place."

THIRTY-SIX

When the conference call ended, **Jeff Gordon received a** cursory briefing consisting mostly of questions put to him by the FBI. Chad and Ike Rudman sat silently and listened while Agent Ortega instructed Gordon.

"You and your colleagues should leave the office now. I'll make the official report to Denver PD," said Ortega.

"What do you call something like this?" asked Gordon.

"Probably best if it's logged as a forcible entry. Maybe intent to commit armed robbery. I'll work that out with the police."

"How much publicity will this generate? We're still trying to get ahead of the media hype from the Leadville thing," said Gordon.

"You've tied into a big fish. These are professionals, and they won't go away easily. You're the victims here, not the perpetrators. We'll do what we can to hush the noise, but we can only do so much."

"Thanks, Agent Ortega," said Gordon. "You can reach me at that number. We want to cooperate in any way we can."

"Better take off." Ortega nodded. "We gotta make this call. We've already got a big time disparity to explain. The media will descend quickly once Denver PD is notified. They'll have a lot of questions. Better if you're not here."

Jeff, Ike Rudman, and Chad Rowley took the stairs to the street level and exited through the back of the building. Since the vending company had already retrieved the delivery truck Rudman arrived in, he accepted an offer from Jeff to transport him wherever he needed to go.

As Jeff's sedan pulled onto the street, a Denver PD squad car signaled to turn in.

"Where are we headed?" asked Jeff.

"If you gentlemen are free for a while, I think we should have a chat," said Ike Rudman. "Then you could drop me at my hotel."

They decided on a small steak and seafood grill near the airport known by Rudman to offer seclusion and better than average fare.

"It's the best I know of at a price a man on a government pension can afford," Rudman offered lightly.

"Which branch of government did you spend your career in?" asked Jeff.

"I've kicked around in various parts of the community," said Rudman. "I know a lot of people but haven't made many friends. How about you, Jeff? How have you earned your living?"

Jeff gave Rudman a short rundown.

As the conversation progressed, the older gentleman skillfully sidestepped questions and repeatedly turned the focus of the conversation back to Jeff and Chad. Chad, who wasn't saying much, observed that Rudman was adept at extracting information from others in the course of what seemed to be innocent conversation, while giving almost no information about himself.

Over dinner in a high-back booth upholstered in rolled leather, the three men talked about the situation that faced them. The lights were dim, the booth was toward the back of the room, and the combination of ambient noise and sound-absorbing decor ensured that they were reasonably safe from listening ears.

"The FBI knows almost nothing about the contractors who made the hit in Leadville," reported Rudman. "A week has passed. Time is running out. If this were a political abduction, we'd have some assurance that the abductors would protect their investment. We have no such assurances in this case."

Rudman stopped to spear a grilled shrimp, which he popped into his mouth, savored, and washed down with a swallow of grape juice.

Chad didn't have much of an appetite. The events of the day and Ike Rudman's prognosis for Sarah and Gwen left him feeling slightly dizzy and set his stomach on edge. The images of bodies on the office floor would not leave him. Whenever he became absorbed in other thoughts, the images were never far away. At the least invitation, they reasserted themselves upon his consciousness.

"We're very fortunate that you showed up when you did," said Jeff to Rudman. "A minute or two later, and this attack could have spelled tragedy."

"Very fortunate," replied Rudman.

"How did you know they were going to strike? Or was it just luck?"

"There's no such thing as luck."

"We'd like to learn all we can from you," said Jeff.

"You've chosen a challenging mission for yourselves," said Rudman, finishing the last of his shrimp and wiping the corners of his mouth with a napkin. "In fact, it's a deadly mission. Knowing what little I do about your operation, I'm guessing that you'll often be outmanned and outgunned by your adversaries. This might be a good time to rethink your whole approach and maybe leave this kind of work to the police and federal agencies."

Jeff stiffened noticeably. "Maybe. I was just wondering if you have a source of information about our attackers—anything we can work on. I'm not planning to start running from them."

Rudman looked steadily at Jeff, then shook his head.

"I was using a technique employed by some of our field agents referred to as fox and lair. The idea is to determine the hunter's prey and then wait at the lair until the hunter arrives. When you know the fox is coming to you, exact timing isn't so vital. However, today was as close as one can imagine. I had just arrived when the hit team entered. They were trained to watch their backs but didn't expect an armed response."

"It's a shame that they weren't taken alive. The authorities could have questioned them about your daughter and Gwen Fong," said Jeff.

It was Rudman's turn to stiffen at the thinly veiled criticism of his actions. He had, after all, saved three lives.

"I see that you don't know a lot about the kind of men we're deal-ing with," replied Rudman crisply. "They don't give out information. They also don't surrender to anyone. As long as they can still generate brain waves, they're deadly. There is only one way to survive a meet-ing with them—the way I survived today."

He stopped talking only long enough to fill his mouth again and continued while he chewed.

"These men probably didn't know anything about my daughter. They may draw their pay from the same bank, but they would have had no connection whatsoever with the earlier hit team. I did what I had to do. There were no other choices."

Rudman continued to push the conversation forward.

"What do you intend to do from here?" he asked.

Jeff hesitated, possibly trying to decide how much he was willing to share with Rudman.

"By noon tomorrow," he said, "we will know how much support we can expect from our Foundation. We may need to scale back our efforts. At any rate, we plan to do everything humanly possible to free Sarah and Gwen."

"You mean well," said Rudman, "and I don't doubt that you have some unusual abilities. But you should see by now that you're no match for your opponents. It's also likely that your efforts will only get in the way of those investigators who are more experienced and better equipped."

It was clear that Rudman meant no offense and that he wished to avoid an open conflict.

"Maybe you're selling us short," replied Jeff.

"Maybe," replied Rudman, "and maybe not. What have you been able to do about finding my daughter and the other woman in the past week?"

"We have deferred to the authorities," was Jeff's polite but some-what heated response.

"Then you clearly are no match for your opponents," Rudman shot back. "They operate outside the law and move much more quickly than the law."

Jeff was visibly rocked by this charge.

"What have you managed to do in the past week?" he asked in an uncharacteristically defensive tone.

"Well, for one thing," answered Rudman, "I know where my daughter is." After a slight pause, "I also know who holds her. In the next twenty-four hours, I'll free her."

"If you know where these women are, have you told the FBI?" asked Jeff.

"This is a matter I prefer to handle myself," responded Rudman. "Too much time has passed. My daughter's life hangs in the balance. Their abductors are not amateurs. They're assassins of the most lethal sort. I can move more quickly than the FBI."

"We want to help in any way we can," Jeff said.

"I need to wrap up some loose ends tonight," Rudman continued. "I will be in Denver until noon tomorrow. If, as you expect, your Foundation withdraws support and you're left on your own, then perhaps there is a role you could play. I don't believe it would be wise to draw your Foundation further into the picture at this point."

When the men finished eating, Rudman paid the bill, and the three men rose to leave.

* * * * *

Near the exit sat a man, eating alone. Seconds after the trio passed his table he dropped a large bill to cover his tab, folded a newspaper under his arm, and waved good-bye to no one in particular. By manner and appearance, this newcomer was no more threatening than an aging techno-nerd. His hair was disheveled. He wore oversized wire-rim glasses. A haphazard row of pens and pencils stuffed his shirt pocket protector. He carried his state-of-the-art phone.

When Jeff Gordon's sedan pulled out onto the street, it was followed half a minute later by an ancient Toyota Land Cruiser sporting a heavy-duty cargo rack, rusted fender wells, and a Colorado license plate.

THIRTY-SEVEN

Julienne Rostetter had wrangled an invitation to dinner from her mother. Ingrid Rostetter had always been a wonderful cook, and this evening's meal was no exception. They dined on braised lamb chops with a refreshing mint sauce. The vegetables were lightly steamed, and of course, there was no dessert. They finished the dinner with a glass of their favorite wine.

Ingrid was in her early seventies, a widow for ten years. She was still active and enjoyed a rich social life. She kept many friends who were younger than she, testifying to her relative youthfulness.

"That was wonderful, as always," said Julienne as they savored the last of the meal.

"Well, I know that you work hard, Julie. It's a pleasure to spend a few minutes with you in the middle of the week."

The two Rostetter women had always been close. Ingrid encouraged and supported her daughter but never pushed. Perhaps that was because Julienne Rostetter had never needed pushing. If Ingrid disapproved of Julienne's present professional pursuits, she never said so openly. She now studied Julienne carefully.

"You seem quiet this evening, Julie. Are things going well at work?"

"About the same," replied Julienne, absently rearranging a few leftovers on her dinner plate with a fork.

Ingrid said nothing further, and Julienne felt the weight of the silence.

"Well, to be honest, this is one of *those* times," said Julienne.

Though Ingrid appeared to be listening intently, she said nothing.
Mom always knows.

"I'm struggling with some conscience problems—and a few minor conflicts at work. Nothing I can't handle," said Julienne with a weak smile. "I just have the feeling that I may have peaked with Fletchner International. Maybe it's time for me to move on. There are a few other things I would like to try."

Julienne was now spindling her dinner napkin and generally looking everywhere but at her mother.

"Julie, you've been working for other people for quite a long time. I'm surprised that you haven't tried to make a go of it on your own. You are so bright and capable. I think you would do very well."

Mom, I swear you can read my mind. Seems like everybody is reading it these days.

"I've certainly thought of that," Julienne responded. "But if I'm honest with myself, I guess I'm afraid. That doesn't sound like me, does it? But I think I've become so good at what I do for other people that I've grown too comfortable. I guess I'm getting soft. I don't even know what I would do for myself."

Again, Ingrid Rostetter allowed her daughter's words and feelings to settle before offering her thoughts.

"Julie, don't be afraid. You're a talented, energetic, resourceful woman. I believe you can do anything you want to do."

"Thank you, Mother." She dropped the napkin in front of her and pushed herself back from the table.

"Thanks for the dinner and the advice. You're a sweetheart. Is it all right if we catch the evening news before I leave?"

"Of course," replied Ingrid. "Let's leave the dishes. I'll get to them later."

Julienne and Ingrid sat through the Toronto evening newscast with hardly a word passing between them. Julienne's thoughts were distant and related to the issues she was trying to resolve at work.

"More on the supposed terrorist attack that occurred a week ago in Colorado," announced the news anchor. "The couple killed in that attack were buried today following funeral services in Boulder."

The story continued for thirty seconds over background footage taken from network coverage of the funeral and burial. Focus was given to the terrorism angle. The upshot was that the motive and responsibility for the attack still remained mysteries. Julienne listened intently because of the possible connection between the story and Fletchner International.

She felt a slight jolt to her system when the footage cut to a head shot of a man filmed at a distance over the roof of his automobile.

"Jeffrey Gordon is director of the Denver-based Freemen Foundation, which employed the murdered couple. He was unavailable for comment on the motives of the attackers."

Jeffrey Gordon.

Julienne watched the brief clip in which Gordon looked directly into the camera before opening the door and sliding into his sedan. She had never seen Gordon nor heard his name, but his face reminded her of a strange dream she had a few weeks earlier. The dream awakened her. It had stayed with her all the next day until she managed to put it out of her mind. She remembered it vividly now.

In her dream, Julienne attended a formal ball with Art Warnock and all of his sleazy henchmen. The Chairman was there as an onlooker. She remembered her disdain at having to refuse the advances of all the men who approached her—until a perfect stranger entered the scene. She couldn't keep her eyes off him. Like Jeffrey Gordon, the man she had just seen on TV, the stranger in her dream possessed a distinctive white lock in the front of his handsome head of black hair.

Julienne didn't consider herself either a sentimentalist or even a romantic. However, she did notice a distinct flutter in her stomach when she saw Gordon on television. She felt herself blushing. Her reaction was unsettling. She would never confess it to another living being, but she knew she was feeling a slight physical and romantic reaction to Gordon.

"Oh, Mother, I've got to go. I'm losing my grip."

Ingrid Rostetter was clearly baffled as her daughter stepped toward the door to leave. But before Julienne could place her hand on the doorknob, the male anchor interrupted the funeral story with breaking news.

"This just in on the Leadville, Colorado killings. Reporting live is Kathleen Taylor of Channel 9 News, Denver."

Julienne turned back toward the television set. Kathleen Taylor stood outside a small business complex in Littleton, Colorado, a Denver suburb. Taylor was an attractive woman in her early twenties. Her well-dressed blonde hair moved slightly in the late summer evening breeze. Julienne could detect almost from the reporter's first word a sort of brassy, pushy quality in her manner and speech.

"This is Kathleen Taylor. I'm reporting to you live from 807 Tyler Avenue in Littleton, Colorado. The two-story building you see behind me houses the offices of the Freemen Foundation, a patriotic watchdog organization. This is the same organization that suffered three deaths in an apparently unprovoked terrorist attack just six days ago in Leadville, Colorado. Two women are still missing and presumed abducted as a result of that attack.

"According to Denver police, at about one this afternoon, two armed men entered the Freemen Foundation offices. Shots were fired and two men were gunned down. Denver police are calling the act forcible entry. The apparent motive was armed robbery. This latest attack occurred on the same day as the funeral services of two Foundation associates killed in last week's attack.

"The spokesman for Denver police department is saying little about today's shooting. There are many details yet to be uncovered. Who killed the two gunmen? Who was in the office at the time? Was anyone else injured or killed? Above all, why wasn't the shooting that occurred about 1:00 p.m. reported to Denver police until after 4:00 p.m.?"

Kathleen Taylor gestured toward the building behind her.

"I spoke with some employees of the insurance company that occupies the building's first floor. They say they were working downstairs at the time of the shooting. They heard no shots and weren't even aware of the shooting until Denver PD responded just a short time ago, three hours later.

"Again, two armed intruders are dead after a shoot-out in

Littleton. We'll return with the rest of the story as more details become available. This is Kathleen Taylor, reporting live from Littleton, Colorado, Channel 9 News in Denver."

Julienne knew instinctively that this attack was more than robbery and more than coincidence. Still reflecting on the two back-to-back news stories, she said good-bye to her mother and decided to return to her office. She was just getting into her car when the mobile phone rang.

"This is JR."

"JR, this is Art Warnock. The Chairman told me to find you. He wants to see both of us in his office, ASAP."

THIRTY-EIGHT

Julienne. Art. Sit," directed the Chairman, gesturing toward two chairs. He was clearly agitated.

"I called you both in because I think it's time for us to settle the unfinished business among us. I don't want any friction between the two of you. I need you both right now."

The Chairman moved about the room. He ranged from the windows in front of them all the way to the back of the room. Julienne had to keep turning in her chair to watch him as he moved. Already seated when Julienne arrived was Hefton Finch, Fletchner International's lead attorney.

"Let's review where we are with this Freemen Foundation thing. First, some of their people who worked for us were stealing information. That's theft. They were breaking the law. So Art invited them back for questioning. But someone got to them first—at Leadville. There was a nasty, tragic attack. Terrible! The people who beat us to the punch were apparently looking for the same parties as we were. Two of their women were kidnapped. Art has been successful in bringing the two abducted women under our protection. I'm assured that they're well and happy.

"I don't care how much you paid to arrange their rescue," the Chairman said to Art. "The safety of these women is worth whatever it may have cost us. I'm pleased that they are safe and that we are now in a position to release them.

"Today, Art sent a couple of investigators to Denver to find the other missing thief. Again, someone beat us to the punch. This time it was someone with a gun. That somebody wasted these two investigators, whom I am assured were decent, law-abiding businessmen.

"Now, it's the somebody with the gun who worries me. I want to know who it was and how it is that he always seems to be a step ahead of us. I need some explanations."

The Chairman sat on the edge of the desk in front of Julienne, looking directly at her.

Julienne was speechless. For starters, the Chairman's interpretation of events was so unbelievably self-serving. Even though Julienne had worked for the Chairman for eight years, she could hardy believe that he was able to say those things with a straight face.

Although the Chairman had forbidden any arguing between Julienne and Art, when Julienne learned that Art had acted without her knowledge or authorization in sending investigators to the Foundation's office in Denver, her deep resentment toward Art immediately ignited. She wanted to lash out at Art and scream a warning to the Chairman that he was being deceived. But she did neither.

She was now all but certain that the Chairman knew what was happening. If Art had acted, he had done so with the Chairman's approval. Suddenly, and with deafening clarity, the voice of reason within Julienne spoke to her.

Woman, you're being set up. You're being moved out. You, Julienne Rostetter—who have always been brighter, quicker, a step ahead of your opponents, always equal to the fast-breaking realities of corporate security work—you're now on the outside.

The Chairman, seeing that Julienne was either unwilling or unable to respond, gave a conciliatory shrug.

"Okay. I think this is what we need to do," he said. "We need to find out who the guy with the gun is. And we need to resolve our differences with this Freemen Foundation. They are nothing to us. A flea on an elephant. Unfortunately, this thing has attracted an unusual amount of publicity. That's not necessarily good for us. Even a flea can annoy if not looked after.

"Julienne, you're our expert on this Foundation. I want you to make contact. Maybe you can start with—," the Chairman waved his hands as if trying to recall a name, "—with their director. The guy on the news tonight. Let's arrange to turn the two women over to him. Make it clear to him that we don't want the RCMP or the FBI involved. This is just a favor we're doing them. We don't want to answer any questions about how these women came into our hands. Find out anything you can from this man that we don't already know. Above all, find out what this Foundation is up to and why it's getting in our way."

"Make arrangements for the hand off somewhere on neutral ground. Be sure they know we're doing them a favor. Have one of our attorneys with you. In fact, have a dozen. Make sure we come out of this clean.

"And watch your back. We have an unknown shooter out there. We'll find out who that is sooner or later. It's time we get this thing behind us so we can get on with business.

"That's it, Julienne," he concluded. "Wrap this up in twenty-four hours."

Julienne rose immediately and started toward the door. A cauldron of emotions boiled within her. She turned back to Art Warnock, who was still sitting with a self-satisfied expression.

"Get the abducted women ready to move," she ordered. "I'll tell you where and when."

Julienne had no intention of involving Art Warnock or his subordinates in this operation. She would turn to her other division head, Celeste Hughes, to accomplish this job. Celeste's corporate acquisitions team was engaged in a highly technical and sophisticated network of industrial espionage. They stole secrets, plans, systems, and prototypes. They kept an eye on the competition and a knife to the competition's jugular.

In contrast to Celeste and her CA team, Art's entire operation was a throwback to the old days of hardball security tactics. Whereas JR considered Warnock a Neanderthal in the industrial security profession, she viewed Celeste as a competent professional. She planned to draw on Celeste's resources to carry out the sensitive mission that lay ahead of them.

* * * * *

After Julienne left the room, the conversation between the Chairman and Art Warnock continued for several minutes.

"Warnock," warned the Chairman, "some of the pieces don't add up. I've told you before, I don't like surprises."

Despite the warning, Art stood his ground. He knew he was playing on a field where there was no forgiveness for errors.

"Sir, I guarantee that I have things under control."

"Okay," replied the Chairman. "I'm going to leave you a little latitude to move. I don't need to know every detail. I prefer not to. Just tell me this, the shooter in Denver, does he—or she—belong to them, us, or somebody else?"

Meeting the Chairman's stare, and without blinking, a hint of a smile crept across Art Warnock's face.

"Let me just say that we're covering our tails on several levels."

"You have definite possibilities, my boy," said the Chairman. "Just don't get too cute with all your machinations, and don't ever dream that you could cross me and survive. You're employed in a very accident-prone occupation."

The Chairman waved Warnock out of the room.

THIRTY-NINE

The last person Julienne Rostetter wanted to meet at the moment was Jeffrey Gordon. She had slept for only a few minutes the previous night amid a continuous round of meetings with corporate attorneys, her own staff, and the ever-unpleasant Art Warnock. Details were hammered out for turning over the two young women to the Freemen Foundation. Because the involvement of Canadian and American authorities was inevitable, a firm groundwork of legal defenses had to be established before any contact was made.

The difference in time zones meant that Julienne was calling Jeff Gordon at 5:30 a.m., mountain daylight time.

"Mr. Gordon, my name is Julienne Rostetter. I'm director of security for a Canadian-headquartered international company. I want to talk to you about the two women abducted from your retreat in Leadville, Colorado, last week."

Julienne's heart pounded inexplicably. She was clearly not herself. She didn't understand where the feelings of vulnerability were coming from.

Gordon listened as she explained to him in her most precise and businesslike fashion that the organization she represented was in a position to serve as a go-between in arranging freedom for the two abducted women.

"Can I talk to the women?" asked Gordon.

"Not yet."

"Are they okay? Are they healthy?"

"Because we're serving as an intermediary, we don't yet have custody of the women. That will happen soon."

"What assurance do we have that this is on the up-and-up?" Gordon asked.

"How many other options do you have?" said Julienne.

"Not too many. Are there any conditions?"

"Yes. This must be done privately, without involving the authorities."

"Why the secrecy?"

"Mr. Gordon, this is a goodwill gesture on our part. We don't want publicity, and we don't want to justify our actions to the authorities. If you can live with that, we'll proceed. If not, we'll leave you to find your own way of rescuing your employees."

"Are you asking for a ransom?"

"No, we're not the abductors. Any conditions the abductors imposed have already been met. No ransom."

Gordon attempted to ask additional questions, but she cut him off. More than once, she reminded him of the conditions for the transfer. The FBI must not be informed until the release had been completed.

"The FBI is already involved," said Gordon. "I'm not sure I can act without their authorization."

"This is a decision you'll need to make," Julienne told him. "The arrangements are extremely delicate. If you delay, or if you're unwilling to abide by these conditions, the opportunity will vanish quickly. The two women might continue to be in jeopardy. I'm sure you don't want that."

"No, we don't. You're right."

"You can't contact me again," she told him. "If you want to take part in this transfer, meet me at the elevator tower on the American side of Niagara Falls at 4:00 p.m., eastern daylight time, today. Come alone. Bring a current passport."

"How will you know me?" Gordon asked.

"We'll recognize you."

"If the organization you work for is above board, why the cloak-and-dagger routine?"

"Mr. Gordon," she replied icily, "we have interests and connections to protect. We're taking great risks. If you want these young women, please do this our way."

Accepting his silence as indication that he was willing to comply, she then hung up the telephone.

FORTY

Jeff Gordon boarded an early-morning flight to Buffalo, New York. He told Ike Rudman he was on his way to a rendezvous that would lead to the release of the abducted women. Rudman convinced Gordon that he also knew where the ladies were being held. He warned Gordon that the proposed release could involve various levels of deception and danger. He suggested that he and Chad provide backup in case all did not go as expected.

"This operation really needs one more body," Rudman explained to Chad after seeing Jeff Gordon off. "Jamie Madero, if you feel you can trust him in all respects."

"He can clearly be trusted," said Chad. "But I'm not sure why we'd need him. He's young and inexperienced."

"That's not necessarily a drawback," replied Rudman. "It may be an advantage. We want someone who will follow instructions exactly. Sometimes people with a little experience try to think for themselves. That's not what we need. Besides, he's immediately available. We're leaving within the hour."

Chad called the mission president. He and Rudman drove to the missionary apartment, collected Jamie, and went immediately to Denver International Airport where a private jet was waiting for them.

The flight gave Chad an opportunity to fill Jamie in on the events of the past week. They were in the air about three hours. Rudman and the flight crew showed them every courtesy. For the first time,

179

Rudman spoke about life in government service. Though he would share no personal information either about himself or about Sarah, he seemed more at ease and impressed the younger men with his command of world affairs.

When they deplaned, they boarded a van and left the airfield without passing through customs.

It was early afternoon when they reached their destination. They had driven deep into the Canadian countryside. Rudman drove the van up a country lane lined with woods on both sides and occasional scattered homes set back from the roadway. These were not mansions, but they clearly gave the impression of being country homes to people of means. The homes lined a small wooded lake that was large enough to paddle or row on but too small for motorboats.

Rudman pulled up to the electrically controlled gate of one of these homes near the end of the lane. He gave two brief, barely perceptible honks on the van's horn. After a delay of a minute or two, the gate rolled open. The van passed through it and onto a circular drive in front of the house.

"Here we are, gentlemen," declared Rudman. "Wait here for a few minutes while I make some arrangements."

"This is not at all what I expected," said Chad to Jamie. "This looks more like a resort than a prison."

"I guess when we get Sarah and Gwen back safely, it won't matter where they've been," replied Jamie.

"That's for sure," Chad muttered. Then, as though he had been waiting for an opportunity to speak, he said to Jamie, "You know, something about this doesn't feel right. What do you make of Mr. Rudman?"

"He's not what I would have expected," said Jamie. "I don't know Sarah very well, but I would have imagined her father to be more like her."

"Yeah, he's a little too hard to have raised a daughter like Sarah," said Chad. "Why do I feel like a sitting duck?"

As he spoke, three men came around the corner of a large garage on the north side of the house and approached the van. An alarm sounded in Chad's head.

"Uh-oh, Bud. I don't like this. Lock your door."

Jamie flipped the lock switch on the sliding side door of the van, and Chad leaped across the seat to secure the driver's side door. All of this was to no avail. With a single crashing blow from the metal butt of a handgun, the large panel window next to Jamie exploded inward, showering him with chunks of safety glass. In an instant, the muzzle of a silenced assault weapon was inserted through the now open window.

"Get out of the van slowly," commanded a voice with a Canadian accent. "Keep your hands up."

Jamie and Chad were thrown to the concrete driveway on either side of the van. Moving with expert precision, their captors bound and blindfolded them, then manhandled them into a cellar through an outside door at the back of the house. There they strapped the captives securely to large steel posts positioned to reinforce the upper floor of the house. The outside door slammed shut with a bang, the sound echoing through the mostly empty cellar. A dead bolt lock slid into place as the door was locked from without.

Jamie and Chad, who had been so recently reunited, were left in darkness, each alone with his thoughts.

FORTY-ONE

As the time approached 4:00 p.m., Julienne sat behind the wheel of a light-colored Ford Expedition, the engine—and the air conditioner—running. From her vantage point in the parking area, she could see the paved paths leading across the park toward Niagara Falls. She could also see six of her own people in various sorts of dress, each busied in some activity thought to mirror the actions of the many tourists coming and going. Julienne and her staff had made some informed guesses regarding the route that Jeffrey Gordon would follow in getting to the rendezvous. They also remained alert for any signs of an FBI presence.

At three or four minutes to four, their efforts were rewarded as one of Julienne's people spotted Gordon stepping out of a rental car several rows away. Julienne watched through the windshield of her sport utility vehicle as Gordon appeared to her right. He walked along briskly among the tourists, making his way directly for the elevator tower. All members of the security team were on an open radio net. She listened as the station reports came in and the team positioned itself according to prearranged plans. Each station covered an avenue of view so that team members didn't have to look at each other or appear to be connected in any way.

One of Julienne's team members, whose overall appearance was similar to Julienne, overtook Gordon from behind. All of the stations went silent, and the reports passing among them ceased. Julienne could hear the heavy breathing of the contact woman in her open mike as she quickened her pace to catch up to Gordon.

"Mr. Gordon," the contact called as she approached him. Julienne saw Gordon stop and turn to face the voice calling his name. She watched as the contact woman gestured in her direction.

"Please follow me. We have a vehicle waiting."

Jeff Gordon hesitated for only a second, as if trying to decide whether this was the woman he was supposed to meet. As the contact woman walked away from him toward Julienne's vehicle, he apparently realized that there had been a change in the plan or that the plan hadn't been fully revealed to him. He followed her.

The contact woman led him directly to the passenger side door of Julienne's Expedition. As they came forward, Julienne listened to the other stations' final reports.

"Station one: Still clear."

"Station two: All quiet here."

"Station three: No activity in the parking lot."

"Station four: Clear here."

"Station five: It's a go."

"Station six: Clear at the tower."

The contact woman opened the door for Gordon. She scanned him with a wand to detect any electronic transmission devices and stepped aside so he could climb up onto the seat. When the team decided to intercept Gordon before he reached the tower and have the initial meeting with Julienne in the car, they had guessed that he would be more likely to enter a car with two women than with men present.

The door slammed. The contact woman entered through the passenger side rear door and sat behind Gordon. Julienne immediately pulled away from the curb. No one spoke while Julienne drove to the exit booth, flashed a parking pass, and entered the stream of traffic heading toward the bridge crossing the river into Canada.

While both Julienne and the contact woman watched for tailing vehicles, Julienne turned her sideways glance toward Jeffrey Gordon. She was relieved to hear that her voice sounded almost natural.

"Hello, Mr. Gordon."

It was a good thing for Julienne that she had her hands on the steering wheel. Otherwise, she didn't think she could control her shaking. She hadn't counted on this man being so handsome in person. She felt a sort of personal magnetism. Her first impression was that he was very clean. More so than the other men in her life. He was clean-shaven and had neatly trimmed hair, a lightly starched white shirt, razor sharp creases in his pant legs, and dress shoes with a shine that you could see your face in. She also noticed that he smelled divine.

She struggled to bring herself under control. After all, this wasn't a date. She had a job to do. She did allow herself to note with a slight downward glance that Gordon was not wearing a wedding band.

"Hello," Gordon replied. "You have me at a disadvantage since I don't know your name."

"Are we alone here?" she asked, sidestepping the question of her name.

"No," Gordon replied. "There is someone in the backseat."

Julienne couldn't suppress a slight smile to his witty response, realizing that the conditions under which they met were as trying for him as for her. "You're right," she replied. "I meant to ask, 'Did you come here alone?'"

"I did as I was instructed," he answered.

They crossed the international border into Canada without incident.

"Mr. Gordon, it will be necessary for us to blindfold you," Julienne said. "We do so for your own safety and for the safety of the women to be released."

Immediately, the contact woman sitting in the backseat reached forward and tied a specially prepared blindfold over Gordon's eyes. It was made of flesh colored material, but it completely shut out all light and vision. His hands were not tied.

As they drove, little conversation passed between Julienne and Gordon. The contact woman in the backseat never spoke. Julienne knew that about an hour of open-road driving lay ahead of them, so she began her planned discussion with Gordon cautiously.

"Mr. Gordon, I understand that you are the director of the Freemen Foundation. Is that correct?"

"Yes."

"I'm told that you are connected with the Mormons."

To her surprise, Gordon answered her question directly.

"As a matter of fact, we have no connection to the Mormon church. We do employ a number of Mormons, but we also employ others. Eventually, we hope the makeup of our force will include a cross-section of belief systems."

"Why have you favored Mormons so far?"

"We had to start somewhere, so we started with the connections we had."

"There's nothing unique in the way Mormon's view the world that makes them the best choices for the kind of work you are doing?"

"Not unique. There are many people in all religions, and possibly those with no religion at all, who share the patriotic values we espouse."

"And what kind of work do you do?"

Gordon didn't hesitate in his response.

"We identify and monitor the activities of organizations that make their money illegally and grow large enough to constitute a threat to society." He quit there without further elaboration.

"Does your organization maintain affiliation or channel funding to one side of the political spectrum or the other?"

"No. Our aims aren't political in nature. They're societal."

"How do you know when an organization is getting its wealth illegally?" she asked.

"That's a good question," Gordon responded. "First, we try to determine how they make their money. If we can do that, it's not too difficult to discover whether the enterprises are legal. However, while it's fairly easy to discover, it's not always easy to prove."

"Suppose you *are* able to discover illegal enterprises—what then?" she continued.

"Of course, we're not a police agency," he answered. "Our intent would be to turn over whatever evidence we can gather to federal or local agencies that could do something about it."

"That's surprising. Once you turn the evidence over to police agencies, do you have the influence needed to see that something will come of your efforts?"

"Not presently, which, I admit, is somewhat troubling. We're not always successful, and we're experimenting with methods for getting the work done."

"I see," she said. "You seem to have paid a fairly high price for something so experimental. Is it something you plan to keep doing in the future?"

"Yes," he answered. "We're just getting started. As we demonstrate success in our mission, we think our donor base will grow. Additional funding will lead to greater influence. It's the same pattern followed by environmental organizations."

"Why don't you leave this kind of work to established law enforcement agencies?" asked Julienne.

"We're not trying to supplant the established agencies. Some of them are serving well—some not. Many are overwhelmed by the flood of illegal activities and just don't have the resources to respond. Our hope is to assist at the grassroots level."

"Doesn't that make you vigilantes?"

"That label has all kinds of negative baggage, of course. But the notion of keeping vigil is a helpful one, if it's done within the law and with honorable aims."

"Isn't that the problem with citizen vigilantes? They mean well in the beginning. Eventually they slip from their moorings and act outside the law. Or they take the law into their own hands." Julienne was pressing what she viewed as fallacies in Gordon's thinking.

"I think you're right," he replied. "But that kind of drift can happen in any organization. Our challenge lies in maintaining a disciplined stance and accountability to a governing board."

"Pardon me if I remain unconvinced," said Julienne.

"I've tried to unveil any mysteries about the Freemen Foundation," Gordon said. "Now tell me about the organization you represent."

Julienne realized she had walked into a trap. Gordon's candor had not been thoughtless.

"I'm sorry, but I can't," she replied.

"How did you come to be in a position to mediate this release?" he asked.

"I'm sorry, I can't tell you that either."

"I see," he said pensively. "Is there anything you can tell me that will help me understand what is about to happen?"

"Only that we have accepted these two women into custody. We're acting as good citizens to arrange for their release."

"I'm sure many people will be grateful for your efforts," he said. "My curiosity compels me to ask whether the organization you represent makes its money legally or not. Would you know that?"

A trillion times in her life, Julienne Rostetter had looked her opponents in the eyes and told them whatever they wanted to hear— or whatever she wanted them to hear—without regard to the truth. Now she was talking to a man who seemed to tell the truth fearlessly. While she couldn't explain her actions, she knew that his honesty obligated her to do the same.

"There are things about the organization I work for that I don't wish to know," she said.

"I see," he said. "You seem to be a bright and decent woman. If you prefer to remain ignorant about its aims and methods, then I have no doubt there's good reason."

"Could you put that in a little simpler language?" she asked.

"Sure—it means that you work for an organization that you can't trust. You're a person of conscience. There's a little war going on inside you. That internal struggle should be resolved quickly. Depending on the organization you work for, the situation could be injurious to your health."

Julienne was completely taken back by Gordon's sudden forwardness. But his observations were offered in the offhand and casual manner one might expect from a hired consultant.

"Are all Mormons mind readers?" she asked with a hint of a laugh.

"No. I guess I'm getting carried away because I'm nervous. And I'm enjoying our conversation," he said. "Have you ever met a Latter-day Saint?"

The conversation had reached, as Julienne knew it eventually would, a point where she would have to choose between satisfying her own curiosity or maintaining exact professional decorum. She knew that the contact woman in the back seat was listening to all they said. She couldn't be sure that the vehicle they were driving was not bugged with listening devices. She also knew she had already said one or two things that might place her job in jeopardy. Perhaps it was pure recklessness on her part; maybe it was an acknowledgment that she no longer had career ambitions with Fletchner International and was ready to make a break; or maybe it was the curious mixture of attraction and interest she felt toward Gordon. Whatever it was, she knew that her next comment would cause her to cross a line into a new frontier from which she could never return. Though it was so unlike her, she did it anyway.

"Actually I have met a Latter-day Saint. A few days ago two of your sister missionaries visited my office."

"Really? And how did you feel about what you heard?" he asked.

"It's interesting that you ask how I *felt*, instead of asking what I *thought* about it. I thought it was stupid. I thought it was unbelievable. I thought it was dangerous."

She glanced briefly at Gordon to see how he was taking her head-on attack. His head was turned toward her as though he could see her through the blindfold. She was grateful to look away to the road again, and when she tried to speak, her voice caught on a hard swallow.

"I wondered how reasonable people could become so devoted to a way of thinking that is so far out on the fringe."

Jeffrey Gordon didn't respond.

"How does that strike you?" she asked.

"I heard what you said," he replied in a light voice. "I thought maybe if I didn't start to argue right away, you would eventually get around to answering the question I asked."

"Which was?" she asked.

"How did you *feel* about what the missionaries said?"

"How did I feel about it? It was—I was unsettled by what I heard. The missionaries were impressive young women. As you did a few minutes ago, they seemed to read my mind. I would think of an objection to their message, and they would answer it before I could voice it."

Nodding his understanding, Jeffrey Gordon then asked Julienne the very question she didn't want to answer.

"Did you feel that what they told you was true? More important, if it were true, would their message meet important needs in your life?"

At that point in the conversation, Julienne turned off the main highway onto a long, straight country road.

"You're doing it again," she said as they resumed speed.

A slight smile crept over the corners of Jeffrey Gordon's mouth.

"I know there seems to be some slight of hand at work here. But there's really not," replied Gordon. "There's very little mystery in this whole matter of seeking for truth.

"Take for example the two women to be released this afternoon. These are fine women. I know them well. They are honest, intelligent, and strong. They are kind in their hearts. They are willing to make sacrifices for others. Huge sacrifices! They would sacrifice their lives for the very truths that the two sister missionaries told you about. They believe above all else in the great plan of happiness instituted by a loving Heavenly Father to bless the lives of his children. All his children.

"These women aren't robots. They haven't been brainwashed, they aren't dogmatic, and they don't act out of blind obedience. All of their goodness—their devotion, their sacrifice—arises from that small warm feeling in the center of their beings that tells them they have found the truth. That inner feeling tells them that what they're doing is pleasing to God—that they have the power to ease the burdens of others and help make others happier.

"I have no doubt that they have suffered tremendously in the past week," he continued. "Even in comfortable circumstances, imprisonment must be emotionally crushing. But I know this: if they're released—*when* they're released—they won't feel sorry for themselves. They won't be bitter or hateful toward those who have abused them. In the midst of their suffering, they'll thank God for their blessings. And all of that," he concluded, "comes from a little voice—a little feeling—inside that says, 'This is true. I am God. You are my daughter. I love you. I have prepared a way for you to be happy—to be fulfilled in this world as well as in the world to come.' "

"If everyone has that feeling," asked Julienne, "why isn't everyone a Latter-day Saint?"

"I don't suppose everyone has that feeling," Gordon replied. "And not all of those who have that feeling can accept other Latter-day Saint teachings or are willing to live them."

"So, I guess that makes those of you who can accept and live it feel pretty special—and pretty smug," she said.

"I'm sorry. I didn't mean it that way," replied Gordon. "But, you wanted me to be honest, and that's what I'm trying to do."

"I don't remember asking you to be honest," Julienne replied.

"No, I suppose you didn't. I guess I just imagined that's what you wanted."

"There you go again," she said in an accusing but not unfriendly tone. "It's a wonder that you don't all make your living reading tea leaves or palms."

"I guess you're right," he said with a laugh.

They turned off the country road onto a gravel-surfaced lane that led up into a small cluster of wooded hills forming a semicircle around a small lake. Julienne had known this remote country spot since her childhood. Set back from the road and isolated by large yards, gardens, and woods were summer homes that, until the present generation, had belonged to the well-to-do of Toronto.

Julienne slowed the vehicle to cut the dust as they passed an elderly gentleman walking his dog along the apron of the road. He wore a woven straw hat, a light shirt open at the throat, cotton knickers, knee-high cotton socks, and open-toed sandals. His dog was a beautiful full grown Irish setter tugging at the leash to explore roadside curiosities. Julienne didn't recognize the old gentleman, though that didn't surprise her too much. Many of the homes along the lane had changed hands in recent years. As a girl she had known every family who lived on the lane. But as the couples aged or passed away, many of their children had sold the properties.

In this secluded spot, where the homes were only occupied occasionally and where residents cherished their privacy above all else, Julienne was certain that the transfer of the young women could be made without notice.

Again the thought came to her, though it annoyed her, that seeing and being in this place where the happiest moments of her life had passed, Jeffrey Gordon would know more about her than she could ever tell him.

FORTY-TWO

The gate to the Rostetter country home was open as Julienne steered her SUV into the drive. She glanced around to see if she could spot members of her security team who were to be conspicuously posted around the interior of the grounds. She could see no one. She tapped the horn two or three times, expecting her security team members to appear and assist in escorting their guest into the house. No one came.

Julienne was about to look over her shoulder at the contact woman in the backseat when she felt the pressure of a gun barrel at the base of her skull. The contact woman, holding the gun, signaled Julienne to be silent. In front of them Julienne could see the overhead door to the carriage house rising. Before the door was all the way up, four black-clad figures stepped onto the driveway and surrounded the van.

Beside her, Jeff Gordon grew uneasy about the unexplained delay and silence.

"Are we here?" asked Jeff Gordon.

"Are *you* here?" he asked again when there was no answer.

Rather than remove his blindfold, Gordon reached over with his left hand until he felt Julienne's hand resting at her side. Despite the certainty that she had been betrayed and that they were both in grave danger, this gentle touch excited a thrill inside her that raised goose bumps on her flesh.

"Did I miss something?" Jeff asked, just as the door beside him was pulled open and a gun barrel shoved into his neck. He reached up to remove his blindfold, but his hand was slapped violently away. No one spoke. Julienne and Jeffrey Gordon were pulled roughly from the vehicle and marched at gunpoint across the porch and into the house.

The Rostetter country home was a great Victorian structure built by Julienne's great-grandfather in the 1930s. She loved this old house. As she stepped across the porch and through the entry door, she recognized everything around her. She had passed countless hours on lazy summer evenings in the grand old porch swing. On the walls inside were pictures of her ancestors and relatives, pictures of her father as a young boy, the family china, her grandfather's hunting rifle, handmade quilts, and crocheted doilies. She knew every piece of furniture and every inch of the house. For Julienne, it was a museum of her own childhood and of the family for past generations.

Entering the parlor with its elegant fireplace, Julienne was stunned to find her nemesis, Art Warnock, his lapdog Mark Hart, and two of Warnock's men scattered throughout the room. They were all armed, as were the men in black who had marched Julienne and Jeff Gordon into the house.

The two young women whom Rostetter and Gordon had come to release were sitting on the sofa. One was a tall, slender blonde who sat upright. The other woman was Asian. She was conscious, but she leaned against her companion as though she might be ill. Both were bound and blindfolded. Their mouths were taped. Their hair was ratted and unkempt. Julienne could see that the women were dirty and uncared for.

Julienne walked straight toward Art Warnock.

"Art, you snake! What are you doing in my house?"

"Shut up, Julienne!" commanded Warnock, striking her hard across the face, snapping her head to the side. "I'm doing the talking now."

The blow stung so badly that it made Julienne's eyes water. She tried to reach up with her left hand to support her jaw that burned with a sudden searing pain, but her arm was gripped from behind her. Mark Hart threw her violently into a nearby chair.

"Well, Julienne," Art continued, glancing around him. "Isn't this one big happy family. You and all of your Mormon friends right here together. The Chairman will be disappointed when he finds out that you were conspiring to blow the whistle on the company and on him personally. He'll feel betrayed. I know he'll be very sad."

Warnock struck her again, this time with his other hand and on the other side of her face.

"That's what I like, Julienne, a woman who can turn the other cheek," he scoffed with a vicious sneer.

"Let's see. Where was I?" Warnock strode over to Jeffrey Gordon, who was now standing with the barrel of an Uzi assault weapon forced up under his chin. Warnock reached up and removed the blindfold from Gordon's eyes. Gordon surveyed the room. His gaze rested on the two abducted women.

"Welcome, Mr. Gordon. Yes, there are your precious Insiders. Unfortunately, you have arrived too late and with too little firepower to do them any good."

At the mention of Gordon's name, the two women sat up straighter. Gwen Fong seemed to come more to life. Warnock, who smiled darkly, did not overlook these obvious signs of hope.

"We understood that you were willing to release these women," Gordon said to Warnock. "I presume that's still true."

"You presume?" mocked Warnock. "Does it look like we're here to release anybody?"

Warnock turned back to Julienne.

"When it's learned that Julienne Rostetter and all of these fine Mormons perished in a dreadful fire, all gone to heaven . . . At least, I suppose *they'll* go to heaven. I'm not sure where you'll be going, Julienne."

"Art, you make me sick," Julienne managed to say, though she could hardly move her jaw.

Warnock slapped her again. Julienne, clearly suffering from this abuse, didn't cry out or look away.

"I don't know your name," came the voice of Jeff Gordon, "but I can see that you're a coward and a bully."

"Is that right?" Warnock wheeled on Gordon.

"And maybe a moron," Gordon added, though he could hardly speak with the weapon at this throat.

Art Warnock threw back his head and laughed a long, harsh, mocking laugh. No one else laughed. Hart smiled awkwardly, looking from Warnock to Julienne and back. The black-garbed warriors were expressionless, doubtlessly thinking that this was not their business.

In the distance, Julienne could hear a dog barking—a big dog. Maybe it was the Irish setter she had seen on its master's leash as she drove up the lane. Things looked bleak indeed, and she found herself wishing that the elderly gentleman, or anyone else, would realize what was happening and call for help.

Then, the irony—the ludicrousness—of her thoughts became clear to her.

I can't believe you. There are no authorities anywhere close. Furthermore, you are the security. You've lost it, girl. You walked into this like it was your first day on the job.

"These women need medical attention," said Gordon.

"Shut up," barked Warnock.

"The manly thing would be to turn them loose," Gordon continued anyway. "If you have a fight, take it up with me."

"Who asked you?" Art exploded. "Shut him up!" he shouted to the Dark Warrior beside Gordon.

On command, the Dark Warrior wheeled Gordon around and drove a fist into his midsection. Gordon sagged to his knees, clutching his stomach.

Julienne tried to rise but was jerked back down into her seat by Hart.

"Don't like to see your friends get hurt, is that right, Julienne?" taunted Warnock.

"You're pathetic."

Warnock slapped her again. Hard.

"This woman is not one of us," gasped Gordon through his pain. "She doesn't work with us and owes us nothing."

"Hit him again!" shouted Warnock.

FORTY-THREE

While Jeff Gordon struggled to recover from the second vicious blow, one of Art Warnock's security detail fell, unconscious, to the front drive of the house next door. The motionless body was immediately dragged into the bushes and left there without the weapon he had carried.

Inside the neighboring house, peering out from behind a curtain, Ike Rudman could see only part of the attack. He stood for a moment, deciding what this might mean. Then his features darkened as he whispered a curse. He anticipated the next move by sliding open the door that led to the cellar from inside the house. Knowing where the planned release of the two women was supposed to take place, Rudman had appropriated this home that stood vacant at the moment. Its close proximity to the Rostetter home would allow him to watch the activities next door and still remain unseen. Additionally, the house had an unfinished cellar that had been used to store potatoes, furniture, and other essentials in years past. The cellar was convenient to his plans.

As he eased down the cellar steps, still in the dark, he removed a weapon from the holster in the small of his back. His eyes gradually grew more accustomed to the dark. He could barely discern the forms of Rowley and Madero, strapped to steel support poles in the open center of the room. He kept to the wall and made his way silently behind a stack of wooden crates where he could see all that might happen without being seen.

He didn't have long to wait. He had been there only three or four minutes, listening in the darkness as the young men squirmed to free themselves, when he heard a tool being inserted against the doorjamb to pry open the cellar door from the outside. He knew there was no way to do that silently. The person outside was muffling the sound with something—perhaps a piece of clothing. Whoever it was, he was not an amateur. With a minor snap, the jamb split apart, rendering the dead bolt useless.

Rudman expected the door to open slowly, and he was not disappointed. As it opened an inch or two, allowing the bright light to stream into the cellar, Rudman's eyes were well enough adjusted to the dark that his dilated pupils could not see any movement beyond the door. Suddenly, the door flew open. The bright daylight burst into the room. Rudman snapped his eyes shut to preserve his ability to see in the dark. They were only closed for a two or three count when the door slammed shut again.

It happened so quickly that Rudman couldn't be sure whether someone had slipped into the cellar, or had popped the door open, seen Rowley and Madero strapped to the poles, and had slammed it shut again. He waited, watching and listening intently. The captives were perfectly silent.

A minute passed. Then two. Three. Perhaps five. Rowley and Madero again sawed away at the cord against the steel posts, trying to free themselves. Because they were blindfolded, Rudman knew they could not have seen whether someone had entered the cellar.

Several more minutes passed. A man of lesser experience would have soon concluded that any danger was past. But Rudman had been too long on the streets and had seen too many mistakes in judgment that had cost men and women their lives. He was not about to do the same. He knew from a lifetime of experience that patience was his dearest ally.

After what Rudman estimated to be eight or nine minutes, he heard others approaching the door from outside. They apparently hesitated as they saw the damaged doorjamb and realized the door had been opened. Again the door flew open, the bright daylight pouring in. This time, two figures leaped through the open door, their assault weapons at the ready. Rudman recognized them as employees of Fletchner International.

Having entered, one of the intruders moved to his right in the direction of the stairs where Rudman was concealed. The other moved along the wall to the left. Rudman counted the seconds. He hoped that if someone else had entered the room minutes earlier, as he suspected had been done, that person would be discovered and neutralized before Rudman was discovered. If the other managed to outshoot the intruders, he would reveal his hiding place in doing so, and Rudman would still have the advantage of surprise.

No sound came from the other side of the room. The intruder on Rudman's side continued to advance. Rudman could see him clearly. He waited in breathless suspense to the very last second before he was sure of being detected. Finally, he squeezed off a shot from his silenced pistol. It struck the intruder with deadly accuracy. The intruder's body fell heavily, his weapon clattering to the floor.

However, before the intruder on the other side of the room could react, Rudman had taken two lightning quick steps forward and was prepared when the man turned toward the noise. Rudman also shot him dead.

Rudman was furious. He knew he had lost the advantage. He moved carefully across the room behind Rowley and Madero, who were craning around, listening hard and trying to determine what was happening behind them. He cautiously rounded the corner, searching every nook and space before him in the shadowy cellar. Several large barrels stood in one corner, and half a dozen hundred-pound bags of potatoes lay on the floor. Rudman searched the barrels meticulously and shot a round into each of the bags of potatoes. Though instinct told him that the danger still lurked somewhere in the dark around him, his reason told him that no one could be hiding in the cellar. At length, he stood upright and stretched out the aching muscles in his back and shoulders. Then he re-holstered his pistol and walked toward the center of the room.

As Rudman stepped to the open cellar door and pulled it closed, returning the room to near blackness, he heard a voice directly behind him that made his heart stop.

"Wie gehts, mein freund?" said a soft voice with an almost friendly ring. "Don't turn around—and don't reach for the gun. Raise your arms over your head."

Rudman's arms came up very slowly. Then instantly, he whirled in the direction of the voice, his right hand reaching behind him for the gun. His hand had just gripped the butt of his pistol when he heard the hissing sound of a silenced weapon and felt an exploding pain in the joint of his right shoulder.

The impact of the shot threw Rudman backward onto the hard-packed, earthen floor. He came to rest on his left side, unable to move his right arm, and writhing in pain. His right shoulder was on fire. Again he tried to grasp the weapon still in its holster with his left hand.

"Don't do it," the man said softly from the darkness. "You're not that good with your left hand. Don't make me end it here."

Rudman was blinded by pain and couldn't lie on his right shoulder. With his left hand, he raised himself up on his knees, trying to keep moving. If he could reach his weapon, he would kill his unseen adversary.

"Turn your back to me," came the voice.

Rudman awkwardly turned himself around, still kneeling, until his back was to Rowley, Madero, and his assailant.

"Now, remove your pistol with your left hand and throw it to your left," the voice commanded.

Rudman couldn't strike from his current position. He had no choice but to comply. He slowly withdrew the gun and tossed it into the corner of the cellar, where it clattered against the concrete wall.

"Now, lie down on your face."

Rudman complied again, with great difficulty. The pain in his shoulder was maddening. His ears were ringing, and he could feel consciousness fading.

"Spread your arms and legs."

Rudman complied just enough to keep from stiffening his opponent's resolve. He knew now that his opponent did not have the will to kill him. Otherwise, he would already be dead.

Don't shoot a man you don't intend to kill.

That rule of thumb had served Rudman well and explained why he was still alive at his age. He was sure this opponent would not live so long. Given any opportunity, Rudman would see to that.

Rudman lay now in silence, his right arm painfully useless. With a moment to think, he tried to pierce the fog of pain and remember where he knew his assailant's voice from. Gradually, pieces fell into place.

Prague.

Brussels.

Budapest.

How many other times he had competed with this opponent in deadly games, he couldn't remember.

Of course you would be here. I knew you'd come. How could you not?

"You have the upper hand," he called out, turning his head away from the musty cellar floor. "Perhaps we can reach an agreement."

Rudman heard sounds of movement behind him, though he could not turn his head to see. He felt himself getting angry.

Anger is good.

Helps me stay focused.

Helps me combat the desire to abandon myself to pain and self-pity.

Helps me find a weakness in my opponent that I can exploit.

There was no response, but he could sense that his attacker was releasing Rowley and Madero.

"How did you escape my search?" he called out.

"Perhaps you should think of retiring," came the reply. "Your eyesight is failing. You looked right at me and didn't see me."

Rudman hissed in anger. Balling his fist, he pounded the cellar floor with his left hand. It hurt. He did it again. It hurt worse. But his head was clearing, and the pain in his shoulder was surrendering to his anger.

"Watch yourself, my friend," Rudman spoke ominously. "I am far from death."

FORTY-FOUR

Jamie Madero felt the cord that bound him to the steel post being cut, unwound, and dropped to the floor.

"Step away from the post," the voice behind him commanded. "And hold your hands still. This knife is sharp."

The tape was cut away from his hands. Jamie rubbed his wrists, but otherwise he didn't move until told to do so.

"Now, young man, you can take the tape off your eyes and mouth.

"Take this piece of cord and walk toward our wounded friend— on his left side. Move around to his head. Stay beyond the reach of his arms. He is very dangerous. Make a loop in the cord and place it around his left wrist.

"Stay far away from him," the voice continued with a note of urgency and warning. "Don't let him grab you."

"He's hurt," said Jamie. "Can I use something to stop the bleeding?"

"The bullet probably crushed his shoulder joint. He's not likely to bleed to death from the wound," replied the man behind. "Let's secure him first. Then we'll take a closer look."

As Jamie leaned forward to place a loop around Rudman's wrist, the wounded man looked up at him. Rivulets of perspiration lined Rudman's face, and his teeth were clenched against the crippling pain he endured.

"Madero, this man is a murderer," Rudman gasped. "If he can stop me, he'll kill you, your companion, and the two women. Resist him. Don't play his game. If he gets his way, you're a dead man."

Rudman winced with every sentence. He didn't cry out, but the excruciating pain was written on his face.

Jamie looked toward the source of the voice. He thought he could barely see the outline of the man holding the gun in the deep shadows.

"He's hurt bad," Jamie hesitated. "He needs help."

"This man is dangerous. He's deadly," came the reply. "Believe me, you are in greater danger than he is. Please do as I say."

Again, Jamie reached forward. Rudman shook his head.

"Don't listen to him. You mean nothing to him. Help me before it's too late," pled Rudman.

"Young man, we are wasting valuable time," came the voice from behind. "I could take this man's life, but I haven't. Now, either do as I say and help me tie him, or stand aside so that I can further disable him."

Jamie thought he knew what that meant. He didn't know who was telling the truth. He reasoned that nothing was to be gained in causing Rudman to be shot a second time. He placed a loop around Rudman's wrist and stepped back, pulling the cord tight. Rudman was strong, and Jamie leaned into the task, wrenching Rudman's arm out straight. The resulting jolt on Rudman's body did cause him to cry out in pain. Then he cursed. Viciously. The outburst startled Jamie, who suddenly felt like he had a tiger by the tail.

"Now, holding onto the end of the cord, pull his left arm down to his side. Stay away from his feet."

Jamie Madero was shaking so badly he could hardly follow the instructions.

"Stay on his left side. Lift up his left foot. Careful! Don't get between me and him."

"I wouldn't think of it," responded Jamie. "Especially if I knew where you were."

Following each instruction with precision so as not to place himself or his companions in greater jeopardy, in just a few minutes

Jamie tied Rudman's wrist to both ankles raised behind his back. It was a terribly awkward position for the fallen man and must have been extremely painful in light of his injury. But Rudman never spoke again. His breathing was shallow and his body quivered. He convulsed in pain each time Jamie applied pressure, tightening the cord.

"Now step away from him and turn your back to me," the invisible man instructed. As Jamie complied, the person now in charge freed Chad and told him to stand by his companion.

"I want both of you to drag him over here out of sight. We're going to use the remaining piece of cord to tie him to the pole."

It was Chad who responded.

"We can't leave him here. He's hurt, and he's a friend."

"He doesn't seem like the kind of person you would choose for a friend," returned the voice. "Please take my word that this man has betrayed you. He's not your friend, but your enemy. That's why you were tied down here. Now, we must tie him and be on our way."

After anchoring the wounded Rudman to the pole, Jamie got his first look at the man who freed him and Chad as the man placed his pistol in the pocket of his baggy pants and stepped toward the cellar door.

Jamie held back cautiously.

"Can you tell us who you are?" Chad said to the stranger.

"Step over here where we can talk without disturbing our captive." Then with his voice lowered to a whisper, the stranger asked, "Who do you think he is?"

"You'd have to ask him," Chad answered.

"I don't have to ask him," replied their rescuer. "I know who he is. I'm just wondering who you think he is."

"He's the father of one of our associates."

"Did he tell you that?" their new ally asked.

"He told us his name and hinted at the rest. However, he did identify himself to the FBI in Denver."

"I guess that explains why you and Jeff Gordon had dinner with him in Denver," the stranger revealed.

"How could you know that from here?" Chad asked.

"Oh, I was there," the man continued. "I've been in and out of the picture since your encounter with the Dark Warriors in Leadville. You believe he's Ike Rudman?"

"It's pretty clear now that he betrayed us," said Chad. "And frankly, I had some difficulty believing him. He's not the man I would imagine to be Sarah Rudman's father."

Jamie nodded his agreement.

"At the same time, the guy has impressive connections," said Chad. "The FBI bought his identity. He flew us here in a private plane and bypassed customs. He's got to be somebody."

"He's somebody, all right," the older man replied. "But he's not Ike Rudman."

"Do you know Ike?" asked Chad.

"*I* am Ike," the other man replied.

The revelation rocked Jamie.

"Then, who's he?" Jamie asked.

"His name is Gerhardt Trautmann. He's an old acquaintance of mine. But not a friend. Trautmann was a member of the East German secret police for years. In the early 1990s, he put himself out for hire and has worked all over the world. For the Russians mostly. But he has also done jobs for the Colombians, some of the African nations, and perhaps others. He's a vicious, deadly man.

"While you were tied to the poles over there, Trautmann added two more kills to his gruesome total. The dead men were hired by the same organization that is paying Trautmann. The same was true for the men he killed at your office in Denver."

"How does he get away with all of this?" asked Chad. "How did he take in the FBI so easily?"

"He didn't take them in," replied the new Ike Rudman. "They played along. I had already visited with Agent Ortega. We were surprised when Trautmann showed up, but he didn't fool either of us. The FBI would have taken him in Denver, but we needed him to lead us to Sarah and Gwen Fong."

"We're only a couple of country boys," Chad said. "With all due respect, what reason do we have to believe that you are Ike Rudman any more than he is? It seems like everybody wants to be Ike Rudman these days. And to be honest," he continued as he looked at the other man attired in knickers and sandals, "you don't look much like a secret agent."

"That's fair. I'm Sarah Rudman's dad. I could convince you of my identity by telling you everything there is to know about my daughter, at least as much as a father can know. Maybe more than most fathers know.

"But in the interest of time—which is critically short—let me tell you what I know about you from my daughter. You're Chad David Rowley. Born and reared in Anaheim. Your father is a respected independent movie producer. Your older brother was killed in a horseback riding accident. You served an LDS mission in the southwest. You're preparing to go to England on a Fulbright scholarship. You enjoy the respect of those around you. And you're in love with my daughter."

Chad extended his hand.

"Sir, if we get out of this alive, I'll come asking for your daughter's hand in marriage."

"If we get out of this alive," replied the older man, "it won't be me you'll have to convince."

FORTY-FIVE

Following their brief conversation about Ike Rudman's identity, the trio turned their attention to the task before them.

"Jeff Gordon arrived about fifteen minutes ago," said Ike. "He was escorted by Julienne Rostetter, chief of security for Fletchner International, and one additional female hand. However, they came in at gunpoint. I would say, for starters, that Rostetter is out of favor with her employer. Jeff Gordon is in serious trouble. They also brought Sarah and Gwen into the house earlier this afternoon. Gwen had to be helped, so I imagine that she's either sick or injured. Until a few minutes ago, the opposition had at least nine men and one woman in addition to our friend Trautmann, who counts for several more on his own."

"He's out of action for the time being," commented Chad.

"You can never count Trautmann out," replied Ike tensely. "Not ever. Maybe not even when he's dead—or when you think he's dead. He's among the most skilled men at his business in the world. He's what we call an entrepreneur. He works alone. His only allegiance is to the person paying his bills. He recognizes no other obligations. As you have already seen, he's ready to kill at the drop of a hat. He'll kill their people as well as ours to fulfill his contract.

"Further, there are two kinds of adversaries at the house next door. Two or three men and a woman belong to Fletchner International. They're highly trained but don't compare with the four Dark Warriors."

"Who are the Dark Warriors?" asked Jamie.

"They are international mercenaries. Hired killers. Extremely dangerous! Possibly part of the same hit squad that attacked you in Leadville and probably hired by Fletchner International. Their mission is probably to bring in those they think constitute a danger because of information you had access to while you worked for them."

"Wouldn't they know that any information the Insiders had would already have been passed on to others?" asked Jamie.

"I'm sure they do. In that case, they'll try to make sure you never cross them again. They'd love to make examples of you to others in their organization of questionable loyalty." Ike shrugged. "It's hard to get inside their minds, but they doubtlessly think they have good reason for doing what they're doing."

"If they're working for Fletchner International, why would they be holding the head of security? Isn't that where their paycheck comes from?" asked Chad.

"I'm not altogether sure what's happening. I recognized Rostetter's number two man, a slimeball named Art Warnock. My guess is that we're seeing a takeover attempt within Fletchner International's security staff. Warnock's probably trying to erase some tactical mistakes he made in killing the Foundation team members in Leadville. But that's mostly guesswork at the moment."

"Is there any hope of getting some help?" Chad questioned further.

"Their move to meet at Niagara and turn north across the Canadian border was very shrewd," replied Ike. "Though the two countries work closely together, there are jurisdictional issues that never seem to go away. Our people are rousing the RCMP as we speak, but I can't say for sure how long it will take for them to arrive. I'm afraid it won't be in time."

"What's the RCMP?" Jamie asked.

"The Royal Canadian Mounted Police. They're the national police force of Canada—the Canadian counterpart to our FBI," replied Ike.

"The plain truth is that we're probably the girls' best hope. We've got to move quickly. Warnock's people may not know yet that you've been freed, but when they do, they may pull the trigger and get out as quickly as they can. They'll come looking for you and their two missing men any minute. What we have to do now is even up the sides."

"How do we do that?" asked Chad.

"We have to remove some or all of Warnock's outside people and destroy their transportation," replied Ike. He signaled toward the door.

"The backyard was clear when I came in. Go out very slowly to your right. Stay low and against the house. Use the concealment of the shrubbery. Cross around behind the garage and wait by the van you came in. It's still parked in the drive. I'll go through the house and make sure it is clear, then meet you in the front. We'll disable the van, move to their yard, and remove some of the opposition. You can help create a diversion that will allow me to get into the house."

With that much of a plan in mind, Chad and Jamie crept slowly out the cellar door into the still-light evening sky, leaving their new-found ally behind in the dark.

FORTY-SIX

"**Try to get Duquette and Edwards on the radio again. They** should have been back here by now. Tell 'em to bring in the others, and let's get the party started."

Art Warnock was ranting. Mark Hart knew well how Warnock's violent temper rose when things didn't happen exactly as he had dictated. Warnock had sent the two men to the neighboring home to bring in Rowley and Madero. Ten minutes had now passed and the men hadn't returned or reported in.

Warnock had revealed his plan of action to the only other person in the room who needed to know—Mark Hart. The plan was simple: Get the five Foundation people and Julienne Rostetter together in the Rostetter home. Stage a conflict that would look like negotiations for the release of the women had gone awry. Leave convincing evidence that the terrorists had murdered those involved to cover their withdrawal. Then burn the house with six bodies inside. The plan would effectively decimate the Foundation and remove Julienne Rostetter as a factor at Fletchner International.

Hart looked away from Warnock to the four captives. Gwen Fong, whom he knew best and for whom he had worked the better part of a year, did not look well. But she was conscious and seemed able to follow events in the room. Hart knew Gwen was an honest, evenhanded person who would shoulder pressure without striking out at others.

She's no weakling.

The other young woman, Sarah Rudman, looked invincible to Hart. She refused to react to Warnock's abusive gloating and sadistic taunts. She remained silent and poised, as though she could still pull an ace out of her sleeve and turn everything in her favor. Hart could not resist respecting her strength and serenity.

Under the right circumstances, she would be a formidable foe.

Julienne Rostetter, whom Hart also knew from Fletchner International, though not well, reacted disdainfully toward Warnock. In turn, her resistance further fueled Warnock's misbehavior. He had slapped her hard across the face several times. But she was unbowed by the abuse and followed the course of events closely.

JR, you're amazing. No matter how outgunned you are, you still act like you're in charge.

Beyond all else, Rostetter's present performance showed that she was a consummate professional and not a criminal. When push came to shove, she resisted lawless behavior even when it threatened her life. Hart had observed her from a distance at her Fletchner headquarters and was never quite sure which way she would fall when the wind really started to blow. Now she was standing in a very stiff breeze indeed, and her leanings were absolutely clear. She was a decent, reasonable person who would not bow to force and who would stand up for the well-being of the helpless.

Jeffrey Gordon was silent, sitting on the floor with his back against a sofa, a gun still at his head. Gordon had tried to defend Rostetter. For this, he had been hammered. He had a powerful build but a quiet manner.

In pain, but not weak, and not beaten.

Hart's own senses were acutely alert. He felt he had to see everything, be aware of everything. His moment was coming, and he knew he would have to act on snap judgments. He listened as Julienne Rostetter railed on Art Warnock, who kept peering out the front window and glancing to the back of the room, where the hallway came in from the kitchen. Warnock impatiently awaited the arrival of the missing guards with the two remaining captives. He had already ordered another outside guard to check the cellar but hadn't yet received a radio reply on what was found.

"Art, I can't believe that you think you'll get away with this," JR said caustically. "This is not television. This is the real world. There are too many people involved, too many details, too many loose ends. You can't possibly cover all your tracks."

Art, if you had an ounce of brains, you'd listen to her. She's right.

"You can still walk away from here," continued Julienne. "Release these people. You and I can fight out our differences. Let the best woman win."

Warnock turned a menacing look toward Julienne. He had hit her hard before and was not above doing it again.

"Let them go," Julienne pressed Warnock. "If your pathetic intellect demands some human sacrifice, kill me. That's what you really want. Or better yet, give me a gun and meet me out in the street."

Hart knew that Julienne was trying to keep Warnock off balance. By drawing his anger to herself, she hoped to distract his attention from other important details so that if something did happen in her favor, she would have a second or two to react while he was refocusing.

Her strategy would have a better chance of succeeding if it weren't for the two Dark Warriors.

The two Dark Warriors stood silently at the edge of the room, amused at Julienne's ongoing harangue. They were doubtlessly amazed that Warnock was willing to put up with it.

"Shut up, Julienne. I'm telling you that for the last time. I'll get to you in a minute. You can be first," Warnock said with finality.

Hart turned his eyes away from Rostetter.

I can understand how her look of disdain must infuriate you, Art. I've tasted that disdain. It can be bitter.

Mark rechecked his watch.

Art, the time to act is long past. Every minute works against you.

Warnock continued pacing.

I'm betting you only have one plan and no backup. You're not the kind of guy who improvises in the field. You're waiting because you don't know what else to do.

Hart surveyed the room once more.

What do these people know about me? Warnock uses me as a convenience. He'd throw me away in an instant, without remorse. I'm nothing to the Dark Warriors. Might as well be an inanimate object. They're trained to squash people like bugs. Rostetter despises me. Shows I'm doing something right. None of the three Foundation people knows anything about me. All in all, nobody will pay any attention to what I'm doing.

Hart felt again for the butt of the pistol under his jacket and visually measured the distance between him and the two Dark Warriors. He knew what he had to do but was unsettled by Warnock's delay.

Let's go, Art. Before I lose my nerve.

FORTY-SEVEN

"**O**kay, I think we're clear here," said Rudman in a lowered voice as he stripped a pair of surgical gloves from his hands. He had slipped quietly out the front door of the neighboring home as Jamie and Chad waited alertly by the van.

"There are no other vehicles in the garage," Ike assured them.

Pointing at the driver's side door, Ike told Jamie to get in and pop the hood latch. When Jamie had done so, Ike lifted it quietly and pulled up the hood bracket, propping the hood open. He then took a flat stiletto from inside his high sock and used it to slice the spark plug and ignition wires. He quietly lowered the hood again.

"This van's not going anywhere soon," he whispered.

They made their way to the back of the property where they found the boundary marked by a high wooden fence that showed signs of being kept in good repair. They helped one another over the fence and followed it along until they reached the adjoining Rostetter property. They entered through a back gate almost hidden by undergrowth. The three managed to push the gate open just far enough to allow them to slide through.

The Rostetter home had a broad covered porch surrounding the house on three sides. Ike and his helpers were viewing the house from the back and could see the kitchen door and windows clearly. To their left was the old carriage house that had been since converted into a garage. Beside the carriage house was a tool shed, also of Victorian design. These outbuildings were partially overgrown with ivy and surrounded by tall shrubbery that would provide good concealment as they worked their way closer to the house.

Unfortunately, they also saw two guards in the yard, black-clad and heavily armed.

"We're going to need a diversion," said Ike. "There's no way to enter the house without alerting the guards. One of you will have to get caught to draw the guards into a position where I can get my hands on them."

"What if they just shoot us down?" asked Jamie.

"I don't think they want to do that," replied Ike. "Unless I miss my guess, Warnock would like to get all of you into the same room with no bullet holes in you."

"I'll go," volunteered Chad. "I'd like to get inside and see how Sarah and Gwen are doing."

Ike gave the younger man an approving nod.

"Don't try to be a hero," he said. "We'll get through this safely if we use our heads, I hope. Act like you're trying to sneak up to the house. Let yourself be caught, and don't try to resist. The Dark Warriors are extremely dangerous. They expect no mercy and extend no mercy. To them, you are only a body standing between them and a paycheck."

With that cheering thought, and on Ike's signal, Chad crawled along the hidden side of a hedge until he reached the corner of the carriage house. He was about midway between the two guards. He rose slowly as though creeping toward the back of the house. One of the guards saw him immediately and started toward him as he alerted those inside and the other guard in the backyard through the open radio net that linked them all.

Ike and Jamie watched the guard approach Chad and saw another Dark Warrior coming to the back door from inside the house. The guard on their side of the yard, whom they hoped to overpower, was a true professional. Instead of watching as his companion took Chad, this guard kept a wide lookout on the rest of the yard, making it impossible for Ike to approach him.

Chad was caught and pinned against the wall of the house. The guard held him there until the man inside came out to assist. The guard in front of Ike and Jamie still held his ground. Ike moaned, "We're going to lose him. Wouldn't you know we'd get a real Marine over here on our side."

Suddenly, Ike clapped Jamie on the shoulder and whispered urgently, "Run for it son. Run for the back door. Make some noise and try to draw the attention of this guard. Go."

Jamie leaped up. By the time he cleared the carriage house and started toward the main house, the guard on their side of the yard had turned and moved toward him. Coming around the other side of the shed, Ike was instantly behind the guard. Before the guard could react or communicate with those in the house, Ike brought him down with the stroke of a gun butt at the base of his skull. In one continuous sweep, he caught the fallen man and his weapon and dragged him into the shrubs where he couldn't be seen from inside the house.

The two guards who marched Chad into the kitchen were still inside. Jamie plastered himself to the wall of the house. Seconds later, Ike joined him, whispering breathlessly, "They gave us a break on that one."

"Wow," replied Jamie between breaths. "You really laid that guy out."

"Let's hope he stays that way for a while," replied Ike, who now moved in front of Jamie next to the open door. "Our boy will be back any second."

As predicted, the storm door swung open, pushed by a black-clad arm from the inside. The guard reemerging from the house never knew what hit him. A chop to the throat kept him from calling out, and a second crashing blow behind the ear left him prone on the doorstep. The pair quickly dragged his body out of sight and resumed their position beside the door.

"Get down on your hands and knees, and crawl past the window," Ike whispered. "Get over to the car in the drive. Watch for other guards in front of the house. Go into the carriage house and try to find something flammable—gasoline, if possible—and some rags. Do what you can to disable anything in the carriage house that can move. Then try to set the SUV in the drive on fire. Here's a lighter," he concluded, pressing a small propane lighter into Jamie's hand.

"How do you know there will be something flammable in the carriage house?" asked Jamie.

"I don't," replied Ike. "We're doing this on faith. Just find something to start a flash fire or cause an explosion—anything that produces some fireworks.

"Be careful. Don't let me down." Ike slapped Jamie on the shoulder and sent him off with his words ringing in Jamie's ears.

"Don't let anyone see you through the windows in the front of the house."

Jamie crawled off as directed. The drive looked clear, so he kept low and rushed to a door on the side of the carriage house. It was unlocked, but the hinges screeched as he pushed the door inward. He held his breath, knowing that the sounds were much louder in his ears than they would be to those at a distance.

He opened the door just enough to squeeze through. Inside, he found a sedan and an SUV loaded with equipment. Both were big and dark—late models. He looked hastily around the interior of the carriage house, trying to be sure there was no one inside guarding the autos. Finding himself alone, he did as Ike instructed.

Jamie peered inside the vehicles and could see that the doors were locked. He was careful not to touch the door latches or any other part of the autos for fear of setting off a car alarm. Moving quickly to a workbench, he surveyed the items on top. He spied an assortment of tools including an old leather awl that had been continuously re-sharpened over the years. This he took and drove it with all his strength into the sidewall of one of the tires on the sedan. The air came rushing out. He then moved on, puncturing the tires on both cars.

Then he searched for gasoline. To his relief, he spied a gas can under the workbench next to a riding lawn mower. He rushed to it, shook it, and then replaced it with a frown.

Empty!

He searched the shelves and work areas. No gas!

Great. Now what?

The thought then came to him to check the gas tank on the riding mower.

Yes!

The tank was nearly full. Grabbing a small garden pail from a nearby shelf, he cut the exposed clear plastic gas line from the tank to the engine. The tank drained with agonizing slowness into the pail. Jamie tried to calculate how much time had passed since he left Ike.

Maybe three or four minutes.

He imagined Ike thinking that he had failed his assignment.

Finally.

Jamie had enough gas in the can to do the job, maybe a half gallon. He rushed to the door. He couldn't see Ike from the door and saw no one in the driveway. Rushing to the front end of the Expedition, he looked in, only to see that whoever had parked it took the precaution of locking the doors.

He crawled under the front end and looked up toward the motor, hoping to see a gas line. He did, but it was metal. He couldn't see any exposed rubber connections. He was stumped.

I've got to do something.

Crawling out from under the car, he spied a large stone beneath a shrub beside the driveway. He hefted it to the side of the Expedition, hardly believing that he had not already been spotted. Grabbing up the gas and rags, he soaked the rags as instructed. Taking a deep breath, he heaved the stone through the passenger side window, smashing it and setting off the alarm.

As the alarm shrieked, Jamie turned the pail upside down, pouring the gasoline into the interior of the Expedition. He draped a soaked rag across the sill of the shattered car window to act as a wick. He ignited it with the lighter Ike had given him. Instantly the gas flared up. Jamie turned and sprinted for the corner of the carriage house. There was a loud pop, and flames engulfed the car.

Jamie had no time to admire his handiwork. Out of the corner of his eye, he saw a woman charge around the front corner of the house, stop for a second to size up the situation, and then lower an automatic weapon and begin firing.

Jamie heard the bullets spraying the side of the Expedition

behind him and striking the surface of the building in front of him. He ducked low and continued to run. As he rounded the corner, he felt a searing pain in his left shoulder. An instant later he felt pain in his left side. He cried out but kept running, plunging into the trees at the back of the yard. Thrashing his way toward the back fence, he stumbled along until he passed through the gate. He paused just long enough to catch his breath and waited to see if he was being followed.

Jamie was breathing so hard he couldn't hear anything else. He peered around the gate again and saw nothing. The pain in his shoulder was shooting down his side and into his leg. Reaching up with his right hand, he felt the moisture in his shirt. Pulling the hand back, he saw that it was covered with blood.

FORTY-EIGHT

Inside the Rostetter home, Mark Hart watched Art Warnock, who had gone wild. Chad Rowley was brought into the room at gunpoint. Warnock, realizing that something serious had gone wrong with his plan, struck Chad repeatedly, demanding to know how he had gotten loose, what had happened to his men, where Madero was, and who else was involved. Chad took the blows silently.

"Tell me what I want to know," Warnock hissed as he stepped to the couch where the two women still sat blindfolded and bound, "or we'll start eliminating our guests right now. Maybe we'll start with our own traitor."

Warnock pulled the blindfold off Gwen Fong's eyes and placed the barrel of his gun in the center of her forehead.

"Do you want to hear her plead? Huh? Beg?" Warnock ripped the tape off Gwen's mouth.

She cried out in pain. Her lips were bloody and chapped from a week of removing and replacing the duct tape used to silence her.

Julienne Rostetter again tried to intercede. Art hit her so hard with his fist that she was out for a moment. As she came around, she again tried to rise, but Mark Hart, standing directly behind her, drew his pistol and placed it at the back of her head. The feel of the cold steel caused her to stop.

On the floor, Jeff Gordon tried to stand and come to Julienne's aid. Without warning, the Dark Warrior standing behind him stepped to his side and whacked him on the back of the head. Having already suffered a concussion just a week earlier, Gordon slumped to the floor.

"How about it, Miss Fong? Want to beg Mr. Rowley for your life? I'll count to three. In that time you'd better convince him to tell me what I want to know, or you get what we gave your friends in Leadville."

Tears streaked down Gwen Fong's face. She looked up beyond the gun at her forehead into Art Warnock's eyes. When she replied, her voice was hoarse from prolonged thirst, and she could barely speak above a whisper.

"You don't frighten me, Mr. Warnock," she said with difficulty. "The only person in any real danger here is you."

"Oh, really?" Warnock croaked. "And who should I be afraid of? You're beaten. In a few minutes you'll be dead." He leaned down right in front of Gwen's face and sneered. "Who should I be afraid of?"

"We're not alone here," she replied. "Those with us are more than those with you. I think it is you who will be dead in a few minutes."

Warnock threw back his head and laughed again, a wicked, hateful laugh. "You people are strange," he said, looking around the room with a sweeping gesture. "You're crazy. You're all about to die."

As he spoke, those in the house heard the smashing of an auto window outside, followed instantly by the shrill car alarm. They saw the female security guard rushing across the porch toward the drive and then heard a loud, hollow pop as the gasoline exploded inside the Expedition. Warnock raced to the front door and threw it open. They could hear the distinct sounds of a silenced, automatic weapon. Warnock yelled back into the room, "Hart, keep them covered. One of you, come with me."

A Dark Warrior hurried forward while his companion stood fast, his automatic weapon covering all in the room. Mark watched the man who remained behind, looking for the slightest break, the blinking of his eyes, any opening that would allow Mark to act. He had only seconds to do what needed to be done.

As if on cue, Chad Rowley lifted himself from the floor and stood directly in front of the Dark Warrior's weapon. With a loud curse, the armed man brought a huge right hand down, crashing it into Chad's neck and shoulder. Chad went down again.

Mark, who still had a pistol to Julienne Rostetter's head, raised the barrel barely above the crown of her head and pulled the trigger. The pistol was not silenced; the report was earsplitting in the small space. The bullet struck the Dark Warrior in the center of his bulletproof chest protector and knocked him backward. Before he could recover, Mark stepped away from Julienne, took aim, and shot him again, this time inflicting a lethal wound.

Hart then checked the hallway behind him and rushing to the front door yelled at Julienne, "Okay, Ms. Rostetter, cut these people loose and get everyone down."

Mark glanced hastily around the doorjamb, trying to see if the porch was clear, when a fusillade of bullets hit the front windows and door. He fell back just in time to avoid all but a grazing wound. He hit the floor and crawled behind the furniture.

The lead poured into the room through the door and picture window. The barrage seemed to last half a minute, filling the room with flying glass and wood splinters. Those inside were showered with debris. The noise was deafening. All they could do was cover their heads and hope no bullet found them.

When the shooting ended, Mark Hart called out, "Move to the back of the house."

But no one could move. Julienne had only been able to loose Sarah Rudman's hands before she took cover. Gwen Fong was motionless. Chad picked himself up off the floor slowly, shaking the debris off his head and shoulders. He had been pelted by a shower of glass shards from the front of a china hutch. He had numerous cuts on the exposed parts of his skin and perhaps under his clothing as well.

Mark paused for a second to inspect the wound on his forearm that was stinging badly and bleeding freely. When he rose, he found himself facing a Dark Warrior standing in the front door; the man's face was twisted into a merciless grin. Mark glanced down for his pistol, still on the floor where he had been lying. With no time to reach it, he knew what was coming. He wanted to close his eyes, but pride and training forced him to defy his enemy to the last instant before death. He met the Warrior's gaze straight on, refusing to look away or even blink.

Behind him, Chad stepped in front of the sofa to provide a human shield for the two women who were still half reclining, Sarah Rudman holding Gwen Fong in her arms.

As though in slow motion, the Dark Warrior's weapon came up. Mark's gaze was riveted to the tightening trigger finger. Seeing the sinews in the finger tightening, he held his breath. He knew his moment had come and braced himself to accept it.

The Warrior's finger gripped the trigger for only a fraction of a second, squeezing off several rounds that flew wild. The Warrior's head snapped backward, and he fell through the door he was entering.

Rousing himself from a violent shudder, Hart spun around to see where the shot that downed the Dark Warrior had come from. Standing across the room was a man whom Hart had never seen before. He was likely in his midfifties, with graying hair, and wearing an unlikely outfit of knickers, long stockings, and sandals. His gun was trained on Hart.

* * * * *

To Hart's left, Chad clutched his chest. Weaving, he fell backwards onto the floor. Sarah reached out at the last second to steady him, but to no avail.

"Oh heaven, please. No!" she choked.

Julienne rushed to Chad's side. Sarah was there in an instant but had to look away as Julienne opened his bloody shirt to inspect the wound.

"I think a stray round hit him in the lung," Julienne said, shaking her head. "We need help, and fast."

Chad was losing consciousness as the two women tried to stop the bleeding. Julienne, who was well versed in first aid, placed a magazine lying nearby against his chest and told Sarah to press her weight against it.

"The lung will try to suck air through the bullet hole," said Julienne. "We've got to stop it or the lung will collapse."

FORTY-NINE

Jamie Madero wasn't bleeding as badly as he had been minutes earlier. His blood-soaked shirt stuck to his side, but he didn't feel faint. After the initial pain subsided, a tremendous rush of adrenalin flooded his system, giving him an unusual feeling of exhilaration. He was no longer afraid. He felt angry and aggressive. It was as though he had faced death and survived—and was now stronger because of it.

Staying low, Jamie crept back toward the house. Parting the boughs in front of him, he saw the woman who had shot him lying prone on the back porch. He skirted left around the toolshed and started toward the carriage house.

As he peered around the corner, he saw one of the Dark Warriors whom Ike Rudman had disabled rising unsteadily to his knees. Without the slightest hesitation, Jamie grasped a weathered shovel handle standing against the toolshed wall. Stepping up behind the partially conscious man, he brought the handle down with all his might. The enemy slumped to the ground again. Jamie shuddered.

Shake it off. This is the real thing. You stop him, or he kills the people you love.

Making an effort to stay calm, Jamie picked up the Warrior's weapon lying not far away. It looked wicked—its stubby barrel capped with a silencer, the magazine extending below the pistol grip. Jamie had no idea how to use it. He grabbed it anyway, walking forward until he could look down the long, covered porch, past the burning Expedition toward the front of the house.

Crouched twenty feet ahead, peering around the front corner of the house with his back to Jamie, was a man in a business suit—a big man. Jamie had never seen him before. As Jamie watched this stranger, he heard a terrible racket inside the house, sounds of shattering glass and the thud of bullets against wood and stone. He could only assume that this man was an enemy. He raised the weapon in his hand. Searching for the safety switch, he fumbled with the weapon for just an instant. When he looked up, the man was facing him, his pistol pointed directly at Jamie's chest.

"Drop the weapon, kid."

Jamie was still pumped and feeling belligerent. He didn't know whether his weapon would fire when he pulled the trigger, but he straightened himself and looked his opponent in the eyes.

"Why don't you come and take it away from me?"

"I don't have time for this, kid. Drop the weapon, or I'll blow you away."

"I'm not a kid. And I don't take orders from you."

Jamie's opponent shook his head once and pulled the trigger. Jamie could see it coming. In a fraction of a second he closed his eyes and pulled the trigger of his weapon. The weapon barely moved in his hands, but he could tell it had fired. Several shots. He braced himself for the sensation of a bullet passing through him.

The expected bullet never arrived, but a deafening blast in front of him assaulted Jamie's senses. He opened his eyes to see his assailant falling backward.

Jamie couldn't tell whether the whole world had gone silent or whether the ringing in his ears was drowning everything else out.

He stood there, stunned, for a few seconds. No one else came around the corner. No one was behind him. There was only Jamie and the man lying motionless in front of him.

Slowly, the realization gripped Jamie that he had killed a man. A man he didn't even know. He could hardly imagine what this might mean.

What if he wasn't an enemy? What if I'm disgraced—turned away from the Foundation? Or worse still, what if I go to jail? I'm a killer.

He shook his head to clear his senses.

Once more he looked around for other attackers. Then he walked forward, the weapon still hanging from his hand, and looked down at the man he had killed. He expected to see a bullet hole, but instead the man's face and neck above his body armor were badly disfigured by the blast. Blood pooled around the man, and Jamie realized that the man's right hand had also been mangled.

He felt sickened. Shock and confusion flooded in upon him. One shot from Jamie's weapon couldn't have caused those injuries. Could it? He looked around again to see what could have caused such injuries.

Still without answers and overwhelmed by guilt, he cautiously looked around the front of the house for the first time. Lying on the porch half inside the front door was the body of another Dark Warrior. The windows of the house were all blown out. Glass and debris littered the front porch.

Jamie could hear no sounds except the ringing in his ears. He felt so alone. Was he alone? Was he the only survivor? He stood frozen at the corner of the house, afraid to look in the front door.

* * * * *

Ike Rudman introduced himself to Hart as Sarah Rudman's father. He stopped short of asking about Hart's identity. He offered no other clues to his own.

Sarah reacted immediately to the thrill of seeing her father. Turning the task of keeping up the pressure on Chad's chest wound to Julienne Rostetter, Sarah fell into her father's waiting embrace.

"Oh, Daddy, I knew you'd come for me," she said. "I knew you'd come. I love you so much."

"What kind of father lets his daughter live this kind of life?" the senior Rudman asked.

"I'll tell you what kind," said Sarah, reaching up with her index finger to sweep a tear away from Ike's eye. "The best father in the world. There was never a better father than you've been to me."

"Never a better daughter," said Rudman. "But I don't like to see you this way. This was way too close."

Their reunion was tender but necessarily brief.

"You take care of Chad, sweetheart. I still have a few important things to do," said Ike.

* * * * *

With three people in the Rostetter house now armed, Mark Hart felt for the first time that he and those with him had a chance to survive. He instructed everyone to stay inside and behind cover until they were able to determine how many of their enemies might still be outside.

Rudman told Hart he had disabled two Dark Warriors outside along with Warnock's female hand. He needed to search them for additional weapons and tie them securely. Hart watched Ike slip quietly out of the room through the kitchen.

What worried Hart most about their vulnerable position was the people now absent and unaccounted for. Foremost on his list was Warnock. Ike Rudman had not seen Warnock outside. With dark approaching, Hart knew the dangers would increase.

FIFTY

Ike Rudman had left the two Dark Warriors crippled but unattended too long. He moved cautiously through the hallway and into the kitchen. He didn't want to find that one of them had revived and reentered the house while he greeted and comforted his daughter. He knew his friends still weren't safe. But his heart was lighter after seeing Sarah alive and mostly well.

Doing a hasty search of the kitchen, he headed for the door to the back porch. This he pushed open slowly with his foot as he searched the porch and backyard with his eyes until he could see the spot where the closest warrior had fallen.

To his surprise, the warrior was sitting, his back to the house, his hands locked behind his head. Fearing a trick, Rudman slowly pushed the screen open further, looking down the porch. There he saw Jamie Madero sitting in a porch chair, ten feet from the captured Warrior, training the Warrior's own weapon on him. Rudman stepped silently onto the porch and could overhear the young man talking to his captive.

"Just give me a reason to shoot. I've already killed one man today. I can do it again if I have to."

Rudman could see that Jamie was wounded. He was startled to hear the youngster say he had killed a man. He hoped it wasn't true. He cleared his throat to announce his presence. Jamie glanced up at him, instantly returning his gaze to the Warrior in front of him.

"I need to talk to our friend," Ike said to Jamie. He reached over and pressed the barrel of Jamie's weapon downward until it was pointing at the ground. The young man was shaking badly. Ike stepped behind the Dark Warrior and hit him again, laying him out on the grass at the edge of the porch.

"He'll be easier to watch that way," Ike said to his young friend. "I suggest you put down that weapon and go inside where you can be with your friends. I'll look after things out here."

"There's nobody else out here," replied Jamie. "Except that guy you put to sleep over by the toolshed."

"Have you seen any movement over there?" Ike asked.

"He came to a little earlier," Jamie said, trying to still his shaking hands. "I put him back to sleep."

"Good man." Ike put his hand on Jamie's right shoulder, trying to get a look at his wounds without drawing Jamie's attention to it.

"Have you seen a big guy out here? Short hair? In a business suit?"

"I saw him," Jamie answered hesitantly.

"Where did he go?" asked Rudman, scanning the yard that was now in deep shadows.

"He's around the house in the driveway. I killed him."

Ike was silent for a moment while he considered this.

"Please go into the house and have that wound treated. We're not out of danger yet. I'll have a look at Warnock—that's the man you think you killed."

"I don't *think* I killed him," replied Jamie, looking up with tears welling in the corners of his eyes. "I *know* I killed him. He's dead. He's really dead."

Ike helped Jamie up and pushed him toward the kitchen door. Then, searching the pockets of the unconscious Warrior, Ike extracted some nylon cord and bound the man's hands and feet. He removed all the Warrior's weapons and then moved on to the next man.

He also bound the female security guard and dragged all three onto the porch, where they could be easily watched from inside the house. Then he walked around to look at Warnock. He stared at the dead man for some time, puzzling over the extensive injuries.

Knowing that all of Warnock's people were now accounted for, he turned his thoughts to Trautmann. It was now fully dark. Ike confessed to himself that he was not excited about going back into the cellar. Trautmann was too dangerous and the risks too great. Although Trautmann was badly injured, he had been badly injured before and survived. He seemed difficult or impossible to kill. Of course, Rudman didn't want to be the person who killed him.

Weighing all the factors, Ike decided against returning to the cellar. He would defend those in the house until help arrived. If Trautmann escaped, then so be it. If he came looking for his targets, determined to fulfill the contract with his client, then Ike would stop him. Having settled on his course, Ike slipped into the shrubbery where he had a good view of the front and one side of the house. When he felt he had things as well under control as possible, he extracted a tiny cell phone from the pocket of his baggy pants and pushed an automatic dial button.

* * * * *

Mark Hart stood to the side of the shattered front window, keeping a watch on the front yard as darkness fell around them. He gazed back into the room occasionally to watch as the small group of survivors cared for one another. There was no panic, no remorse. No profanity. No expressions of anger or talk of revenge. Even Julienne Rostetter, who had likely not known any of these people until earlier in the day, moved about among them as though they were members of her own family.

Though the danger had not completely passed, perhaps the sweetest moment of the day for Mark had come just minutes earlier when Julienne Rostetter stepped beside him and spoke softly.

"Hart, I have no idea who you are. But I'm willing to admit when I'm wrong. I'm sorry that I misjudged you, and I'm certainly glad you were here today. Thanks."

Hart just nodded in response.

"Of course, my attorneys will contact you about my hearing loss," she added with a raise of her eyebrow.

* * * * *

Chad Rowley still lay on the floor, now with a couch pillow under his head. He was in and out of consciousness. The external bleeding was mostly stopped, but Julienne gave Sarah little hope.

"I'm sure his lung is filling with blood," Julienne whispered to her. "If you have any influence with a higher power, you'd better use it now."

FIFTY-ONE

Sarah Rudman sat beside Chad on the floor, dabbing perspiration from his forehead. She still pressed firmly on the magazine held against his chest.

He lay silently, looking up at her through partially open eyes.

"You're a beautiful woman," he said.

"Now you're starting to worry me," she said, sweeping her hair behind right ear with a finger. "You're getting delirious. I'm a mess. I hate for you to see me like this."

"Never," he replied. "You take my breath away." He winced in pain.

"Funny," said Sarah, leaning near to him. "You hang on. When you're better, I'll show you what it means to be breathless."

Chad managed a half smile. "I'm feeling better already," he whispered.

Sarah leaned over and kissed him at the corner of his mouth.

"It's such a relief to see you safe," he said. "I'm sorry it took us so long to get to you."

She nodded. "I knew you'd come. But it was hard. Terribly hard."

She glanced over at Gwen, who had practically roused herself from the brink of death.

"I figured you were busy." Sarah smiled. "I thought you might have taken up golf. Or maybe you were dating somebody else. Didn't have time for me."

"Right," said Chad with another deep and bubbling cough. "Never happen."

"Hang on, Chad." She kissed him again.

"I finally discovered your secret," he said. "All I have to do to get a few kisses is arouse your pity."

She touched one of the cuts on his face lightly.

Chad smiled, then groaned, a deep rumbling in his chest. His eyes glazed over as he began to drift away.

Sarah felt the sudden grip of panic.

"Chad, no!" she shouted.

Julienne reached immediately to Chad's throat for a pulse.

"We're losing him," she said in alarm.

Sarah was sobbing. She reached up to wipe away her tears with the back of her hand.

"Chad, please!" she cried, the tears coursing down her cheeks. "You promised me. Please don't leave me. I love you, Chad."

* * * * *

Minutes later, the beleaguered Insiders and their newly found friends heard sirens approaching in the distance. An involuntary cheer went up throughout the room.

It's about time.

Mark felt the burden of responsibility lifting from his shoulders. He heard murmurs of, "Thank heaven," and "Oh, yes, yes, yes!"

It took a few more minutes before a fire truck arrived, and then a second. The firemen set to work, immediately extinguishing what was left of the Expedition. Paramedics put a chest tube in Chad Rowley and started an IV. The RCMP finally arrived and established control of the house, the neighboring house, and the grounds.

* * * * *

Long after dark, two sleek, black Apache helicopters set down in a clearing a quarter mile up the lane. They bore the white circular insignia of the Central Intelligence Agency. They were on the ground only long enough to load seven passengers, including two litters, before heeling into a stiffening northerly breeze and coming around to a course that would carry them south toward the international border.

FIFTY-TWO

Celeste Hughes could feel the noose tightening. She really didn't want any part of this, but she had little choice. For fifteen minutes, she sat listening to the Chairman expounding on the present crisis in torrents of quiet rage. He didn't shout at her. Didn't throw things. Didn't make threats. He didn't express his rage in words but in subtle body language.

Even though Celeste didn't know him well, his intentions were perfectly clear to her.

"The matter was badly handled," he said, his back to her, hands in his pockets, gazing out over the dark Toronto skyline.

"The fault was mine. I foolishly misjudged some of my most trusted people. It's difficult to tell how much this little fiasco will cost us. Be assured that it will be in the tens of millions by the time we pay all the legal fees."

He turned and strolled along the windows, still gazing outward. Celeste couldn't tell whether he was talking to her or just using her presence as an opportunity to talk the matter through with himself.

"Art Warnock was a moron. He was inflexible. He had no finesse. Never understood the word *patience*. Certainly never tried it. He was a bull—and a bully. Treated his people like dogs. It's not surprising that he got bit. His departure was unfortunate but necessary. On the other hand, he had qualities that are absolutely essential to success in your line of work. I admired the man's willingness to go for broke."

"Julienne Rostetter, in contrast, was wonderful. Smart. Great sense of timing. Good head for strategy. But she was weak and hampered by conscience. Now she has committed the unforgivable sin: she has betrayed me. She may think she can walk away—but she can't. She has been part of the inner circle. If she is sleeping well tonight, it's only because she doesn't know me as well as she thought she did."

The Chairman sat in the great leather chair behind his desk, steepled his hands in front of his face, and looked over them at Celeste.

"Julienne can join the Mormons, go into a convent, try the witness protection program. It doesn't matter. I have eyes everywhere. She'll never have a minute of peace again, until one of us is dead."

He leaned back, gazed up at the ceiling, and slowly swiveled around to look out the windows behind him again.

Celeste had not said a word. She also hadn't missed a word he said. She felt her palms moisten with perspiration. Gently wiping her hands against her skirt, she reminded herself that she didn't want to hear any of this. While she had no affection for Julienne, Celeste also didn't want to become trapped in Julienne's former position. But, right now, she had no idea how to avoid it.

"The person Fletchner International needs to head security is a combination of Julienne Rostetter and Art Warnock. He or she must be ruthless, but flexible. Unrelenting, but patient. Visionary, yet doggedly practical. Decisive, but teachable. Organized, but innovative. Obedient, yet self-motivating. Because I couldn't find all of the needed qualities in one person, I thought I could bring Julienne and Art along together and have everything I wanted. I miscalculated. Art is gone. Julienne must go. And I am back where I started."

Finally, the Chairman turned and looked directly at Celeste. He had a piercing gaze. She felt briefly that he was reading her thoughts. With a look of weariness not at all typical of him, the Chairman inhaled deeply and then blew it out slowly.

"You're not that person, Celeste. And you know it. Like Julienne, you're inclined to be decent. I don't want decent people around me. I want effective people. But you're the best I can do."

The Chairman never asked Celeste if she wanted the job—which she didn't. He simply dictated to her the next steps she would take in moving Fletchner International forward.

"First, find Julienne. We don't need to act too quickly regarding her. Keep a close eye on her. I want to reach her instantly when the right time comes. We need to let the dust settle for a few weeks— maybe a few months. The same for the three Mormons—Rowley, Rudman, and Fong."

"Find anyone in our organization who is a Mormon. Get rid of them. Warnock underestimated them. That explains why he's probably answering to their God as we speak. We don't want to make the same mistake again. They are the enemy. Arrange some financial support to their opponents.

"Find out where the RCMP is holding Warnock's people. They must not be allowed to talk. We've already lost too much ground. I'm counting on you to do the damage control. Don't let me down, Celeste. Stay where I can reach you. Good-bye."

With that abrupt dismissal, Celeste Hughes left the Chairman's office, feeling her knees shaking as she walked toward the elevator. Once inside, she leaned against the wall and closed her eyes, trying to catch her breath.

Oh, Celeste. Why didn't you resign yesterday?

FIFTY-THREE

After their nighttime helicopter extraction from the Rostetter summer home in southern Ontario, the Insiders and their friends were airlifted to Washington DC. With the exception of Ike Rudman, all members of the party were hospitalized. Jeff Gordon, Julienne Rostetter, Sarah Rudman, and Jamie Madero were treated and released. They were transported as guests of Ike Rudman to the headquarters of the Central Intelligence Agency in Langley, Virginia.

While the investigation of the attacks in Leadville, Denver, and Ontario fell principally within the jurisdiction of the FBI and the RCMP, the CIA offered to host an interagency collaboration because of the involvement of Ike Rudman and Gerhardt Trautmann.

The Foundation associates spent three additional days in secure debriefing rooms, answering questions. During the final session—with everyone present except Chad Rowley, including representatives of the FBI, RCMP, and legal counsel for the Foundation, as well as Julienne Rostetter's personal attorney—the entire affair was summarized and made a matter of record. Julienne Rostetter was granted legal immunity in return for her cooperation and willingness to testify in an investigation of Fletchner International. Mark Hart, who had been instrumental in freeing the abductees, worked undercover for Canadian authorities. Federal authorities were searching for a Los Angeles–based private investigator named George Kilgrow, known to Jamie and Chad as Cufflinks. Gerhardt Trautmann, assassin and subject of an international manhunt, had escaped once more.

"It would be wrong for me to raise any false hopes at this point," Ike explained. "It's doubtful that there's enough solid evidence to make charges stick to Ramon Fellini, Chairman of the Board of Fletchner International. Mr. Fellini has been around the block a few times. He gets cagier with every scrape he survives. He'll claim that Art Warnock was acting on his own. There's nothing in the Rostetter or Hart testimonies to disprove that. And, in a measure, I think that's accurate. Warnock was almost certainly Trautmann's client. I think Fellini will walk from this investigation. Next time around, he'll be even harder to get close to. It's not going to be easy to bring him down."

There was a murmur of disappointment among the Insiders.

"Furthermore, we don't yet know how extensive his international connections are. Information about affiliate organizations provided by Gwen Fong will help. We're running an Interpol check on those organizations now. You can be sure that you have hooked into one of the biggest fish in the pond.

"Let me share a few of our findings about the death of Art Warnock," Rudman said as he wound down his report.

Jamie blanched every time the event was mentioned.

"We know how Warnock died," continued Rudman, "but it's hard to say who—or what—killed him. Jamie, you were there. We know that you've assumed the blame for the killing. It's true that the weapon you were holding was fired, probably when you pulled the trigger. However, no bullet from that weapon was found in Warnock. In fact, he wasn't killed by a bullet wound of any kind. The bullets you fired missed him completely."

Rudman looked around at the group while that information sank in.

"Warnock died when the weapon he attempted to fire exploded in his hand," Ike continued. "The autopsy showed that a portion of his right hand was missing, and the right side of his head was massively injured. Analysis of gun fragments found near the body shows that the weapon was sabotaged. A powerful explosive was either loaded into the gun as a dummy round or inserted into the chamber.

It definitely wasn't the result of gunpowder from one round exploding. The blast was much too powerful for that. And the explosive residue proves the tampering.

"As to who was responsible, we can't say yet, and we may never know. Possibly someone in Warnock's own organization wanted to get rid of him. Maybe Fellini. Maybe one of his underlings.

"For our purposes, the most important conclusion is that you didn't kill him, Jamie."

* * * * *

Standing near the foot of Chad Rowley's hospital bed, Jeff Gordon informed his friends that the Foundation board had reaffirmed their support. Operations would resume, but there would likely be some important changes.

"We—rather I—seriously underestimated the lethal intents and abilities of our enemies. I shudder at the thought of what it has cost us. However," Jeff continued, "I assure you that we'll never be caught unprepared again. While Ramon Fellini and others like him are getting stronger, so will we. We've gained some valuable experience. Our determination is stronger. At any rate, we've survived."

Then glancing around at those in the room, he added, "With a lot of help from our friends."

EPILOGUE

When Jamie Madero wrapped up his summer internship with the Freemen Foundation and headed home to Winslow, Arizona, he left many friends behind. But he didn't necessarily know where to find them. Most of them disappeared soon after the shootout in Ontario and the CIA debriefings in Virginia.

Mark Hart was the first to go, then Julienne Rostetter, Gwen Fong, and Ike Rudman. The remaining Insiders vanished. When Ike arrived in Denver, traveling with Jeff Gordon, the pair picked up a few files from the now vacant Freemen Foundation office that sported a For Lease sign.

They had left Chad Rowley in a Virginia hospital. The outcome of his life-threatening chest wound was still uncertain. Sarah was at his bedside when Jamie said his good-byes. He knew Chad wouldn't remember his visit but hoped that Sarah would.

"Jamie, you've earned a spot on the team," said Jeff Gordon as they sat in the Denver airport awaiting their separate flights. "Things in the Foundation will be in a state of flux for a while. Eventually we'll settle into our new home and build from there. You can come back to work each summer on an internship basis until you graduate, if that interests you."

"Will I be able to stay in touch with the other team members?" asked Jamie.

"Yes. The best way to do that is to contact the Foundation office."

Jeff handed him a business card.

"This phone number will always work. Destroy the card as soon as you've memorized it," instructed Jeff.

"When you call, identify yourself by this three-digit number."

He wrote a number on the back of the card.

"The number will get you to a voice recorder. Leave your call-back number, and we'll get back to you. You can reach me or any of the Insiders that way."

In a serious tone, Jeff continued, "I know you understand how confidential these arrangements are. The lives of your friends could depend on safeguarding their whereabouts."

"I would never put our friends in danger," said Jamie. "I admire them all. I care about them."

He paused, looking at his hands folded in his lap.

"Chad has been like a brother to me," he said. "There's no one I'd rather be like."

Jeff nodded.

"I understand. And I think you'll be like him. He's about as good as young men come. He got that way by paying his dues."

"What do you mean?" asked Jamie.

"He learned to serve by filling a full-time mission. He got himself an education. He's always improving himself. Everything he does deepens his character," said Jeff. "You'll be wise to follow his example."

"Yeah," Jamie replied. "I guess that's where I need to go."

"I hope you'll keep us up to speed regarding your activities and plans," said Jeff. "We'd love to have you join us when you finish your degree."

The two friends parted with a handshake.

Jamie returned home to something of a hero's welcome. He had two dandy scars from his wounds in the shoot-out. He couldn't attend a family gathering on his mom's side without lifting his shirt so all the kids could get a firsthand view of a gunshot wound.

When the dust settled, Jamie decided what he wanted to do with his life. He needed a degree to have any chance of a career with the Foundation. But he also remembered his brief conversation with Jeff

Gordon about paying his dues and becoming the kind of man Chad Rowley was. After a few short months and an additional semester at NAU, Jamie was called as a full-time missionary for The Church of Jesus Christ of Latter-day Saints.

* * * * *

Elder Jamie Madero walked down the Terminal 2 concourse at Phoenix Sky Harbor International toward gate 13 and his flight to Salt Lake City. He had lingered outside the passenger security area until the very last minute, saying good-bye to his mom and the crowd of family members and friends who came to see him off to the Mission Training Center.

Jamie was dressed like a missionary—shirt, tie, and standard name tag. His nerves were aflutter. Was he afraid of the step he was about to take?

Afraid is too strong a word. I'm a little nervous about something new. That's all.

Passing gate 2, he realized he had cut himself too short on time. His gate was a long way down the crowded corridor ahead. He was about to break into a trot when a familiar face came into view, the face of a strikingly attractive brunette, midtwenties, very classy.

Elder Madero slowed his pace to look directly at the woman. He couldn't say for sure that he'd ever seen her or the man she was with. But he felt he knew her.

His change of pace seemed to catch the woman's eye. He thought her eyes also lighted in recognition. She carelessly swept the hair behind her right ear with a finger.

Jamie's breath caught in his throat.

Could she be—?

Was he looking at Sarah Rudman? The couple didn't change direction but seemed to slow a bit so that their path would intersect his in just a few more steps.

Is that you, Sarah? Chad? Doesn't look like 'em, but they can look almost any way they want.

On impulse, fighting off his nervousness about missing his own flight, Elder Madero stepped right in front of the couple.

"Excuse me," he blurted out with less polish than he had hoped for. "I feel I know you. You remind me of a friend—Sarah Rudman."

How could they not recognize him, considering his appearance and the name tag on his pocket? An awkward pause followed before the woman spoke. Her voice was not at all familiar.

"I'm sorry, you must have mistaken us for someone else."

Jamie took a step backward to let them pass.

"Sorry," he said. "Didn't mean to trouble you."

"No trouble," she said. "We're the Guymons. Our home is near Seattle."

With an effort to salvage some dignity from the ill-fated encounter, Jamie turned to the man. Instinctively, he extended a hand.

"It's a pleasure to meet you," he said.

Mr. Guymon took the hand firmly and gave Jamie a soft nod and a wink and then loosened his grip. He never said a word.

Jamie turned to sprint down the concourse. Seconds later, he stopped cold. Whirling around, he searched the crowded concourse for the Guymons. They were gone.

The gate attendant was just closing the gate door as Jamie arrived breathless.

"That's my flight. I've got to get on there," he said, puffing.

"They've closed the door but haven't pushed back," she replied. "Let me see if we can get you on."

"All right, Mr. Madero," she said after a moment on the phone, "you're good to go. Better hurry down there."

Reaching his seat, Elder Madero's emotions were tumbling. It was the wink. Chad's eye print. Jamie hadn't thought of it since Ontario. And Sarah's habit of pushing her hair back. He had seen them. He knew it. He ached to have been so close but not able to spend a second with them. Give them a hug.

They recognized me. Sure they did. But they couldn't acknowledge me publicly. They're still hiding.

"Can't cut it any closer than that," said the man sitting in the window seat as Jamie buckled into his.

"Sure can't," replied Jamie.

"You're a Mormon missionary, right?"

"That's right."

"Are you coming or going?" asked the gentleman.

"Going," said Jamie. "I'm headed for Chicago. My name's Elder Madero. What's yours?"

"Can't tell you or you'll send somebody out to visit me."

Jamie laughed. "It could be the best visit you'll ever have."

His seatmate smiled. "Could be."

DISCUSSION QUESTIONS

1. Jamie Madero wants to become a man like Chad Rowley. Jeff Gordon tells him he'll need to pay his dues to become like Chad. Did this story remind you of dues you need to pay to reach important goals?

2. Aside from the drug cartels of Columbia and Mexico, can you think of other criminal organizations that threaten the foundations of free government and could be considered "secret combinations"? Is there anything we can do to slow their growth?

3. Do you think there's a place for organizations like the Freemen Foundation in our society? Why or why not?

4. With which of the characters do you identify most closely? What about that character reminds you of yourself?

5. Were there any surprises in the story that you didn't see coming? In retrospect, do they make sense to you?

6. Julienne Rostetter's encounter with the Insiders of the Freemen Foundation—and with Jeff Gordon—changed the course of her life in some significant ways. What do you think lies down the road for Julienne?

7. Why do you think Sarah Rudman ran from Chad Rowley's romantic advances early in the story? Did that tendency on her part change as the story progressed? How? Why?

8. The old rivalry between Gerhardt Trautmann and Ike Rudman was reignited in this story. Both men have survived lengthy careers in a very dangerous occupation. In what ways are they alike? In what ways are they different?

9. What do we learn from this story about the risks of confronting evil?

10. If you were writing the next chapter in this story, what would you like to see happen?